# COLD SKY

DALTON SAVAGE

BOOK 3

L.T. RYAN

WITH

BIBA PEARCE

*For information contact:*

contact@ltryan.com

http://LTRyan.com

https://www.facebook.com/groups/1727449564174357

## THE DALTON SAVAGE SERIES

*Savage Grounds*

*Scorched Earth*

*Cold Sky*

*The Frost Killer*

Join the L.T. Ryan reader family & receive a free copy of the Rachel Hatch story, *Fractured*. Click the link below to get started:

https://ltryan.com/rachel-hatch-newsletter-signup-1

Love Hatch? Savage? Noble? Maddie? Get your very own L.T. Ryan merchandise today! Click the link below to find coffee mugs, t-shirts, and even signed copies of your favorite L.T. Ryan thrillers! https://ltryan.ink/EvG_

# ONE

THE HOMELESS MAN wheezed as he scrounged through the trash can. His asthma always played up this time of year. Something about the change in seasons. It wasn't bad enough to worry about, and nothing a bottle of cheap bourbon wouldn't fix, or at least take his mind off. Same thing, really.

He found a half-eaten sandwich and squinted at the sell-by date. Tomorrow.

*Sweet.*

Stuffing it into his pocket, he did another deep dive and came up with a lipstick-marred cigarette, practically untouched. The wife having a last desperate puff before going inside to cook dinner for her family. Lawyer, power dresser, probably kicked ass in the courtroom, then came home to be knocked around by her coke-snorting banker husband. You never knew what went on behind closed doors.

But he did.

He knew a lot about this neighborhood. More than he should. Because he was a watcher. To survive on the streets, he had learned to keep his eyes and ears open. Living in the shadows, just like in his military days, except without the guns, grenades, and anti-tank missiles. Still, a backfiring car or the rumble of a truck could catapult him back there. In his head, he'd never really left.

If you were going to be a bum, this was the best area. Wealthy, middle-class, educated folk. Even the kids addressed him with a degree of respect when they addressed him at all, which wasn't often. Mostly they just walked around him and went on their way, eyes glued to their phones. Instagram, Tik-Tok. Double tapping their lives away. To him, a double tap had a different meaning. Neither meaning was good.

He wasn't ignorant. He knew what was going on in the world, even if he opted not to be in it. He read the news, usually a day late, but often the newspapers were the only thing keeping him company through the night. That – and the watching.

The lady with the new fake tits was having an affair with the landscaper. Every Tuesday morning, they were at it like rabbits while her husband was at work. Never bothered to draw the living room curtains, never made it up to the bedroom. He wasn't complaining.

The high school kid in the big house around the corner climbed out of her bedroom window and down the trellis at least three times a week. She caught the number eleven bus downtown. He didn't know where she went, but she got back around two, three o'clock in the morning. Sometimes a little drunk, sometimes stoned. He couldn't always tell which.

Elderly Mrs. Caraway in 375 made him coffee in the morning. Sometimes they chatted about the weather. Her rheumatism played up worse than his asthma. He liked Mrs. Caraway. She was a kind soul, still believed in the good in people.

He snorted. She hadn't seen the blood-strewn terrain of a battlefield. Landmines exploding all around, nowhere to turn. The chaos, the destruction. Soldiers turned into animals, intent on killing each other. For what?

He cleared his throat and spat in the gutter, before shuffling onwards, toward the end of the road. It was a dark night, no moon.

Only the streetlamps and a glittering parade of shops beyond the intersection illuminated the path. That's where he'd bed down for the night. An undercover delivery entrance around the back of the grocery store offered shelter in case it rained. They kicked him out in the morning, when the first trucks rolled in, but they didn't seem to mind too much. He hadn't been warned off yet.

It was a block before the intersection when he saw the boy. No, not boy. Teenager. Kid must be about eighteen, nineteen. He was slim and kinda geeky looking with glasses and a collared shirt, but he walked with a jaunty stride, hands thrust in his pockets, head up and shoulders back, like he was happy about something.

The homeless man flattened himself against a dark hedge. Old habits. Thankfully, he was too far away to be seen, and had the added bonus of being sandwiched between the two properties. The street was deserted, everyone safely tucked away in their Benjamin Moore living rooms. Cars were parked in carports and driveways, the engines cold. Only a gray tabby idled across the road, its luminous eyes probing the boy.

"Where ya goin', kid?" the homeless man muttered as he watched the teenager stroll down the street as if he didn't have a care in the world. He didn't recognize him, so he was almost certain the kid didn't live around here. Was he on his way to or back from a score? Nah, he didn't look like a user. Dealing? Maybe. He could have some stash hidden in his pocket. Soliciting? Nah, not in this area. A decade of relying on his gut instinct told him something was off.

The kid checked his phone. Right pocket. From his hiding place, the homeless man saw the screen light up, momentarily casting the boy's face in a fluorescent green glow. Then it flicked off, and the darkness moved in again.

Approaching vehicle headlights drew the homeless guy's attention. And the boy's. The kid followed them with his eyes, until the SUV was close. Black, sleek, with the sheen of a new vehicle. He squinted at the make. Hyundai.

Not a sound came from the car's engine. It snuck up like a sharpshooter, camouflaged and as silent as still air, but moving ever closer. The kid stepped onto the pavement to allow it to pass, but it didn't. Instead, it pulled over and the driver's window slid down.

The homeless guy strained to see through the veil of darkness, but the window was on the other side of the car, and he didn't have a good enough line of sight. Frowning, he remained glued to the darkness, watching.

A muffled voice carried over the still night air. "Get in."

To his surprise, the kid opened the passenger door and slid in. That's when the homeless man noticed there were no license plates. They'd been removed. Squinting, he tried to see through the windshield, but it was tinted, and the night was too dark. He could only make out the vague silhouette of the driver's head.

A couple of seconds passed before he heard a muffled bang, and the interior of the car lit up like a firecracker had gone off inside. Except it wasn't a firecracker. The homeless man began to tremble. He recognized that sound only too well. That was a handgun, a 9mm, like a Glock or a Sig Sauer, and it had discharged in that vehicle.

Eyes wide, he waited to see what would happen next. Had the kid shot the driver, or the other way around? He didn't recall the kid carrying a weapon, and he could usually spot someone who was carrying. His question was answered when the passenger door jerked open and the kid dropped out, like a sack of potatoes. He landed on the hard tarmac, shoulder first, rolling onto his back. He wasn't moving.

The SUV took off with an indignant screech.

*Shit.*

Had that really happened or was this one of his flashbacks? He rubbed his eyes and looked back at the street. The kid was still there. Motionless. The homeless man couldn't tell where he'd been shot, but it didn't matter. He knew a dead body when he saw it. There was no coming back from this.

The phone was probably still in the kid's pocket. Usually, he'd take advantage of an opportunity like that – the latest iPhone fetched a couple hundred bucks on the black market – but not tonight. That phone would be hot. If he took it, it might be traced back to him, and he did not want to be messed up in this. No way, man. A black kid killed in an upmarket white neighborhood. Hell, the shit was going to hit the fan in a big way, and he wanted to be nowhere near when it did.

The homeless guy moved on, toward the parade of shops in the distance. As he did so, he trained his gaze on the windows overlooking the street. The last thing he wanted was to be identified by one of the residents as a witness, or worse, a suspect. It was too easy to pin the blame on the homeless bum. Happened all the time, especially if the bum had mental health issues and knew how to fire a weapon. But there were no lights, no featureless faces staring down onto the street.

The homeless man looked back at the kid. He fought the urge to check on him, make sure he was dead, even though he knew he was.

In his head, he'd already planned his escape route. He'd cut across the kids' play area to Dahlia Street, and from there, loop around the high school to Alameda and head toward the downtown area. No way was he sleeping around here tonight. It was too close to the crime scene, too easy to be found. And questioned.

*No, officer, I swear I didn't hear a thing.*

He wasn't a very good liar. Didn't need to be where he'd been. There was nothing more truthful than war. No mixed messages there. It was either shoot or be shot. Things were black or white. Not like civilian life. Here, there was nothing but mixed messages. The world was gray. He couldn't cope with that at all.

*Don't do it. Keep moving,* his head told him.

The soldier inside him made him pause. He hesitated, looking left and right one last time before stepping into the road. The kid wasn't moving. Eyes shut, mouth open in a silent scream, hands clenched over a gaping stomach wound. Gut shot. There was no rise and fall of his chest.

The homeless man felt for a pulse. It was as he'd thought. Nothing. His chest constricted. What a terrible thing to happen. The kid was so young, but then when was old enough to die? Twenty? Thirty? Fifty, like him? He took a shaky breath and straightened up. Not his problem.

He kept walking. By the time the kid's body was found, he'd be long gone.

# TWO

SAVAGE WAS SITTING in an armchair bottle-feeding baby Connor on his lap when his phone rang. Balancing the bottle with one hand, he reached over the arm of the chair and picked up the phone.

No caller ID.

"This is Savage."

"Dalton Savage, will you accept a call from the Colorado State Penitentiary?"

For a moment, his brain froze. Who'd be calling him from a correctional facility?

"Sir? Do you accept the charges?" the voice prompted.

Only one way to find out. "Um, yeah. Sure."

For a fleeting moment, he thought it might be Rachel Hatch, the one who got away. She had gotten herself into some sticky situations, but she'd always managed to get herself out of them. He hadn't heard from her since she'd left Hawk's Landing and wasn't expecting to either. Particularly now that he and Becca had moved in together. Strangely, he found he was holding his breath as he waited for the call to connect.

A deep male voice said, “Detective Savage? Is that you?”

*Detective Savage?*

He hadn't been called that in a long time. Not since Denver. The caller obviously didn't know he'd moved on. There was no point in correcting him, not until he knew what this was about. “Speaking.”

“This is Dewayne Simmons. I don't know if you remember me, but –”

“I remember.”

How could he forget?

“I need you to come and see me.”

Savage heard shouting in the background and a loud clang, followed by a loudspeaker spewing out orders. The normal prison soundtrack.

It had been years. Why was Simmons calling him now? Then he got it. There must have been an appeal, something to cause him to get in touch.

“If this is to do with your case, I have no control over that.”

“It's not. It's to do with my baby brother.”

“Your brother?” He closed his eyes, allowing himself to slip back into the past. In his lap, Connor gurgled contentedly.

THE SNOW FELL *onto the unmarked Crown Vic, getting thicker by the minute. It no longer melted on the hood. Showed how long they'd been here.*

*Waiting.*

*The parking lot was already several inches deep but looked better for it. Cleaner. The snow covered up all the trash, the stains, the debris. Wiped it all clean.*

*Burger King was busy despite the weather, but then it was five-thirty on a Friday night. Commuters came in hungry and left with greasy smiles or bulging brown paper bags. Either way, they were happier than when they went in.*

*A van pulled up in front of the store, blocking their view of the door.*

*"Is that them?" Christenson asked, leaning forward. "I can't see. Is that them?"*

*The passenger door opened and a stocky guy holding a gun and wearing a ski mask jumped out.*

*"Shit! It's them. Let's move!" Savage was first out of the car, racing across the street to the restaurant. Christenson followed, coming up beside him as they paused alongside the door.*

*Peeking around the corner, Savage could see the perps waving their guns around. The customers got down onto the floor, some crying, some screaming, others glancing furtively at the exit.*

*"Don't move!" the stocky man yelled, his gun in the air.*

*The tall one went straight to the counter and jumped over it. "Open it," he demanded, waving at the cash register.*

*The terrified cashier did as he was told.*

*"In here!" He held out a canvas bag. The cashier loaded bills into the bag.*

*"Now." Savage nodded to his partner, and they entered the restaurant. "Denver PD. Freeze!" Savage pointed his gun at the tall guy behind the counter. Two white eyes stared back at him, through the slits in the mask.*

*"Put your weapons down!" Christenson yelled, his service pistol trained on the stocky perp. "Nice and easy."*

*Except it wasn't nice and easy. Nothing was ever nice and easy.*

*The tall thief knew he had the advantage behind the serving counter. He spun with the grace of a dancer and took off through the kitchen.*

*Shit.*

*Savage started to go after him, but Christenson hurdled over the counter, shouting, "I've got this." His partner was younger and fitter, having been a track star in college. Savage let him go. He adjusted his aim to the stocky one.*

*"Don't be stupid." Savage kept his voice even. "Put the gun down."*

*The perp glanced around, looking for a way out, but there was none. He was scared. Scared meant unpredictable.*

*"Game's up," Savage said. "There's nowhere to go. Put it down."*

*The perp eyed the entrance, his eyes huge behind the mask.*

*"Don't do it," Savage warned. He never for a minute thought the guy would go for it. It was a suicide mission. Yet, the perp ran for the door, his only thought to escape. It opened automatically, letting in a blast of cold air.*

*"Stop!" Savage heard the plea in his own voice. He couldn't let the guy get away. Savage gave chase, except the perp reached the door, then spun around, and aimed at Savage.*

*Time slowed. The man's finger tightened around the trigger.*

*Savage fired.*

*Three shots. Bang. Bang. Bang.*

*Deafening, accurate. Center mass, like he'd been trained.*

*The would-be shooter stumbled backwards onto the slushy pavement, dropping his gun. A woman screamed. Savage heard sobbing.*

*He approached the perp, kicking away the gun. He heard the dull clunk as his boot made contact. It didn't sound right. Frowning, Savage bent down to inspect the weapon. His heart sank. The kid had been holding a pellet gun.*

*Around him, the snow continued to fall, but it couldn't wipe this clean.*

EVEN NOW, Savage's chest constricted at the thought. Horror, guilt, remorse all washed over him afresh. Not that he'd ever let those feelings go, having instead learned to bury them. The passing of time had helped. Six years was a long time. But not long enough, apparently.

He remembered the kid's mother at the trial, sobbing. Her son was dead. Justin, his name was. Savage hadn't been able to look at her.

Next to her was another woman, Dewayne's mother. She'd been fighting to hold back the tears. Clutching her hand had been another kid, much younger. Dewayne's kid brother.

"What about your brother?" Savage asked, his voice gruff.

"He was shot and killed last week. Gunned down in the street, in a swanky, white area. He bled out in the gutter." Savage could hear the disgust spewing down the line.

He cringed. "I'm sorry to hear that."

"The cops aren't doing a damn thing about it."

"I'm sure they're investigating."

"My mama says they haven't even been round to offer her condolences. Nobody's asked any questions, nothing. They ain't doing shit about it."

Savage didn't know what to say. "I'm sorry for your loss, but what's this got to do with me?"

"You gotta help me, man. You gotta figure out who did this."

Stunned, Savage fought to reply. "You know I don't live in Denver anymore. I'm not part of Denver PD."

"I know, man. That's why I'm calling you. You don't have to answer to these dickheads."

"I can't just leave everything and go up to Denver. I have responsibilities here. Besides, I've got no jurisdiction there."

"You know this city, man. You know it better than anyone. And I know you felt bad about Justin. At the trial, you – "

"That was a long time ago. Things have changed."

"No, man. Nothing's changed. That's my point. Nothing's fucking changed. Someone's gotta pay for what they did to Kenan. I can't do it 'cos I'm stuck in here." Bitterness, frustration, desperation – it was all there in the uneven pitch of his voice. The unspoken words echoed down the line.

*Thanks to you.*

Savage shook his head. Connor stirred, but he adjusted the bottle and the baby carried on suckling. "I don't know what you expect me to do."

"Help me. You shot Justin. Now you need to help me find out who killed Kenan."

Justin had been a kid when he'd died. Just nineteen. The guilt threatened to choke him. "It was a clean shot," Savage growled. "Your buddy pulled on me."

"A pellet gun!"

"You were both involved in other robberies." He had to justify it somehow. It couldn't only be about that one night.

"Believe whatever you want, but you know that wasn't us. I didn't kill that woman."

"I don't know that, Dewayne."

"Then why did you say what you did at the trial?" The phone made a beeping sound. Time was running out. "Why did you ask my lawyer for an extension?"

"Look, I've got to go. I'm sorry about your brother."

"Come on, man. You *owe* me."

"I've really got to go."

A loud beep signified the call had ended.

"Who was that?" Becca poked her head into the room. Her expression changed to a frown. "Dalton, you've gone white. Are you okay?"

He shook his head as if to clear it. It didn't work. His brain felt fuzzy. "Yeah, I think so." Out of all the people he knew, Dewayne Simmons was the last one on earth he'd expected a call from.

"Here, let me take him."

Connor had fallen asleep, the bottle still in his mouth. Savage passed the sleeping baby over to his mother and stretched his neck. Tension had made his shoulders seize up.

"I'll be right back."

She took Connor to his room. It was his bedtime. Savage remained unmoving, lost in the past. He heard Becca walk back down the hall, do something in the kitchen, then come into the living room. She was holding a glass of wine. "Okay, I'm listening."

He dragged himself back to the present. "It's nothing. A blast from my past, that's all."

"From Denver?"

"Yeah." He glanced over at her. "How'd you know?"

"What other past do you have?"

He managed a thin smile. "Fair enough."

"Who was it?"

Savage hesitated, not knowing where to start. "A convict, someone I put away a long time ago. He's serving life for armed robbery."

"That's a hell of a sentence for armed robbery." Becca was astute. A clinical psychologist, she ran her own clinic in Pagosa Springs that helped challenged youth, some of whom had been involved in or were victims of crime. She was no stranger to the law.

"It was a series of robberies. Carried out by two guys. During one of the robberies, they shot a woman leaving a restaurant. It was a senseless act of violence and this guy Dewayne went down for it."

"Did he kill her?"

"He says not."

She nodded slowly. "What happened to the other guy?"

Savage hesitated. "I shot him."

Becca gazed at him for a long moment, her clear blue eyes resting on his face. "By accident?"

"He pulled on me first."

A soft exhale. "Then you had to shoot him, right? Or he'd have shot you."

"Not exactly." Savage looked away. "The kid was carrying a pellet gun. I didn't know it at the time."

Becca said nothing.

"I thought it was real." He ground his jaw. "I've replayed it a thousand times in my head. Every time ends the same. Crazy thing—when I see it in my mind, I can't see his face. It's just a dark void where it should be."

She leaned over and squeezed his arm. "That's your brain's defense system at work. What you're describing is typical of people who suffer from post-traumatic stress. What you're describing is called traumatic memory suppression. It's the mind sheltering you from the guilt of taking another's life."

"Doesn't seem to be working. I still feel it, face or no face."

"That's because you're a good man. One who will never take lightly the burdens of your profession. The split-second life and death decisions you're forced to make can take a lifetime to process."

He placed his hand over hers. "Thank you."

"For what?"

"For always listening and never judging."

"It's not in my nature to judge. Besides, you make it easy." Becca placed her lips on the top of his head. "I love you, Dalton Savage."

He felt the tenderness in her words. He felt the truth behind them. She wasn't placating him. Her insight came from a depth of knowledge. And knowing all of that didn't change the fact that he did blame himself. Who else was there to blame? *He* was the one who'd pulled the trigger and killed that boy. Not anyone else.

Him.

"What did Dewayne want?" Becca broke into his self-recriminations. "That's his name, isn't it? The man who called you?"

Savage gave a tight nod. "He wanted me to help figure out who killed his kid brother."

"His brother's been shot?"

"Yeah. I remember him too. Scrawny kid. He was at the trial. Must have been about thirteen at the time."

She shook her head, confused. "How long's Dewayne been inside?"

"Six years."

"That's a long time."

"He's got a lot longer to go. He's lucky the state abolished the death penalty."

"Thank God." Becca closed her eyes briefly. She wasn't a fan of capital punishment.

"His kid brother would have been about nineteen now." Same age as Justin when he'd bled out on the pavement outside the burger joint.

*You owe me.*

"What are you going to do?" Becca asked quietly.

He shrugged. "Nothing I can do. Dewayne's brother was killed in Denver. I don't have any power there. Not anymore."

"You have contacts."

"It's not my job to find his brother's killer. Denver PD has to do that."

She frowned. "Then why did he call you?"

"I don't know. He doesn't trust the police, I guess. Can't say I blame him."

"But he trusts you? The man who killed his partner and put him in prison?"

Savage shrugged.

"What aren't you telling me?" Becca tilted her head to the side.

Savage looked down at his lap, not sure what to tell her first.

"Dalton?" She could read him like a book.

"Dewayne always insisted he didn't kill that woman."

Becca's eyes narrowed. "There was a trial, right? I mean, he was convicted by a judge and jury."

"Yes, but it wasn't as clear as that, despite how it looked. There were four robberies in total. The perps wore ski masks so even though they were caught on camera, it was difficult to see who they were."

"The boys were charged with all four?"

"Yeah, they were caught at the scene of the fourth robbery. The MOs were identical. They hit the restaurants just before closing, held the cashier at gunpoint, and stole the takings for the day. Height and build of the perpetrators matched."

"Well, there you go."

Savage gnawed on his lower lip.

Becca's eyes narrowed. "You believed him when he said he didn't do it, didn't you?"

He sighed. "I thought it was worth looking into. Dewayne said they were hired for the fourth job, and only that job. According to his testimony, they didn't do the other heists."

"Is it possible they were set up?"

"Maybe. He could have been lying, but I thought we should look into it."

"What did his lawyer say?"

"He agreed, if only to stall the verdict, but the judge refused to grant a continuance. A jury convicted him of first-degree murder in a little under three hours."

"Fast forward six years and now he's asking for your help?"

"Yes."

"Do you want to help him?"

"I don't know if I can."

"That's not what I asked."

Whimpering came from down the hall.

Savage spread his arms. "In an ideal world, maybe. But not now. I can't leave you and Connor."

She gave a little nod, and without saying anything else, got up and walked out of the room.

# THREE

SAVAGE SHUDDERED as he stared up at the large, solid, brutalist building with its horizontal rows of hard, tinted windows surrounded by gray concrete. This was where he'd worked every day for ten years. The headquarters of the Denver PD Homicide Division. He never thought he'd come back here.

Even the air outside felt the same. Frigid tentacles pricking his skin, making his eyes water. That faint tinge of smog coating his nostrils. The metallic taste of fumes drifting over from the congested streets. And above all, the unrelenting slate-gray sky.

He didn't want to be here, but before he went to the prison to visit Dewayne Simmons, he needed access to the official case report. With everything digitized on the Denver PD server, Savage could've called the records division and tried the "official business" route, but it was likely to raise some red flags and draw unwanted attention to the personal nature of his inquiry. Even in his current position, the release of case files to an ongoing investigation were typically done so with a supervisor's approval or that of the detective assigned a primary. All of these roadblocks left him with one choice. He needed to speak to Manning.

May as well get this over with.

Sucking in a deep breath of cold air, he strode into the building.

The duty sergeant in the lobby was a youngster, early twenties and probably not long out of the academy. He signed Savage in and then asked him if he knew where he was going.

Savage confirmed he did. He could probably get to his old department blindfolded. The elevator gave a familiar squeak as it took off and again as it stopped on the fourth floor. Sounds that had been engraved into his subconscious.

The homicide division was always busy. Uniformed police officers and detectives, along with a handful of civilian administrators, moved around the haphazardly positioned desks with practiced precision. A sidestep here, a little twist there. Organized chaos.

The air of urgency hadn't changed, either. Frantic tapping on keyboards, urgent voices on telephones, hurried footsteps as the admin staff rushed from office to office, all punctuated by the splutters of the printers as they spewed out warrants, police reports, and forensics.

He didn't miss it at all.

"Well, I'll be – ," came a shout, as a heavyset detective lumbered out of his chair. "If it isn't Dalton Savage! How the hell are you?" He strode across the open-plan squad room and shook Savage's hand.

"Kramer, good to see you."

"Heard you were Sheriff in some backwater?"

Kramer had always been a bit of a dick. "Something like that."

"What are you doing back in the mile high city?"

"Here to see Manning." Savage looked around but couldn't immediately see his old colleague. "Is he around?"

"Your old partner's in with the LT. Shouldn't be too long." Savage nodded.

Lieutenant Sarah Hagan.

She'd been promoted to lieutenant a couple years before he'd left, but her rise had been meteoric. Top of her class in the Police Academy.

Five years in Vice. Four in the Special Victims Unit, which took guts, and two in Homicide. There had been rumors that she was a bit too friendly with the Deputy Chief of Police, but Savage knew that to be untrue. He knew, because she'd hit on him.

They'd just closed a big case and were celebrating at The Depot, the local cop watering hole. It was the end of the night. He was several beers and a couple tequilas down, but Hagan was worse. She could hardly stand upright. He offered to get her a cab, so they walked out together, her hanging onto his arm, slurring her words. Once outside, she tried to kiss him. "That'sh an order, Detective."

He'd pulled back, shocked. She was an attractive woman, but she was also his boss. They'd worked cases together. He reported to her.

She'd gotten angry. "What'sh wrong? Haven't got the balls? What kind of man are you?" Cutting remarks to hide her humiliation. He hadn't taken them personally. It'd been the tequila talking.

The cab had pulled up in the nick of time. Savage opened the door and Hagan ducked into it, sending scathing glances his way.

The next day she'd refused to talk to him. Nothing. Not one word. At the very least he'd expected her to brush it over or laugh it off. Instead, she'd sent him hostile glares and blatantly ignored him. The woman knew how to bear a grudge.

Things hadn't improved with time. He'd gotten assigned the worst cases, given the crappiest tasks. When he'd tried to talk to Hagan about it, thinking it might help to clear the air, she'd reprimanded him. Didn't he know who he was talking to? He ought to watch himself or she'd report him. He'd be out of a job faster than you could say 'gross misconduct'.

It'd gotten so bad, his colleagues began to comment on it. "What did you do to piss her off?" A knowing wink. "She's got it in for you, buddy." A sympathetic chuckle.

Eventually, he left the department. It'd taken two years, but when he'd found himself, a top tier detective, investigating muggings in Platt Park, he knew it was time to call it quits. That was four years ago.

"Dalton, how's things?" Detective Sanchez asked.

"Good, thanks." Savage shook his hand. Joaquin Sanchez had been a good, but ambitious cop, intent on moving up the ranks. Savage was surprised to find he was still in Homicide. "You?"

"Not too bad." Perhaps there was nowhere to go with Hagan at the reins.

A couple other detectives eye-balled Savage. He didn't recognize them. Four years wasn't that long, but high turnover was rising among law enforcement agencies across the country, and Denver PD wasn't immune. The climate had changed. Those who joined the ranks seemed less inclined to make a career of it, and those who did often sought job shifts within the department. Whether it was that people were now conditioned to short burst, instant gratification embraced by the app-based social media influence or the job itself, the debate could be argued either way. One thing was certain, the culture was different.

Savage scanned his surroundings, feeling out of place, a relic of a past whose years of dedicated service had faded into oblivion. Many of the old crew had moved on, either into retirement or out of the department, transferring to another agency in the hopes the grass was greener and likely finding it wasn't. The room was filled with degree-holding, fresh-faced officers, who saw the job as nothing more than a steppingstone to greater things. He could see it in the way they carried themselves. He recognized it in the look in their eyes. They weren't lifers, not like Manning and himself.

An office door opened, and Lieutenant Hagan appeared. Slim and toned with a runner's body, she looked professional in a black trouser suit with a red blouse underneath. Her dark hair was shorter than he remembered, in a fashionable pixie-style cut. The only reason he knew that was because Becca was thinking about having it done and had shown him several photographs of models sporting the same style. Personally, he preferred Becca's hair longer, but it wasn't his choice to make. She'd look good either way.

"Dalton." Hagan stared at him, her lips puckered into a fishy pout. "What are you doing here?"

"Good to see you too, Sarah." He used her first name knowing it would piss her off. Why shouldn't he? She'd used his. Plus, she wasn't his boss anymore.

Sanchez sniggered as Savage had known he would. Hagan colored and was likely winding up for a scathing retort when Manning stepped forward from behind her.

"Dalton, good to see you!" He pumped Savage's hand. Made a big song and dance of it, letting the tension dissipate. "Let's go grab a coffee."

Manning put his hand on Savage's shoulder and herded him out of the bullpen before Hagan had a chance to say anything else.

"Already causing trouble? You only just got here." His ex-partner chastised him as they walked down the hallway to the canteen.

Savage grinned. "Sorry about that. Hagan and I have never seen eye to eye."

"I remember. Why is that?"

Savage fixed his gaze ahead. "Beats me."

Manning didn't look convinced. "Coffee?"

"Is it still that industrial strength stuff?"

"You betcha, but it puts hair on your chest."

Manning filled two cups from the half empty pot and came back to the table. Savage studied his old friend, impressed by his appearance. "You're looking good, Clint."

"Yeah." He rubbed his flat stomach. "I've been working out."

When Savage had left Denver PD four years ago, Manning had been paunchy and slow on his feet, but then he had fifteen years on Savage, so that was to be expected. Now, he looked fit and agile. Even his hair was neater, slicked back, probably to hide the bald spot on his crown.

"How come?"

"Trish has started this new fitness regime and I've been going to the gym with her. I'm lifting weights for the first time in my life." He grinned. "I actually enjoy it."

Savage chuckled. "It suits you. You look years younger."

Manning took a sip of his coffee, grimaced, and put it down again. "Heard you had a kid?"

"Yeah, his name's Connor." Savage couldn't help the grin.

"Thought you looked a little tired."

Savage chuckled.

"Congrats, man. I'm happy for you."

"Thanks."

"How are things in La Plata County? You find that biker dude you called about a couple months back?"

"I did." Manning had provided some background on a case Savage had been working back in Hawk's Landing. The subject of his investigation had originated from Denver. Savage didn't elaborate, though. "How's Trish and the girls?"

"Great." Manning smiled. "Both girls have left home now. Can you believe that?" He shook his head. "Amanda is married with a kid on the way, while Summer is training at the police academy downtown."

"Wants to be a detective like her old man?" Summer was his youngest, if Savage remembered correctly. A bright, practical girl with a no-nonsense attitude. She'd make a good cop.

"Something must have rubbed off." Manning smiled proudly.

"How does her mother feel about that?"

"You know." He shrugged. Trish lived for the day Manning hung up his badge. Not many cops managed to stay married, such was the pressure of the job, but somehow Clint had. It was one of the things Savage admired most about him.

Manning leaned back in his chair. "So, what can I do for you? You were a little cryptic on the phone."

"I know, sorry about that." Savage scratched his head, then took a scalding sip of his coffee. "Remember the Burger King robberies?"

"Yeah?" Manning drew out the word, a curious expression on his face.

"Dewayne Simmons got hold of me last week and asked me to look into his little brother's death. You know about Kenan Simmons?"

"That's why you're here?" The other man's gaze became guarded as he leaned forward, setting his cup down on the table. "To look into Kenan Simmons's murder?"

"What can you tell me about it?"

"Nothing. Dalton, that's not your case. Hagan has a team on it. She's not going to be happy with you poking your nose into her investigation."

Savage sighed. "I know, but I owe the kid, Clint. He doesn't think justice is being served. He says the cops haven't even been around for a statement. Is that true?"

Manning looked sheepish.

"Is it true?" Savage leaned forward over his Styrofoam cup.

"It's complicated," Manning said. "An African American kid from the wrong side of the tracks shot in a rich, predominantly white neighborhood. Nobody wants to touch it."

"It's still a homicide. What's so complicated about that?"

"You know how it is. Things have been tense around here for a while now. We've got to be careful what we do, how we act. There's a spotlight on the police. This case has the potential to turn into a shitstorm."

"That doesn't mean you shouldn't investigate it."

"We are investigating, but carefully. Everything has to be done by the book. It takes longer."

"Maybe I can help. Get the ball rolling."

"I don't think so." Manning stared into the black abyss of his coffee. "Hagan isn't going to allow that."

"Can you at least get me the files on the shooting?"

Manning hesitated, clearly conflicted. "If I'm caught giving you information on an active case..."

"I'm still in law enforcement. It's not like I'm a civilian."

His ex-partner gave a reluctant nod. "There isn't much, but I suppose I can print off what we have."

"Thanks, Clint." Savage took another sip of coffee. "I also want to take another look at the Burger King burglaries."

Manning frowned. "Now why'd you want to do that? The case was closed six years ago. *You* closed it."

"For old time's sake."

His friend shook his head. "If it matters that much to you, I'll get the folder from the basement. It'll be less suspicious than printing the whole damn thing in the office."

"Thanks, man. I owe you."

"Yeah, you do." He glanced towards the office. "I gotta go. Meet me this evening at The Depot, and I'll give you the files. How does eight o'clock sound?"

Savage nodded. At eight o'clock on a Monday night, it wouldn't be busy.

---

SAVAGE WALKED into The Depot and looked around. The western-style bar had remained unchanged in the ten plus years Savage had been going there, and the last four years he'd been away had made no difference at all.

It looked like something out of an old cowboy movie, but Savage found the dim lighting and hazy warmth strangely comforting. A haven amidst the cold, awkward atmosphere of the precinct. Country and western music played from a jukebox in the corner, while a neon pink 'The Depot' sign, from which the bar had gotten its name, still hung above the bar.

"Hey Rich." Savage greeted the smiling bartender.

Richard Spader had been the manager for as long as Savage could remember. He looked exactly the same, too. Jeans, checked shirt, backwards cap. Some things just didn't change. They'd all unloaded on Rich at one time or another. The corpse found in the dumpster. The kid who'd OD'd in the crack house. The hooker beaten to an inch of her life. Rich was a good listener, and he'd heard it all.

"Well, I'll be damned." The bartender grinned. "If it isn't Detective Dalton Savage. How the heck are you?"

They shook hands. "It's Sheriff now."

"Sheriff. Glad to see you're moving up in the world." He gestured to the beer on tap. "What can I get you?"

Savage ordered, then went to join Manning who was already halfway through a Miller Light. "You want another?"

"I'm good. Just one for me tonight. Trish is cooking."

Savage glanced around to see who was there. Being a Monday, the bar was virtually empty. A group of off-duty officers sat in the corner laughing, while an old-timer nursed a beer at the other end of the bar. Nothing to worry about.

"Here's what you asked for." Manning slid two manilla folders across the bar.

"Thanks." Savage dropped them into the rucksack he'd brought along, just in case. The off-duty officers paid them no attention. The old-timer didn't even glance up. "Can you give me a run down?"

Manning shifted on his stool. "It's pretty straightforward. The kid was found in the street after a 911 call alerted the authorities. He'd been shot once in the gut. Bled out in minutes."

"What was he doing in Wash Park?"

"Nobody knows. He didn't have any stash on him, wasn't armed, didn't look like he was selling anything, including himself."

"Cellphone?"

"It was locked. We're going through the records. Nothing flagged as suspicious yet. He was a popular kid, most of the calls he made or received were from friends."

"No one from the area?"

"Don't know yet. We have to look up all the numbers to see where they're registered. It takes time."

Everything took time. "How many men are working on it?"

"Two. Gordon and Vialli."

Savage shook his head. He didn't know them. "Competent?"

"Yeah, but rookies. The LT figures if it all goes to hell, she can blame them. They're shit scared to do anything other than research at this point. Nobody wants to be thrown under the bus."

That's what Dewayne meant when he said nobody was doing anything.

"Any noise from the kid's family?"

"Yeah, for sure. The whole Five Points community is in an uproar, and who can blame 'em? I'm surprised they haven't rioted. Guess they're waiting to see which way this thing breaks."

"It's always been a powder keg ready to blow."

"Who can blame 'em? Not like we've got a stellar track record in bringing closure. You remember the old saying, a body drops and you got five more pointing in the opposite direction."

"Five Points. Different rules for a different life."

"Maybe so. Doesn't change the facts. One of their own has been killed. If we don't give them the justice they seek, they'll be taking matters into their own hands. And that's something we can't afford."

"Underserved communities don't typically trust the cops to get the job done. Simple as that. History has given them good cause not to."

"What you gonna do?" Manning asked.

"Talk to his family, for starters."

"You're gonna go to their house?"

"I know his mother, remember?" Savage had spent a long time talking to her during the trial. A strong woman, she'd worked as a seamstress for a local dry-cleaning company, raising her two kids on her own. He admired that.

"You put her eldest son away."

"I know." Still, he had to try. Mrs. Simmons had understood he'd made a judgement call based on the circumstances, even though the rest of the community blamed him for killing Justin and putting Dewayne behind bars. The sad thing was Mrs. Simmons spent her whole life trying to shield her sons from violence. Now Dewayne was serving life and Kenan was dead.

Savage winced, as if a knife had turned in his gut. Life could be tough.

*You owe me.*

Yes, he did. And he was determined to do what he could to bring Kenan's killer to justice.

For her.

# FOUR

SAVAGE SHOWED his ID and was ushered through the razor-topped gate of Colorado State Penitentiary's Maximum Security Division. Under the watchful eye of the guard tower, he walked up the paved path toward another gate, this one set at the bottom of a high concrete wall. Looking up, he felt like a character out of *Honey, I Shrunk the Kids*. The wall was at least forty feet tall, while the building beyond was five stories of sheer concrete. Grim and foreboding, it looked exactly like what it was, a secure correctional facility housing the most dangerous and high-risk offenders in the state.

Savage went through the security checkpoint and was told to leave his phone and keys, along with any other personal belongings in a locker. He could collect them on the way out. Then he was searched and finally allowed to proceed through a swivel door into a waiting area. He took a seat.

It had been six years since he had watched Dewayne Simmons leave the courtroom in handcuffs. A life sentence with the possibility of parole after twenty-seven years. That was a long time by anyone's standards. Dewayne had only served six so far. Savage wondered how it had affected him. Six years was already a long time for a scrawny, nineteen-year-old kid.

Savage's name was called, and he was led down a narrow, sterile corridor that smelled faintly of detergent to a large visiting area. This was where the prisoners met friends and family, but since Savage had arrived before general visiting hours, he and Dewayne would have the place to themselves.

It was a plain room filled with small tables, each with two chairs on either side. Everything was bolted to the floor. There were no pictures on the cream-colored walls, no windows, and no decorative touches. It was functional and emotionless. Perhaps it had to be that way to counteract the tears, sadness, and desperation expressed in the room.

Savage didn't have to wait long. The steel door leading into the bowels of the prison swung open and a giant of an African American man was led through.

Savage stared up at him. "Dewayne?"

Gone was the lanky, nervous kid, and in his place stood a massive, muscular, tattoo-covered prisoner. His arms were the size of a wrestler's, while his torso was so thick it looked superhuman. Veins bulged in his forearms and neck. He'd grown to at least six four and towered above the prison guard. The ankle and wrist chains clanged as he shuffled to the table.

"Thanks for coming," the inmate said.

The guard pushed him down into the chair. Dewayne shot him an annoyed look but sat anyway, resting his thick wrists on the table. The tattoos and prison-yard physique gave him a sinister air, threatening and dangerous.

*Don't fuck with me*, was the message, loud and clear.

Savage gave a stiff nod. The two men stared at each other for almost a full minute until the guard disappeared and left them alone. In the corner of the room, a camera mounted to the ceiling flashed red. There were eyes everywhere.

"I'm sorry about your brother," Savage said. "I remember Kenan. He was a good kid."

Grief flashed across Dewayne's face, but he controlled it well. His massive hands clenched, then relaxed. "Thanks."

"What happened?" Savage nodded to the raw scabs on the knuckles of his left hand.

"Someone was disrespecting me, that's all. Can't let that shit slide inside."

Savage nodded.

"In here you gotta earn respect."

It was clear Dewayne had done what he had to in order to survive. He was here for the duration, he couldn't afford to be soft. Savage knew what it was like inside. He'd interrogated enough prisoners and ex-cons, seen video footage on the prison wings, and heard stories that would make your hair stand on end. A violent, aggressive environment, where an accidental jostle could mean getting shanked in the exercise yard.

"Tell me what you know." Savage dispensed with the small talk. He didn't have long, and what more could he say? *Hey, sorry I got you locked up. How are you coping?*

"Kenan was shot and killed in Wash Park. That's a white neighborhood. A *wealthy* white neighborhood." Dewayne emphasized the word like it was something bad. Washington Park – or Wash Park as it was called locally – was characterized by wide, tree-lined streets, beautiful houses, and large yards and gardens. It was a suburban picket fence dream.

"You know what he was doing there?"

"Nah, man. That's what I need you to find out. It don't make sense. He had no reason to be there."

"Dewayne, I have to ask, was Kenan into anything illegal?"

Dewayne's powerful forearm muscles twitched, but he remained calm. "No way. My mama raised him right. He didn't do drugs and he wasn't a gangbanger."

Savage nodded. It wasn't that he didn't believe Dewayne, but dealing drugs could be one reason Kenan was in that area. It was possible Dewayne hadn't known that about his brother. It wasn't really something you spoke about in conversation. He'd confirm that with Mrs. Simmons when he spoke with her.

"When last did you see your brother? Did he ever visit?"

"Sometimes." The deep voice trembled. "I saw him last week. He was in a good mood. I asked him how he was doing, he said he'd got a new job. He was making money, helping put food on the table."

"You know what he was doing?"

"He was kinda vague about that, but I got the impression he was doing odd jobs for a local businessman. Some bigshot property developer. Helping out on building sites, running errands, making coffee, that type of thing. I was proud of him. It was his first real job, ya know?" Dewayne swallowed over the grief and blinked back tears. He was barely holding it together.

Savage nodded. "Do you know who he was working for?"

"A man called Guy Hollander."

Savage thought he'd misheard. "Guy Hollander?"

Dewayne frowned. "You know him?"

A surge of adrenaline made his pulse quicken. "You could say that."

*Guy freakin' Hollander.*

Of all the gangsters in Denver, it had to be *him*. Hollander had been the man responsible for flooding La Plata County with Pink Soda, the lethal drug that had killed a couple of kids and sent plenty more to the hospital.

The DEA had cracked down and gotten most of it off the street. The public safety warnings had worked. Nobody wanted to buy a kid-killing drug. The price plummeted and batches of crystals were found in drains and sewers all over the city.

Still, Hollander had never set foot in Hawk's Landing. He'd gotten his minions to do his dirty work for him. A psychopathic thug called Jonny Star had been his point man, while a heavy-fisted women-abuser named Kushner had been the enforcer. Savage and his team had brought them both down before he'd gone on paternity leave.

"How?"

"Let's just say we've got history."

"From your cop days?"

"It doesn't matter." Savage paused, thinking. If Kenan had been mixed up with Guy Hollander... Had the kid witnessed something that had got him killed? Working for a guy like that, Savage wouldn't be surprised. Secrets coursed through that man's veins.

"Odd jobs, did you say?"

"Yeah. Kenan didn't go into detail." Dewayne's gaze darkened. "You think this Hollander had something to do with his death?"

"I don't know. All I know is he's not a nice guy."

Dewayne frowned as the door opened and the guard returned to take him back to his cell. He placed a beefy hand on Savage's wrist. "What do you know about him?"

The guard hauled him to his feet.

"Detective Savage, what do you know?"

"I'll talk to you soon," Savage promised, as the guard pulled him away.

"Tell me," pleaded Dewayne, but the heavy door closed on his words and Savage was left alone in the visitors' room.

SAVAGE WANTED to run what he'd discovered past Manning, but his ex-partner would still be at work, and Savage had one last stop to make before he went back to his motel.

Mrs. Simmons lived in Five Points, a culturally diverse neighborhood northeast of downtown Denver. Home to many jazz clubs, theaters, and restaurants, it drew visitors from across the city. Back in the day, it had been the epicenter of the civil rights movement in Denver, and that spirit of activism was still alive and well. Evidence of that could be seen in the graffiti sprawled on the walls. He passed a raised fist with the letters BLM inside, and a slogan that said, "No Justice, No Peace."

Well, he was here to administer that justice.

As he pulled up outside Dewayne's mother's house, Savage noticed several people staring at him. Some through windows, others out on the street. Some furtively, others outwardly curious, even threatening. They wouldn't know who he was, wouldn't remember him as the detective who put Dewayne Simmons away – at least he hoped not – but they recognized law enforcement when they saw it. And here, that was never a good thing.

Mrs. Simmons opened the door in her nightgown, a scarf wrapped around her head. It wasn't quite six o'clock yet, but she looked ready for bed. Savage was willing to bet she'd never gotten out of it.

"Mrs. Simmons, it's Dalton Savage. I used to work for Denver PD. Your son Dewayne asked me to investigate... the shooting." He couldn't bring himself to say Kenan's name. Not in front of his grieving mother.

A tear rolled down her lined face and his heart went out to her. One son in prison, the other dead.

"I'm so sorry for your loss."

She gave a tired nod and turned around, leaving him at the door. As it was open, he stepped inside and closed it behind him.

Mrs. Simmons tottered down the hall and into the living room. It was as sparsely decorated as he remembered, if a little more worn. Still, it was cozy and well lived in. You could see two active boys had grown up here. Scuff marks on the legs of the coffee table, worn patches on the couch, soda stains on the carpet that she'd tried to scrub out but couldn't. Evidence of happier times, of life.

She gestured for him to take a seat, and he did. "You want coffee?"

"No thanks. I won't take much of your time. I'd just like to ask you some questions about Kenan, if you're feeling up to it."

She hesitated, then gave a little sigh. "Ask your questions, sonny. I don't know how much use I'll be." Dewayne's mother was nothing like the woman he remembered. Back then, she'd had a sparkle in her eye that her hard life hadn't been able to erase. There'd been strength in her sinewy arms, a bounce in her step. Now she was nothing but a shell. The last six years had seen to that.

He ground his teeth. Even the most stalwart people got worn down eventually. Losing both sons would do that to you. For a split second, he wondered how he'd feel if it were a teenage Connor taken away to prison. Or worse, gunned down in the street. The pain that sliced through him was so intense, he caught his breath.

Savage let it out, refocusing. "When was the last time you saw Kenan?"

Her features pinched with sadness. "The day he died. He told me he was going to run some errands."

"Did he say for whom?"

"No." A desolate shake of her head.

"Did you know he had a new job?"

It changed to a nod. "He was happy about that."

"Do you know who he was working for?"

"A businessman in the city. How he got that job, I'll never know, but he was earning good money."

Savage nodded. He was willing to bet that Kenan's errands weren't strictly legit, but he didn't say that to the boy's mother. Rumor had it that Hollander had his grubby fingers in a lot of very shady pies.

"He was shot in Wash Park. Had Kenan ever gone there before? Did he know someone who lived there?" Another shake of her head. The details didn't matter to her. He wasn't coming back, that's all she cared about.

"Okay." This was a dead end. She didn't know anything, and was too consumed by grief to remember, even if she did. Savage got to his feet. "I'll leave you in peace now, Mrs. Simmons –"

"You shot Justin."

He stared at her. She was looking at him as if seeing him for the first time. Like the synapses in her grieving brain had somehow connected and shaken her out of her stupor.

"That's right. I'm Officer Savage."

"You put my boy in prison."

He grimaced. "Your boy robbed a burger joint, Mrs. Simmons." He hoped they weren't going to rehash what happened six years ago.

"That might be true, but he didn't shoot that lady." She seemed to be looking straight through him, into the past.

"Then who did? Because according to the CCTV tapes, it was your son and his friend."

"Wasn't them," she reiterated, shaking her head. "They were both home with me when it happened. I told the judge that, but he didn't believe me."

Unfortunately, Dewayne's mother hadn't made the most reliable witness. She'd almost pleaded with the judge about her son's innocence, and it just made her look desperate. The jury hadn't bought it. Neither had the state prosecutor.

"Unless we can prove it, there's nothing I can do."

"They never found the gun."

He glanced back at her. "No, they didn't. That's right."

"You find the gun, you find the shooter."

The gun was probably long gone by now. Six years later. Sold, destroyed, filed down, thrown in the river. It would be impossible to find. He was the first to admit there'd been holes in the case. The men in all four robberies had been wearing masks, making it impossible to identify them. All they had to go on was height and weight. A so-called expert had come in to analyze the way they walked, their gestures, and so on, and declared the same perpetrators had committed all four robberies.

Experts weren't infallible. It was circumstantial, at best.

Not to mention the pellet gun. Why the hell had Justin had that? Where were the real guns? Where was the weapon used to kill Helen Ridley? The prosecution had claimed the defendant had disposed of it after the shooting, which is why they'd used pellet guns in the fourth and final robbery.

Then there were the alibis for the first three robberies. Dewayne and Justin claimed they'd been at Mrs. Simmons's house at the time of the third robbery, when Helen Ridley had been fatally shot. The first and second were less clear. They'd professed to be out with friends. Doing nothing in particular. It was sufficiently weak to be true.

"Only the guilty need alibis," Dewayne's defense attorney had told the jury, but it had fallen on deaf ears. Their minds had been made up.

Savage had asked Dewayne's lawyer to request a continuance. Time to verify the boy's alibi and dig deeper into the other robberies, but he'd been denied. The state prosecutor was up for re-election and wanted to close this case before they went to the polls. Dewayne's fate was sealed.

"I can't reopen the case, Mrs. Simmons. I don't work for Denver PD anymore."

She looked at him over her glasses. "You don't?"

"No, I'm a Sheriff now."

Confusion clouded her face. "Sheriff?"

"That's right, ma'am."

"Then what you doin' here? Why you helping us?"

"Dewayne asked me to."

Her eyes narrowed. "You always do what a man you put behind bars asks you to do?"

He had no answer for that one.

She nodded slowly. "You believe him, don't you? You know he didn't kill that lady. You know it as well as I do."

# FIVE

SAVAGE STOOD in the street where Kenan had been shot and turned around in a slow circle. It was wide and leafy like most of the roads around here, flanked by expensive houses with well-tended lawns. He held the case folder Manning had given him. It contained the ME's report, a forensic analysis and crime scene photographs.

Savage surveyed the blinding white facades, neat shutters and mowed lawns. Suburban bliss. From the corner of his eye, he caught the movement of a curtain, the flick of a blind. Which of these onlookers had made the 911 call?

According to the report, it had come in at nine minutes past 2 a.m. on Wednesday morning. If the medical examiner was correct, Kenan had only just been shot at that time, which meant there was a good chance that whoever placed the call had seen the shooting.

He'd studied the file in depth over breakfast at a diner near his hotel. The boy had already been dead when the ambulance arrived at the scene. He'd lost too much blood and could not be saved. The ME put the time of death between midnight and 2 a.m.

The positioning of the body piqued Savage's interest. He carefully examined the diagram, comparing the meticulously drafted sketch to one of the photographs taken at the crime scene. Both sources indicated that Kenan was discovered lying on his back. It seemed to be an accurate depiction of the crime scene.

Savage had read the reports. Forensic analysis of the blood spatter revealed something intriguing, the absence of radial dispersion, suggesting that Kenan had not been killed in that spot. The blood spatter was concentrated solely on the body, with no evidence of it on the surrounding asphalt. If he'd been murdered where the sketch and photographs indicated blood would've been found outside of his body.

He scrutinized the photograph in his hand, focusing in particular on the gunshot wound to the abdomen. The ballistics report indicated the shot was taken at close range. No shell casings, or bullet fragments were located at the scene. Using only the entry and exit wounds, it was determined likely to have been a .40 caliber round. Without a firearm to compare it to, everything was open to interpretation.

Savage was certain of one thing. Forensics told the tale. Kenan was definitely killed somewhere else and finding it would be critical.

"He was shot somewhere else and dumped here," Savage muttered, as he stared at the dark stain on the ground. This was where he'd bled out. He gazed up and down the street. Why here? In upper-middle-class suburbia?

Something about the 911 call was strange too. The caller had used a stolen cell phone registered to a finance guy living nearby. The financier had told officers it had been stolen a couple of days prior to the murder. He hadn't known exactly when, but he'd suspected the perpetrator pickpocketed the device while he was walking toward the mall. What kind of person uses a stolen cell phone to call in a dead body? A thief with a conscience? Savage wished he had a transcript of the call, but that had been left out of the file. As soon as he got back, he'd get Manning to request it.

The police had tried tracing the phone, but it was off. Probably destroyed by now.

A shadow appeared at a window opposite to where he was standing. He could tell by the silhouette that a woman was staring at him.

That was as good a place as any to start. He strode toward the house, and the shadow disappeared. Undeterred, Savage rapped on the front door. Three times. Hard. It left the person inside with little doubt that he'd seen her and wanted to talk.

The door opened a crack. A woman with a chic blonde bob gazed up at him. "Yes?"

"I'm Sheriff Savage." He held up his ID. She wouldn't know he was out of his jurisdiction, not unless she looked really closely at his card. "You are?"

She squinted at the card, then back at him. "Veronica Halston."

Pocketing his ID, he said, "Veronica, I'd like to ask you a few questions about what happened here last week."

She brushed a hand through her hair. "This isn't a good time. I'm about to go out."

"It won't take long." He didn't budge.

She sighed and opened the door. He saw she was wearing leggings and a T-shirt that said, 'Strong is the new skinny'. "Okay, but you'll have to make it quick. I have a yoga class at eleven."

Savage noticed a gym bag and a bottle of water by the door. He gave a curt nod and stepped inside. "Thank you."

They went into a wide living room decorated with sheer curtains, spot lighting, and a great arching floor lamp. She gestured to a salmon-colored leather sofa and a matching armchair. "Please, sit down."

Savage eased his long frame into the armchair feeling like he was sinking into a conch shell. Veronica gazed questioningly at him.

"Were you home last Tuesday night?"

Veronica got straight to the point. "You mean the night of the shooting?"

"Yes." Technically it was Wednesday morning, but for ease of questioning he stuck to Tuesday night.

"We were all here," she confirmed. "My husband, my daughter, and I. But none of us heard anything. That's what I told the officer who came by the next day." Denver PD would have sent a couple of juniors to canvas the neighborhood. "It was late, and our rooms are on the other side of the house overlooking the garden."

"You didn't hear a shot, or a loud bang?"

"Nothing like that." She shook her head and made a tutting sound with her tongue. "This is normally such a safe area. I still can't believe there was a shooting right outside on our street. I worry about my daughter going out now."

"I'm sure it's an isolated event, ma'am."

She didn't look convinced. He got the feeling there was something she wasn't saying.

"Did something else happen?" he pressed.

"Of course not." Too quick. She glanced at her wristwatch, impatient to leave.

"Did you know the man who died? Kenan Simmons."

There was a pause.

"*I* didn't know him, no."

His pulse escalated. "But you know someone who did?"

She gave a dramatic sigh. "Okay, I should have told this to the other officer, but I only found out two days ago. Claudia from down the street saw a young African American man walking back from the bus stop with Silvia's daughter." She rolled her eyes. "Isobel is, how should I put it – troubled."

"Troubled?"

"She's going through that rebellious phase. Sneaking out, smoking pot, even got a nose ring. You know how young girls these days are." He didn't, but he got a good visual from what she'd said.

"Is it the same man who was shot?"

"I don't know. She said it was, but, you know..." A shrug.

Savage decided he didn't like Veronica Halston very much.

"Could you give me Claudia's address?"

"Sure." She walked over to a bureau and opened a drawer. Taking out a small notepad and pen, she wrote down the name and address, tore it off, and gave it to him.

*Claudia Dorrington. 239 Oleander Crescent.*

---

THE OLEANDER after which the street had been named was brown and shriveled, and the petals lay like rotting confetti on the sidewalk. They were beginning to smell too, but he guessed the Public Works Department would send a street sweeper along to suck them up and dispose of them. Perhaps they'd clean the blood stain off the road too? Residents like Veronica Halford wouldn't want to be reminded of what had happened here.

Claudia's house was larger and grander than Veronica's. Victorian in style, it stood majestically at the end of the street as if casting a watchful eye over the neighborhood. The doorbell chimed inside the house as Savage pressed the small button. He waited for some time before the front door opened.

"Can I help you?" asked a robust woman with a short, cropped hairstyle and capable expression.

"I hope so. I'm Sheriff Savage. I'm investigating the shooting that occurred here last week. Are you Claudia Dorrington?"

She nodded. "Oh, yes. That was terrible. I still can't believe it."

"I believe you knew the victim, Kenan Simmons?"

"Was that his name?"

Savage nodded, his face impassive. Claudia made no attempt to let him into the house so he asked, "Can you tell me how you knew him?"

"Well, I didn't know him, not really. I mean I saw him once, walking Isobel back from the bus stop. I noticed because... Well, you just do, don't you?"

Savage didn't comment. "How do you know it was the same person?"

"I saw his picture in the paper and it looked just like him."

Savage sighed. He could be going down a rabbit hole here. Eyewitness accounts were notoriously unreliable. Still, so far it was his only lead.

"Where does Isobel live?"

"Bougainvillea Close." Savage was detecting a definite theme here.

"Number?"

"403. But she won't be there now. She's at school."

"Which school would that be, Mrs. Dorrington? What's Isobel's last name?"

"George Washington School. It's Isobel Drake."

That was all he needed.

---

ISOBEL DRAKE WOULD HAVE BEEN PRETTY if it wasn't for the nose ring, pink hair, and smudged makeup that made her look like she'd been punched in both eyes. Dressed in a black, tight-fitting skirt and a heavy metal T-shirt, she was a perfect example of a rebellious teenager.

Surprised at being taken out of class to speak to a member of law enforcement, she was subdued and wary. Her brown, kohl-rimmed eyes fixed on him as he perched on the edge of the desk in the empty classroom they'd been allocated. He noticed her eyes were an unusual almond shape.

He studied her, unsure how to begin. Teenage girls weren't his forte. "I'm sorry to disrupt your lesson. This won't take long."

She shrugged. "Take your time. I'm in no hurry to get back."

He took a photograph of Kenan Simmons from the police file. Wearing jeans, a T-shirt, and a smile, he looked happy and carefree. The complete antithesis to the crime scene photo hidden behind it in the folder. "Do you know this man?"

She stared at it for so long, her eyes watered. Or maybe it was tears. Then she blinked and looked away. "No."

*Liar.*

He chose to ignore that reply and push on. "Someone saw you two walking home together from the bus stop. Were you friends?" She kept her eyes fixed on the side wall, her even white teeth gnawing at her lower lip. He waited, letting the silence draw out. Eventually, she gave a little nod.

"I'm sorry for your loss," he said quietly.

She sniffed. The heavy make-up was probably supposed to make her look hard, like she didn't care. But to Savage, she appeared vulnerable.

"Were you close?"

"It's not what you think." Her voice was hoarse.

"What was it then?"

"We were friends. I met Kenan at the Community Center. I work there on weekends."

He raised an eyebrow. Isobel didn't strike him as being community minded. It just went to show how little he knew.

"He was taking a computer class." She rubbed her eyes, smearing them even more. "I was helping out. One of my teachers gives the class."

"You get paid?"

She nodded. "Not a lot, but it helps."

Savage was beginning to like this misunderstood girl with her pink hair, huge dark eyes, and hidden facets.

"Where's the Community Center?"

"Congress Park. It's not far from here." She paused, as if in thought. Savage waited, sensing more to come. "Kenan came up to me after class one day and asked a question. We got talking. Turns out we had a lot in common."

"How so?"

"His brother was in prison for armed robbery. My father did a stint for fraud. I know what it's like having a family member inside." She talked like an old pro. Still, the stigma must have been great. Perhaps that's why she'd dyed her hair and got piercings. If you give people a reason to dislike you, they might not focus on her convict father.

"He's out now? Your father, I mean?"

"Yeah, he got out ten months ago." She wrapped her arms around her body like she was hugging herself. "It was strange. We had to get used to having him back again."

"That would be an adjustment."

She nodded. "Anyway, the night Kenan was shot... We'd been out. Nowhere special, just a club near where he lives. Kenan caught the bus back with me, to make sure I was okay. He was a gentleman like that."

Or he really liked her.

"Did your parents know?"

"That I went out? No way. It was a school night. They'd kill me if they found out."

"Is that why you didn't tell them about Kenan?"

"They'd just assume he was a bad influence. He wasn't. It was my choice to go. That wouldn't be fair to Kenan."

Savage studied her. Stubborn chin, pouty mouth, determined gaze. She was a good kid. Pity her folks didn't see it. "Talk me through what happened once you got back."

"There's nothing to tell. Kenan walked me to the back and waited while I climbed back up the trellis and in the window. Then he left. I waved as he walked down the street."

"You saw him walk away?"

"Yeah. He waved back."

Savage scratched his head. None of this made sense. Kenan did have a reason to be in Wash Park. Isobel. So why was he shot?

Could it have been a random attack? A case of being in the wrong place at the wrong time? Except Kenan wasn't shot on the street. He was shot in a house or a vehicle and then thrown out onto the street. That didn't signify an impulsive shooting. That signified premeditated murder.

Savage thought for a moment. "Was he meeting anyone after he left you?"

"I don't know. If he was, he didn't tell me. I thought he was going home. I went to bed and the next thing I know, the whole neighborhood is freaking out because someone was shot. I only found out the next day that it was Kenan." She gulped back a sob.

Savage frowned as he processed this new information. Something had happened after Kenan had left Isobel. But what?

"I'll let you get back to class now." Savage got to his feet. He needed to think about this. None of it made any sense. "Thanks for your time."

She gave him a long look. "You will find out who did this, won't you? Kenan was a decent guy. He didn't deserve what happened."

Savage couldn't agree more.

# SIX

DENVER PD WAS STRANGELY quiet when Savage arrived later that afternoon. A shooting at a business park and a seven-vehicle pile-up on the freeway meant the department had their hands full. Only Manning and the admin staff were left at the station.

"Hey, Dalton. Come into my office. Take a seat."

Savage grinned. Manning's "office" was a four-by-six cubicle on the far side of the squad room by the window. At least he had a view, if you could call it that. Austere gray buildings surrounding the street below. Savage remembered looking out at a view just like this one for nearly ten years. How could Manning stand it? He thought about the pretty town of Hawk's Landing, the rolling landscape and the distant ice-capped mountain peaks, hazy in the morning sun, and felt a pang of longing so strong it made his gut clench.

"How are you getting on?" Manning interrupted his thoughts.

"Okay, but I need everything you got on Guy Hollander." It was time to get down to business. Savage wanted to solve this case and get back to La Plata County, where he belonged. Where Becca and his son were. Denver wasn't his home anymore.

Manning frowned. “Hollander. Now there’s a name I haven’t heard for a while. What’s he got to do with this?”

“Kenan Simmons worked for him.”

“You’re kidding me?”

“Yeah, according to his brother, Dewayne, the kid was doing odd jobs, running errands.”

Manning pursed his lips.

“Also, can we get a copy of the 911 recording?”

“Wasn’t there a transcript in the file?”

“No, I couldn't find it.”

Manning shook his head. “One of the team must have it. They’re probably working the witness angle. I’ll get them to send another copy over.”

Savage pulled up a chair.

“You’re not going to find much on Hollander,” Manning continued. “I know he’s got a reputation, but he keeps his nose clean. We’ve looked into him several times over the years, but nothing's stuck. His businesses are legit, he’s big on philanthropy, and does a lot for the community. He even donates to the Police Benevolent Fund, and I think he plays tennis with the captain.”

“Sounds like an all-round nice guy,” Savage smirked.

“Honestly, man. I’m serious. You won't dig up any dirt on him.”

Savage didn’t reply. Instead, he pulled his chair closer to Manning’s. “Let’s do a search anyway.”

They spent the next half hour going over Guy Hollander’s criminal history, looking through Denver’s internal report system. They did a secondary search for any complaint or non-criminal incident report mentioning him. There were a few instances, but as Manning had said, nothing that would directly connect him in any way.

In one report, an auto shop owner accused Hollander of stealing from the company. Selling off the assets, as he put it. “One of Hollander’s businesses owned over 51% of the company, so he had every right to sell the equipment,” Manning pointed out.

In another, Hollander had allegedly threatened a man's family. "Turns out the guy owed Hollander money and couldn't repay."

"Loan sharking?" Savage asked.

Manning shrugged. "Not according to the detective on the case. Hollander gave the guy a job in one of his companies so he could pay off the loan. It was all above board. A misunderstanding, the guy said."

Savage grunted. He scanned the notes attached to the last report and saw the investigating officer was none other than Zebadiah Swift. "I see Zeb was in charge of this case."

"Why does that name ring a bell?"

"He was the cop who took out that shooter at the mall back in 2012. The escaped fugitive."

"You've got a good memory."

"I was there, remember?"

"Oh, yeah." Manning frowned as he thought back. "Didn't you have a standoff with the perp?"

"Zeb arrived just in time," Savage said grimly. That had been a damn close call. The shooter had had Savage and a member of the public pinned in the parking lot. A couple more seconds and they would have been dead. Zeb snuck up from behind and shot the fugitive in the head. Game over.

Manning rubbed his stubble. "Wasn't Zeb investigated by Internal Affairs? I seem to remember something about missing drug money?"

"There was an internal investigation, yeah."

"I can't remember the outcome."

"Zeb was cleared, but he resigned after that." They hadn't found the money, but the general consensus was that Zeb had taken it.

"What happened to him anyway?"

"He lives in La Plata County now. Runs a trailer park."

"I see you're still here, Dalton." Hagan's frosty voice rang out from across the squad room. Savage swore the temperature decreased several degrees.

He got to his feet. "I was just leaving."

"Solved the case yet?" There were some sniggers from a group of detectives who'd walked in with her.

"I'm working on it."

Hagan frowned. "Go home, Dalton. We've got this. This is not your case."

"I spoke to the victim's mother." Savage walked up to Hagan and stopped in front of her. He was so close he could smell her perfume. "Something your guys forgot to do. Did you know Kenan Simmons was working for Guy Hollander?"

Hagan's eyes narrowed. "Leave Hollander out of this. He had nothing to do with the kid's murder."

"You can't know that until you check him out. Does he have an alibi for the time of the shooting? Has anyone even questioned him?"

"I'm warning you, Dalton. Back off. Hollander is a respected figure in this community."

"Doesn't mean he's not involved." Savage strode past her out of the room.

Behind him, he heard her snap, "Clinton, I don't want him back here or I'll arrest him for interference. You got that?"

Savage didn't hang around to hear his friend's reply.

---

WHEN ZEB eventually answered the phone, he sounded tense and out of breath. "Yeah?"

"Hey, it's Savage." He'd called several times over the last hour, but this was the first time the ex-cop had answered.

"Savage. Man, this isn't a good time."

"Something wrong?"

The man's panting filled the line before he continued. "I've got a situation here."

Savage frowned. "What kind of situation?"

"Billy Ray just beat up on one of my girls."

"Shit. Is she okay?"

"No, she's not fucking okay. I'm waiting for an ambulance."

"I'll call the sheriff's station and get them to send someone over."

"Why can't you come out? Still on daddy leave?"

"I'm in Denver."

More heavy breathing.

"Is Billy Ray still there?" Savage asked.

"No, he got the hell out once he realized what he'd done. He's holding up at Mac's Roadhouse." The Roadhouse was an outlaw biker bar on the Durango Road owned by Rosalie Weston, who also happened to be the President of the Crimson Angels Motorcycle Club.

"Is he one of theirs?"

"Yeah."

Zeb also rode with the Crimson Angels from time to time. A recreational member, as he put it, except Savage knew there was no such thing. It wasn't that type of club. You were either in or out. This put Zeb in an awkward position. A lot depended on how the girl was doing.

Savage hesitated. "Is she going to make it?"

"I don't know. She's unconscious. He did a number on her."

"I hope she makes it," Savage murmured, "or Billy Ray is going to be up on a murder charge."

"You don't have to tell me." Zeb knew the drill.

Sirens filled the background.

"I'll send one of my deputies over to take your statement and follow up on the girl. Give her an opportunity to press charges."

"Sure." He sounded weary. "Oh, what did you want to ask me?"

"Call me later, once you've seen to the girl."

Zeb grunted a reply and hung up.

For a small town, Hawk's Landing had more than its fair share of action. He hoped his deputies could handle this one. Rosalie and the Crimson Angels weren't going to hand over one of their own. Not unless there was an actual warrant out for his arrest. Sighing, he placed a call to the Hawk's Landing Sheriff's Office.

Sinclair, answered.

"Hey, it's Savage. I just spoke to Zeb out at Hidden Gem trailer park. Get someone over there now!" He told her what had happened.

"On my way. Thorpe is at Mrs. Ballentine's farm. Her chickens escaped again. She's convinced someone is deliberately releasing them from the coop." It all sounded achingly familiar.

Suddenly homesick, Savage decided to give Becca a call. "How are you and Connor doing?"

"We miss you."

His chest constricted. "I miss you guys too."

"How's Denver?" She sounded inordinately far away.

"Same as always." Cold. Dirty. Depressing. But he didn't tell her any of that. After all, it had been his choice to come here.

"Have you spoken to Dewayne?"

"Yeah, I visited him at the correctional facility. He gave me a lead. Remember I told you about a man called Guy Hollander? He was involved in that construction project out near the reservation."

"I remember," she replied, quietly. "What about him?"

"Kenan worked for him."

She was silent before saying, "Do you think this Hollander was involved in his death?"

"It's an angle I'm looking into."

"Be careful, Dalton," she said, a note of anxiety in her voice. "Promise me you'll be careful."

"I will. Don't worry." He frowned. It wasn't like Becca to let her emotions get the better of her. "Hey, are you okay?"

"I just don't like you being so far away. I've got a bad feeling about this. Maybe you should come home." Before he'd left, she'd said she was okay with it. That she could manage a week or two without him.

"Don't worry. I'll be fine," he said. "I owe it to this kid to figure out what's going on. I owe it to his family."

She sighed. "Just take care, okay?"

"I will."

# SEVEN

IT WAS NEARLY midnight when Zeb sent a message. "You awake?"

Savage immediately called him back. "How's your girl?"

"Stable." Relief filled the other man's voice. "Looks like she's going to make it."

"That's great news. Has one of my deputies spoken to her?"

"Yeah, Suzi's decided not to press charges."

A heavy silence descended. "I see."

"She's scared, Savage. Those guys are her best customers. She rats on them, her career is over."

Some career, whoring for Zeb. "Maybe that's a good thing."

"She'd be out of work. You know girls like Suzi. Small town, no real skills. What else would she do? At least she's getting paid and can put food on the table. This way she still has a choice."

Zeb had a point. These girls were local, some even lived at the trailer park. They made good money working for Zeb, and he ran a tight ship. His girls were clean, and he looked after them. As far as favorable working conditions went, it was right up there.

Savage sighed.

"Now what the hell are you doing back in Denver?" Zeb asked. "I thought you'd left that place behind. Nothing but bad memories there."

He was right about that.

"Remember that kid I shot in that Burger King robbery?" His throat tightened just saying it.

Zeb had still been around at that point, although working in a different department. "You put the other one away for life."

"He asked for my help."

"From beyond the grave?"

"No, dumbass. The one in prison. Dewayne Simmons."

Zeb chuckled and despite everything, Savage felt the tension ease, just a little bit.

"His kid brother was shot in Wash Park last week. Bled out on the street."

"Jesus."

"He wants me to look into it."

There was a brief pause while Zeb assimilated the details. "Wash Park?"

"Yeah."

"Wasn't Dewayne Simmons – ?"

"Yeah. He's from Five Points."

"What was he doing there?"

"That's the mystery. Nobody knows, and Denver PD are shit scared to do anything in case it snowballs. The Five Points community is demanding answers, and rightly so."

"Sounds like trouble," Zeb muttered. "Maybe you should leave this one alone."

"I can't. I promised Dewayne."

"It's not your fault his buddy died, Savage. You do know that, don't you? He pulled on you. How the hell were you supposed to know it wasn't a real gun? Any one of us would have done exactly the same thing." Savage knew he was right, but that didn't make it any easier to stomach.

"Kenan, the kid brother, worked for Guy Hollander."

The silence dragged out for longer. Eventually, Zeb said, "Now I *know* you should leave it alone."

"What can you tell me about him?"

"He's bad news, Dalton. Seriously, you don't want to mess with him."

"He might have nothing to do with the shooting," Savage said. "I just want to rule him out."

Zeb cleared his throat. "Guy Hollander and shooting are terms that often go hand in hand."

"That's why I need to know what you know."

Zeb sighed. "Okay, here's what I can remember. Hollander turned up in Denver about ten years ago. You were in Homicide back then so you wouldn't have come across him. I was in Organized Crime and he was a newcomer, fresh on the scene and causing waves."

"In what way?"

"Just ripples at first. He was from Philly, I think, and had money. I don't know where it came from, but he set himself up as a kind of venture capitalist, investing in local projects – for a share of the profits, of course. Then the rumors started. He'd muscle in on burgeoning businesses and start selling off the assets, stripping the companies. When the owners complained, he'd withdraw funding, leaving them with a bankrupt business. Most foreclosed, some he bought out and sold. One guy, a father of five, put a gun in his mouth and ate a bullet."

"Couldn't Organized Crime do anything about it?"

"It was all above board. His business interests were legit. There was nothing the local business owners could do. Of course, Hollander had other companies too, everything from venture capitalism to community investment. He did a lot for local charities, ingratiating himself with the mayor and other local politicians."

Savage wondered why he'd never heard of him before this year. He supposed ten years ago he'd had his hands full in the Homicide Division and after that, he'd quit the force for the greener pastures of Hawk's Landing.

"By the time I left, he was playing golf with the Police Commissioner. They belong to the same country club."

Savage was beginning to understand Hagan's reluctance to disturb that particular viper's nest. As Commanding Officer of the Homicide Unit, she answered to the Division Chief of Investigations. From there it was a few short steps to the Chief of Police.

"Every now and then a dead body would turn up that we linked to one of his organizations, but nothing was ever proven. Hollander is a smart man, Dalton. He has people to do his dirty work. Loyal people. Even if he was involved in your boy's shooting, there won't be any evidence. You're wasting your time."

Savage contemplated this. "No one is untouchable, Zeb."

"I think you'll find this guy is the exception."

Savage muttered a quick goodbye to the other man, then sat in his hotel room and scowled at his phone. Zeb's words pissed him off. No one was above the law. Or if they were, they damn well shouldn't be. What the hell were they all doing otherwise? Wasting their goddamn time? He ground his teeth.

*Too bad, Mr. Hollander. Your life is about to get up-ended.*

Savage still hadn't forgotten the role the mobster had played in disrupting his quiet county town earlier in the year. Bringing in lethal drugs that'd harmed the kids, attempting to take over the local drug distribution network, going after the Crimson Angels' Mexican connections. All of which other people had taken the fall for. Jonny Star, Hollander's point-man in Hawk's Landing, had been arrested with the rest of his thugs bringing drugs across the border. Kushner, his enforcer on the construction site, had gone down for murder. Douglas Connelly, who'd gone to Hollander for money to fund his venture, had lost everything. It was time Hollander learned his actions had consequences.

---

THE NEXT MORNING, Savage went to visit Derek P. Edwards, the auto shop owner who'd accused Guy Hollander of destroying his business. The retired mechanic lived in a single-story bungalow in Arvada, a quaint, old-American style town twenty minutes from Denver.

As Savage pulled up, he spotted a man of about sixty mowing the front lawn. The shock of white hair showed no sign of thinning, and the man's lean, wiry build pushed the lawn mower across the grass with ease. He stopped the mower and glanced up as Savage got out of the car.

"Mr. Edwards?"

"Who wants to know?" Tanned, rugged skin, with wrinkled eyes that were used to squinting into the sun. Edwards wiped his hands on his jeans.

"I'm Sheriff Savage. I'm investigating a homicide on behalf of Denver PD, and I'd like to ask you some questions about a man called Guy Hollander."

His face turned thunderous. "That bastard."

Savage gave a sympathetic nod. "I heard what happened."

"He destroyed me. I lost everything because of that crooked scumbag. My business, my house. My wife." Stormy eyes glared at Savage.

"I'm sorry. Will you tell me what happened?"

He swiped a bead of sweat from his forehead. "What's the point? Ain't nothing you can do about it."

"I'm just trying to get a feel for who Mr. Hollander is."

"A ruthless criminal is who he is."

"Can we go inside?"

Edwards gave a curt nod, spun around, and marched into the house.

Savage followed.

It was cooler inside, not that it was a particularly warm day, but the sun was out, which was a change. The interior was practical and functional with wooden floors, a shoe rack in the hall, a plain light fixture in the ceiling, but Savage could see it lacked a woman's touch.

There were no pictures on the walls, no vases of flowers or hall cabinets covered with photo frames.

Edwards led him into an equally sparse kitchen and gestured for him to sit down. It was neat and clean, with no dirty dishes in the sink. Savage pulled out a chair from under the kitchen table and sat down, while Edwards got two beers out of the fridge. He offered one to Savage.

"No thanks. I'm on duty."

That was nonsense of course. He wasn't on the clock, he answered to no one but himself out here. Still, force of habit wouldn't let him drink while he was working.

Edwards had no such qualms and pried the lid off the bottle before taking a long pull. Mowing the lawn was thirsty work. He set the drink on the table and lifted his gaze to Savage. "What you want to know?"

"Tell me about how you met Mr. Hollander?"

"He came to me. Somehow, he knew I needed money, and he approached me with the offer of an investment in exchange for a share in the company. He'd be my silent partner."

"And you agreed?"

"I was at a critical stage in the business that demanded cash. I was expanding. So yeah, I said yes. The bank had turned me down for a loan, so I jumped at the chance." He sucked air through his teeth as if the recollection made him cringe. "I was stupid."

"Why is that?"

"I didn't do due diligence. I took him for his word. He showed me a portfolio of other businesses he'd invested in through his company." He frowned. "Apollo Investments, they were called. They appeared sound, so we signed a contract. I gave him a percent of the business for a hundred-thousand-dollar investment."

"What happened next?"

"I began expanding. Bought more land for another site, purchased more equipment." Savage nodded to keep him talking. "Except someone else wanted the land we'd bought and was offering more. Twice what it was worth, in my opinion. Hollander sold it straight away. The money didn't go into the business, it went into his pocket. When I complained, he told me to consider it his first repayment. That's when I began to realize what kind of guy Hollander was." He glanced down at his weathered hands and dirty fingernails, stained with decades of motor oil and grease.

"It got worse. He began buying expensive equipment from suppliers who trusted me to pay on credit. When I couldn't, he assured me he had it covered. But in reality, he was selling off the new equipment and pocketing the money. He's a thief, Sheriff Savage. Plain and simple."

"Did you try to take legal action?"

"I tried, but I couldn't afford the legal fees. Also, as a shareholder, he wasn't without rights. I knew it would be pointless going to court. He had me over a barrel."

Savage grimaced. "So, you sold the company?"

"I had to declare bankruptcy. Hardest thing I ever did. I walked away from a business my father built from the ground up, thanks to that dirty bastard."

"I'm sorry to hear that." How Guy Hollander lived with himself, Savage had no idea.

"My wife left me because all of a sudden we had no income. She'd become used to a certain standard of living and wasn't prepared to slum it with me." He shook his head. "The real shock was realizing all I was to her was a paycheck."

Savage looked around. "You seem to have gotten back on your feet."

"Barely. I grew up here in Denver, so I got a job as a hiking guide in the mountains. They're filled with hiking trails, as I'm sure you know. In my spare time, I worked as a mechanic, fixing cars. Last year, I bought this place. It's nothing compared to the house I used to have, but it's comfortable and I get by."

Savage gave an admiring nod. Edwards was nothing if not resilient. What happened to him would have felled most people. Some would have turned to drink, given up on life, on trying to earn a living. Ended up on handouts from the government or turned to crime in order to survive. But not Derek P. Edwards. He'd worked two jobs until he'd gotten back on his feet.

"Again, I'm sorry for what happened." Savage said tightly. "Hollander shouldn't have been allowed to get away with that."

"Damn right he shouldn't have, but that's how bent the politics is in this city. He's got police officers, lawyers, even judges in his pocket."

Savage studied him. Edwards looked like a smart guy. A resilient guy. "You don't strike me as the type of man who'd give up that easily."

Edwards grew somber. "A week after I contacted a lawyer, my daughter got run off the road. She narrowly escaped with her life. I couldn't say it was Hollander for sure, but they never caught the asshole who did it. I took it as a warning. After that, I figured it was better to walk away."

"I understand."

Edwards clenched his fists on the table. "If it was just me, I'd have gone after the bastard, but family is too important to mess with. I have two daughters."

Savage nodded. He got it. In fact, maybe he'd do the same under the same circumstances. Then again, maybe not. Hollander deserved taking down, but Savage wasn't sure he was the guy to do it. He didn't have that long in Denver, and his main focus was Kenan's murder. Not Hollander's criminal network. But if the two somehow aligned, then things might be different. As of right now, he had no proof Hollander was involved in Kenan's shooting.

Savage had a feeling that if he kept digging, that might change.

# EIGHT

GUY HOLLANDER WAS HAVING a bad day. That damn kid's murder was all over the six o'clock news. They were protesting in Five Points. The community wanted answers. They wanted to know who'd killed the boy and why the police weren't doing anything about it.

Thankfully, his name hadn't been mentioned. The last thing he needed were the dicks coming around and questioning him – not at this strategic point in his business.

Turning to his stunning executive assistant, he said, "Susan, we didn't have that kid on the system, did we?" A failed model, he'd recruited her right out of business school. Unlike most models, she actually had a brain. He paid her a good salary, more than what she was worth, but then it wasn't really her expertise he was paying for. It was her loyalty.

Hollander liked to look at beautiful women. Looking was fine, but he never allowed himself to touch. That wasn't to say he wasn't tempted. But an affair would give his enemies ammunition. It would put everything he'd worked for, everything he'd built, at risk. So, despite many propositions from the women he employed, he always declined.

"No, sir. He was a casual employee. We never put them on the system."

"Casual employee" was the name given to the staff employed in the illegal parts of Hollander's business empire. The drug running, the racketeering, the prostitution. They were all off the books. Of course, he wasn't directly involved in any of those aspects of the business, but he did demand regular updates from his Board of Directors – the men he hired to oversee those activities.

Speaking of the Board, Lenny "the Lizard" Musgrave had been involved in some freak multi-vehicle accident on the freeway and Hollander was still waiting to hear if he'd survived or not. The hospital wasn't giving out any information on the victims, not until they'd identified them and informed their next of kin.

The fuck-up was that Lizard had been transporting the proceeds of last night's illegal betting racket out of the Ridgewater Casino. If the cops confiscated his vehicle and found the funds, Hollander's name was bound to come up in the investigation. He was part-owner of the casino.

Hollander went into the office and closed the door. That would not go down well with the Caruso brothers. They didn't appreciate fuckups.

There weren't many people Guy Hollander feared in this world, but Frank Caruso was at least one. Even as kids, Frank had scared him. It wasn't just his mean streak, although that could be pretty bad. No, it was the emptiness in his eyes. The total lack of empathy. Hollander suspected his friend might be a bona fide psychopath. He remembered once, they'd found a dog lying on the road. It had been hit by a car. Hollander had wanted to take the poor thing to the vet. He liked dogs. But Frank had told him to leave it. It was dying anyway, there was nothing the vet could do to save it.

So they'd stood there for nearly an hour and watched this animal die. The incident had affected Hollander, giving him nightmares. He'd been ten years old. Frank, on the other hand, had a strange smile on his lips the whole time.

One of the reasons Hollander had left Philadelphia was to get away from Frank. The city wasn't big enough for the both of them. Hollander was smart. He had big dreams. Dreams that involved running his own empire one day, and not answering to Frank.

Sitting in his high-end leather desk chair, Hollander swiveled so he could gaze out of the floor-to-ceiling window behind him. The view from up here was pretty spectacular. Towering skyscrapers stabbed at the sky, blinding when hit by the sporadic sunshine, while behind them, the snow-capped peaks of the Rockies reminded him of the city's unique position nestled amidst the majestic mountain range.

Dominating the skyline, the iconic Republic Plaza stood tall and proud, its sleek, glass-clad structure reaching a height that commanded attention. As the tallest building in Denver, it symbolized his own ambition. Unfortunately, he'd only achieved part of that dream.

Sure, he ran his own empire here in Denver, but he still answered to Frank. They were partners, as Frank liked to remind him. One couldn't survive without the other.

As much as he hated to admit it, it was probably true. Frank had advanced him the money to set up his own show here in Denver. Without that, he wouldn't have met Selma, his wife, or been able to ingratiate himself with the creme de la creme of Denver society.

Hollander often wondered why Frank had ever befriended him. Why he'd stood up for him when the other kids had bullied and made fun of him. Frank was strong and athletic, good looking too. Attracted a lot of women. But he wasn't smart. Not genius-level smart like Hollander.

Sure, Frank had street smarts, and a geeky younger brother, Romano, who took care of the accounting and administrative sides of the business. Hollander liked Romano, but the kid was too soft. Didn't have what it took to be part of the Caruso crime family and consequently lived in his brother's shadow.

Hollander often thought about that day in the playground when

Frank had come to his rescue. He figured it was because Frank saw something in him that he wanted. Or needed. Hollander didn't kid himself into thinking Frank had done it because he'd felt sorry for him. Frank didn't feel. Period. No, Frank had known early on that if he was going to take over his father's criminal empire, he needed Hollander's brain to do it.

Now they were partners. Till the end.

Hollander called the hospital again. The anxiety was giving him an ulcer. He popped an antacid as he waited. Finally, he was put through to a doctor. "Hello, I believe you're enquiring about Mr. Leonard Musgrave?"

"That's right." Hollander found he was holding his breath. "I'm a family friend."

The hammer fell.

"I'm sorry to have to tell you that Mr. Musgrave died this morning." The doctor's voice lowered. "His family have been notified of his passing."

*Shit.*

Hollander was so pissed that he hung up without saying goodbye.

He sat there, massaging his forehead, thinking. It was imperative he get that car out of the police lot, before the forensic techs got their hands on it. A crash that size, it would take days to clear up. They'd have criminalists analyzing the scene. The vehicles involved would be impounded at the police lot. Once they were done at the crash scene, they'd move on to the vehicles to determine if anyone had been at fault. He knew how these things worked.

Hollander figured he had twelve hours at the most. The cops hadn't found the money yet, or he'd have heard about it from his contact in the police force. Of that, he was sure. It was hidden in a secret compartment in Lizard's Beemer.

Hollander looked out over the city. His city. Eventually, he came up with a plan. Picking up his cell phone, he called Roberto, his right-hand man.

"Boss?"

"Come down to the office as soon as you can. There's something I need you to take care of."

# NINE

THE BUDGET HOTEL had thin walls, and the incessant, high-pitched whine of a kids' TV program from the room next door was getting on his nerves.

Savage focused on the documents spread out over the bed. These weren't Kenan's case files. These were from the Burger King robberies, six years earlier. He took a deep breath. Going through the files was like ripping a band-aid off an old wound. Steeling himself, he picked up the first report, an outline he'd written before the fourth and final robbery.

Three burglaries. Each at a different Burger King in the area. Always the same MO. The two perps would arrive just before closing, armed and wearing ski masks. They'd enter the restaurant, hold up the cashier and whoever else was inside, and demand the takings of the day. The terrified cashier would empty the till and hand over the money, after which the perps would back out, race to their vehicle, and speed away.

It'd worked seamlessly for the first three robberies, until they ran out of Burger Kings. With only two more restaurants in that location, the Denver cops had split up and lay in wait. Savage and his new partner – a capable youngster named Christenson – staked out the one in Hilltop, while Leland and Cortez covered Quincy Avenue. One of them had to get lucky.

Owing to the timing and nature of the crimes, Savage had been convinced it was an inside job, but hadn't been able to prove it. None of the Burger King employees had a criminal record, and when interviewed, they'd appeared genuinely shocked by what had happened.

Helen Ridley, a single mom with two young kids, had been shot during the third robbery. The circumstances around her death were bizarre and even now, Savage didn't understand why she'd had to die.

The taller gunman, who the prosecution had been adamant was Dewayne Simmons, had dragged her out into the parking lot and shot her in the head at point blank range. There'd been no cops nearby, nobody to stop them. A clean getaway. So why had he shot her?

"A cold-blooded killer," the state prosecutor had said. "Total disregard for human life."

Maybe he was right. About Dewayne though, he wasn't sure.

Savage moved on to his final report, written the day after the fourth robbery. Short sentences, minimal description. His fragile mental state was evident on the paper, in the words he'd chosen, in the perfunctory way he'd explained what had happened.

He skimmed through the first page of the report, trying not to relive the events in his head, until he got to the last few paragraphs.

The suspect moved toward the door, as if attempting to escape. He turned and aimed his weapon at me. In the few seconds I had, I determined he was going to shoot, so I discharged my weapon three times in line with police protocol. The suspect fell to the ground outside the restaurant. I checked for signs of life, but there were none.

Not once did Savage mention the pellet gun. That came later, in the ballistics report. Reading it, he winced as the lines blurred in front of his eyes.

*Umarex Glock 17 Gen3 CO2 Air Pistol. This pellet gun is an officially licensed replica of the Glock 17 Gen3 semi-automatic pistol. It is a CO2-powered air pistol that shoots 4.5mm steel BBs.*

He should have spotted the difference. The Glock CO2 Air Pistol was available on Amazon for under a hundred bucks, for God's sake.

Christenson – who'd run track in college – had managed to apprehend the suspect, Dewayne Simmons, and bring him back in cuffs. When Dewayne had seen what had happened to his friend, he'd gone berserk. It had taken both police officers to restrain him.

"You bastards. You shot him! What the hell is wrong with you?" Tears ran down his face. "It wasn't even a real gun."

An icy chill sliced through Savage as he remembered those words, and even now, his stomach knotted thinking about it. A damn pellet gun. He'd killed a kid holding a pellet gun.

Backup had arrived soon after that and taken away the distraught Dewayne. Justin, his friend, had been checked over by paramedics, but there'd been nothing they could do. He'd died almost immediately when Savage's bullets had ripped his chest apart.

That's when he'd gone outside and thrown up.

Savage exhaled slowly. His hands were shaking. The memory was raw, like it'd happened yesterday, not six years ago. The theory that time heals all wounds was a load of bull. Time healed nothing. It just placed a thin veneer over the top. You could fool yourself into thinking it didn't matter, that you were over it, but in reality, it was all still there, festering just below the surface.

He flung open the hotel window and took several deep breaths. The air had a metallic tinge, thanks to the evening traffic, but he sucked in great mouthfuls anyway. Slowly, the shaking subsided.

If he could only go back in time and do things differently. Maybe if he'd taken more time to study the suspect, to analyze the weapon he was holding, he'd have realized it wasn't a real gun. Except it had all happened so fast.

Dewayne running off like that, Savage switching to cover Justin. The kid's desperate attempt to flee. How he'd pointed the gun at Savage. How his hand had tensed around the trigger. If it *had* been a real gun and Savage had hesitated, he'd be the one in the body bag. He couldn't have taken that chance. He'd been trained not to. Savage sighed, turned away from the window. There was no point in wondering 'what if'. It had happened, and now he had to live with it.

Needing some fresh air, Savage went downstairs and got himself another to-go coffee from the diner next to the hotel. Taking it back to his room, he thought about the other three robberies. Dewayne's defense attorney had tried to convince the jury that his client and his friend had only taken part in that one job. That they'd been hired by an unknown mastermind who'd promised them half the proceeds. A fifty-fifty split.

No one believed him.

Savage pulled out the expert witness's report on the height and stature of the two men. As far as he could remember, that had been the deciding factor in Dewayne's trial. In all four robberies, there'd been one tall and one medium-height man. Always wearing ski masks. According to the expert, Dewayne and Justin's builds, heights, and gaits matched those of the men who'd committed the other three robberies. There'd been no doubt in his mind that they were the same perpetrators.

Except Savage and Christenson had been in their car right outside the fourth Burger King to be robbed, and they hadn't even seen Dewayne go inside. He'd been hidden by the van. There was no way the camera in the parking lot could have picked him up. Justin had been the one to run around from the passenger side of the van, and even then, how the expert could tell anything in under two seconds of footage was beyond Savage's comprehension.

A disc lay amongst the papers. It had a date on it. Savage ran his fingers over the label, too faded to read. It didn't matter. He knew the date this took place. The footage of Helen Ridley's murder, the one Dewayne Simmons was serving a life sentence for.

Savage had no way of viewing the disc in his hotel room, but he knew someone who could help.

• • •

CLINTON MANNING LIVED with his wife Trish in Sunnyside, just northwest of Denver. Surrounded by Union Pacific Railroad lines on the east, Interstate 70 to the north, Federal Boulevard to the west, and 38th Avenue to the south, it was a commuter's dream. It was also affordable and had easy access to the Highlands and the mountains, where he knew Manning liked to hike. His ex-partner had lived there as long as Savage had known him.

Trish opened the door. She looked exactly how Savage remembered, if a little older. But she still had that casual elegance that he admired, along with intelligent dark eyes and a wide, open smile. "Dalton. Clint told me you were in town."

"Hi Trish." He kissed her on the cheek and followed her into the house, then stopped and looked around. "Looks a lot different in here."

Trish laughed. "We've had some renovations. Works well, don't you think?"

They'd knocked out a wall and combined the living area and kitchen, creating one long open-plan space. It was lighter and more inviting now. "It looks great."

Pointing outside, she said, "Clint's on the back porch. I'll leave you two to talk. I'm in the middle of cooking dinner."

Savage nodded and went out the back. Manning sat on a wicker chair, surveying his back garden. The back porch had also been extended, stretching into the garden. A shiny grill stood to the side, waiting for a warm weekend to be fired up. The grass was bright green and recently trimmed.

"I like what you've done with the place."

Manning grinned and got to his feet. "Thanks. Getting ready for my retirement."

Savage nodded. Manning had been on the job a long time. He was one of the oldest serving detectives in the squad. It was getting late though, so Savage got straight to the point. "I need to borrow a DVD player. I want to look at the old footage of the Burger King robberies."

Manning chuckled and shook his head. "I'll have to dig it out of the garage. We put all that stuff in there after the kids left. We stream everything now. Crazy, eh?"

"Yeah." Savage didn't stream anything. He was old-school that way. Although Becca liked a good psychological thriller on Netflix.

"You want to stay for dinner?" Manning nodded to Trish. "We're having pot roast."

"You're more than welcome," she called from the open kitchen window. "There's plenty to go around."

"I'm good, thanks."

"Your loss." Manning walked into the house. "Grab a beer. I'll be right back."

# TEN

KENAN... Hollander... Dewayne.

*I didn't do it. I didn't shoot her.* Dewayne sobbing as he was led away.

*I have a bad feeling about this, Dalton.* Becca shaking her head, looking at him warily.

Savage woke in a sweat. For a minute, he didn't know where he was. Then he blinked, and the room came into focus.

Denver.

The time on his phone said 6:30 a.m. Groaning, he contemplated going back to sleep but in the end, swung his legs over the edge of the bed and sat up. The events of the last few days were playing through his head on a loop. There was no off switch. He may as well get up and start working.

After a quick shower, he took his laptop down to the surprisingly busy hotel dining room where the breakfast buffet was located. Then again, the guests consisted mostly of young professionals, sales personnel, or those traveling for business. Breakfast and coffee at this hour would get them to the office in time for their 9 o'clock meetings.

Savage helped himself to the buffet, filled up a cup of coffee, opened his laptop, and began researching Guy Hollander.

An hour later, he was still reading all about Hollander's charitable works, his philanthropic ventures, and how much he'd done for the community. On paper, Hollander appeared to be a model citizen.

*Nobody's that clean*, he thought as he scrolled further down through the search results. Strangely, there was no mention of Hollander prior to 2010, when he'd first appeared on the Denver scene. Savage recalled Zeb saying he'd come from Philadelphia, arriving in Denver with money. That's how he'd set himself up as a venture capitalist.

Savage typed "Guy Hollander Philadelphia" into the search bar, but the only result was a photograph of Hollander supporting the Denver Broncos against the Philadelphia Eagles at Empower Field. Nothing abnormal there. Savage didn't recognize the other two men in the picture, but the caption below reported them to be local politicians.

He continued his search but there was absolutely no mention of Hollander prior to when he'd arrived in the city. It was like he hadn't existed before 2010. Savage leaned back, allowing his eyes a break from the bright laptop screen. Could Hollander have changed his name? Or had he just been a nobody in Philly and arrived in Denver to start over? There was no crime in reinventing yourself. Savage had done exactly that in Hawk's Landing. A fresh start. A chance to be somebody different. Somebody better.

Then again, maybe Hollander wasn't from Philly and Zeb had got it wrong. After all, it was only Zeb's recollection, and that was probably based on rumors. Savage thought about Hollander's attempt to muscle in on the drug trade in La Plata County. He was expanding his business, looking for new opportunities. That much was clear.

*Not in my county*.

Hawk's Landing had its drug problems just like everywhere else, but Savage liked to think they were contained. He knew all the players, and the chess board was smaller than most. The Crimson Angels brought in the stuff from Mexico, then Kevin Handsome and his network of reprobates distributed it to the local street dealers who sold it on to the users. It was a manageable amount, nothing too hectic. A profitable sideline for the Angels MC, but not their main gig.

Savage stretched his neck, trying to iron out the crick. The hotel bed left a lot to be desired. Also, the neighbors had watched television for half of the night.

Outside, it had started raining. Great big splotches fell against the windows, then ran down in thick rivulets. Umbrellas mushroomed and people ran for shelter. More people squeezed into the dining room to escape the deluge. The windows started misting up.

He thought of Becca and Connor in Hawk's Landing and quashed the desire to get in his car and head south. A few more days. He'd give it until the end of the week. If nothing happened by then, he'd consider going home.

In the meantime, he needed to speed things up. There was no point sitting around waiting for Hollander to make a move. It was time to shake the tree and see what fell out.

---

GUY HOLLANDER ENJOYED his weekly tennis lesson. It was when he unwound, worked up a sweat, and focused his mind on hitting the ball with topspin and precision across the court. He didn't think about the business or its problems, the dinner party his wife had planned for that night, or his next meeting with Frank Caruso.

"Follow through," his coach yelled as Hollander hit a killer forehand cross court. "That's it!" The young tennis pro smashed it back, but Hollander managed to get there, his racquet connecting with the ball and sending it whizzing down the side of the court, inches from the line. Back to the ready position, he bounced on his toes as he waited for the return. That's when he spotted a tall man descending the stairs to the indoor courts, walking toward him.

His coach hit the ball deep. Caught off-guard, Hollander saw it flash past in his peripheral vision. He frowned and lowered his racquet.

"Mr. Hollander," the stranger said. "Can I have a word?"

Hollander stared at the stranger. The salt and pepper hair, rugged complexion and broad shoulders looked vaguely familiar, but he couldn't place him.

Then it hit him.

It was that sheriff from Hawk's Landing. The derelict backwater where he'd sent Jonny Star to muscle in on the drug trade.

What a disaster that had turned out to be.

It could have been so lucrative too. Apparently, this outlaw MC gang was bringing in quality product direct from the Mexican cartels and distributing across the county. Pure, high-grade stuff. Not like the shit they got here.

Since his business was expanding, he wanted in on some of that action. A connection with the Mexicans would have been vital, not to mention favorably looked on by the Carusos. They'd never managed to get that level of purity from the Columbians. It had all been going well until the goody-goody Sheriff, got wind of it. A small-town hick with a bee in his bonnet about keeping his town clean. He snorted. Like any town was drug-free!

Hollander studied the man striding toward him across the court. All he'd seen was surveillance photographs of the Sheriff taken by Jonny's men, and they hadn't done him justice. In person, he was much more impressive. Less of a hick than he'd thought. Sure, he wore jeans, a button up shirt, and cowboy boots – totally out of place at the Country Club – but there was an intelligent gleam in his hazel eyes. Hollander had underestimated him once. He wouldn't do it again.

"Who's asking?"

The gleam got brighter. The Sheriff knew that Hollander knew exactly who he was. Still, they had to play the game. He never laid all his cards on the table.

"Sheriff Savage from La Plata County."

"You're a ways out of your jurisdiction, aren't you, Sheriff?"

"I'd like to talk to you if you can spare the time."

He glanced at the tennis coach. "Let's take a break, Brock. Meet you back here in fifteen?"

The kid sauntered off, racquet resting over his shoulder.

Hollander turned back to Savage. "What do you need?"

His curiosity was genuine. He had no idea what Savage was doing in Denver, let alone at the club. All he could think was that the conscientious sheriff wanted to make sure Hollander had no plans to return to Hawk's Landing. Well, he needn't worry on that front. There was no way in hell he was ever going back to that one-horse town. He'd find some other way to work with the Mexicans. The opportunity would arise in time, and he would be ready to take advantage of it. If not Hawk's Landing, then some other rural dump. Hollander was a patient man.

"I want to talk about the murder of Kenan Simmons."

Hollander's pulse skyrocketed. Sweat prickled on his forehead that had nothing to do with the exertion from the tennis lesson. He cleared his throat. "I have nothing to say about Kenan Simmons, other than what a tragedy it is that –"

"You know who he is though, don't you?"

Hollander scowled. He hated being interrupted. "Of course I know who he is. It's been all over the papers since it happened."

"And, of course, he worked for you."

There was a pause as Hollander tried to work out how the hell Savage knew that. Nobody knew that. The kid must have told someone. He clenched the racquet. "I think you're mistaken."

"Not according to his mother and his brother, who both say Kenan told them he had a new job. Working for you."

Hollander stiffened. "What are you implying?"

"Nothing. I was just wondering in what capacity Kenan was employed by you."

"I told you." Hollander fixed his gaze on Savage. "He wasn't."

"Right." Savage nodded, but held his gaze as if to say, *So this was how we're going to play it.*

Hollander shrugged. "I don't know what else to tell you." There was no cause to worry – yet. There was nothing on paper. No employment contract, no payroll. Just a verbal agreement and cash payments. No proof. Kenan's family's word against his. Rather, the word of a convicted felon and his grief-stricken mother against an upstanding businessman and personal friend of the Chief of Police.

Hollander knew it, and he knew Savage knew it too.

"Good making your acquaintance, Sheriff." Hollander tilted his head. "You take care now."

# ELEVEN

SAVAGE STOOD AT THE WINDOW, gazing out at the gray drizzle. Hollander wanted to play games. Fine. They'd play.

Disgruntled, Savage called Manning, but the call diverted straight to his voicemail. Strange. Manning never turned his phone off. Cops were always contactable, especially when on duty. He tried again and got the same result.

Concerned, he called the precinct. He got Sanchez. "Hey, is Clint there?"

Sanchez, usually chirpy and upbeat, hesitated. "Um, no. He didn't come in today."

"What happened?".

"I shouldn't really say, but since it's you –" He took a breath. "He's at the hospital. His wife was assaulted last night."

Savage's heart skipped a beat. "Is she okay?"

"I heard it was pretty bad."

"Which hospital?"

"General."

Savage hung up, grabbed his jacket, and ran out the door in under a minute.

---

DENVER GENERAL HOSPITAL was a level one trauma hospital in the Lincoln Park neighborhood and consisted of one main building with multiple secondary buildings covering everything from urgent care and outpatients to maternity and mental health.

Savage pulled into a vacant spot, made sure his Sheriff's ID was on the dash, and darted toward the hospital.

He flashed his badge at the receptionist. "I'm looking for a patient, Trish Manning?" He took a moment to catch his breath. "She came in last night. Assault."

The receptionist consulted her computer. A few swift keyboard strokes later and she nodded. "Ward 11B. Fourth floor."

He took the elevator, gritting his teeth as it creaked to a stop on every floor on the way up. Finally, the doors wheezed open and he dashed out. Where the hell was Ward 11B? He glanced around, finally seeing a sign listing the different wards.

"Can I help you?" a nurse asked.

He shook his head and headed down a long, sterile corridor. 11B was in a high dependency ward with four beds in a row, beige curtains dividing them into cubicles. Savage poked his head into each until he found Manning. The Denver PD detective sat beside his wife, head in his hands. Trish lay unmoving in the bed, attached to a machine by several wires and tubes. Savage had never seen his colleague so drawn and tense. He didn't even look up as Savage entered.

Trish's face was black and blue, and she had a nasty gash on her forehead. Her left eye was swollen and puffy, and there was dried blood in her hair and on the side of her face.

"How is she?"

Manning glanced up, his eyes hollow. "Don't know yet. The doctor said she's got a concussion, but we don't know if there's any internal bleeding. They're going to do some scans this morning."

Savage placed his hand on Manning's shoulder. "What the hell happened?"

Manning gulped over his words. "She was attacked after she got home last night."

"In the house?"

"Outside. A man with a baseball bat. He did a number on her. She was barely breathing when our neighbor found her and called an ambulance." His voice cracked. "Doc says she's lucky to be alive."

"I'm so sorry." Savage studied the unconscious woman. She looked frail and weak lying there, connected to the beeping machine. "Do you know who's responsible?"

Manning shook his head.

"It couldn't have been random." Savage frowned. "Was she mugged too?"

"Not that I can tell. Her purse was found beside her. Wallet, everything untouched."

Weird.

Savage shook his head.

"I know what you're thinking," Manning said. "That this is connected to a case I'm working on, but you're wrong."

"There must be a reason."

"Don't you think I've been racking my brains? I've been going crazy trying to figure out who would want to hurt me, but there's nobody."

Savage thought for a moment. "Bust any gangbangers lately?"

"Not for a couple of months. I mean, it could be one of Big Benny's guys, but I don't see it. It doesn't feel like him. He's not smart enough to send someone after Trish."

"You sure about that?"

"I'll check as soon as I get back to the station, but it's slim."

Savage nodded. It didn't sound like Big Benny was responsible, whoever he might be. "Can I do anything?"

"I'm going to wait for the results of the scans, and then I'll talk to Hagan." Manning gazed contemplatively at his wife. "I've decided to take early retirement, Dalton."

Savage arched an eyebrow but allowed his old friend to go on.

"It's what Trish wanted. She's been patient long enough. After this..." He stared at her face, so pale against the pillow. "I owe it to her."

"She's going to be fine," Savage said. "You know that right?"

"Yeah." Manning's voice was flat.

"Trish is a toughie. She must be to have stuck with you for thirty years."

Not even that got a chuckle.

Savage waited while they took Trish down to radiology for her scans. Manning was quiet, having withdrawn into himself, so Savage busied himself by drinking copious amounts of bitter black coffee and thinking about his meeting with Hollander yesterday. Now wasn't the time to bring it up with Manning.

Hollander was a sly devil. He'd pretended not to know Savage, even though he'd recognized him almost immediately. Then he'd denied that Kenan Simmons had worked for him. There were only two possible reasons for that. One: Hollander was involved and didn't want anyone to know. Or two: he was afraid it would lead to unwanted questioning, and he didn't want to draw attention to his business. Maybe both.

*You take care now.*

Was that Hollander's idea of a threat? Two could play that game. If Hollander thought Savage was just going to back off, he could think again. Things were just getting interesting.

Walking back to the waiting room, Savage overheard two nurses talking.

"My son got into a fight at school the other day. Teacher called me to come and get him. He got suspended. He told me he was standing up for this other kid, who was being bullied. Can you believe that? He did the right thing and got suspended for it."

The lightbulb went off as he re-entered the waiting room.

"You know, there is one possibility we haven't considered." Savage handed Manning a coffee in a polystyrene cup.

His ex-partner looked up. "What's that?"

"This could have nothing to do with you. It could be that someone had a beef with Trish."

Manning gave an incredulous stare. "She's never hurt a soul in her life."

"Has she been acting strange lately? Anything seem out of the ordinary?"

"No, Dalton. I'm sorry, you're way off base with that one."

He let it slide, but he considered talking to Trish when she woke up. Something could have happened that she hadn't told her husband about. Something inconsequential, that had led to a physical retaliation.

He'd just sat down when Manning's two daughters arrived.

"How is she?" asked the eldest, displaying a noticeable baby bump. Her hair was pulled back into a messy bun, her face was pinched with worry.

"We're still waiting."

The youngest daughter ran straight into her father's arms. "Is she going to be okay, Dad?" Manning hugged her, his face tense. Savage felt the love radiating off his ex-partner and understood why he wanted out. Nothing was worth jeopardizing his family.

Savage was hit by a pang of longing and excused himself. They needed some privacy and he needed to hear Becca's voice.

"That's awful," Becca said, once Savage had told her what had happened. "I'm so sorry to hear that." She'd never met Manning or his wife, but her empathy and natural concern for others told him she meant it. "Is she going to be alright?"

"We're still waiting to hear."

Her voice was cautious. "Do you know who did it?"

"Not yet."

"You will be careful, won't you?"

"Always."

She hesitated. "I miss you, Dalton."

"I miss you too." More than she knew. "I'll be careful, I promise. As soon as I've figured out who killed Kenan, I'll be back in Hawk's Landing."

Becca didn't bother asking how long that would be. "Be careful, Dalton."

"I will."

After hanging up, he went back to Manning to say goodbye, but overheard his youngest daughter saying, "You don't think it had anything to do with that incident outside the charity shop?"

Manning frowned. "What incident?"

"You know, the guy who was abusing his girlfriend."

Savage joined them. The girls noticed him for the first time.

Manning nodded in his direction. "This is my old partner, Dalton Savage.

He nodded at the girls. He had met them before, but they'd been a lot younger back then, and wouldn't remember him. "Any news yet?"

The eldest, Amanda, offered a tentative smile. "Mom is going to be okay. The doctor just let us know."

"That's great news." Savage felt a weight lift and could only imagine how relieved his friend was.

Manning had regained some of his color. "There's no internal bleeding. It's just a bad concussion. She's going to be fine. They're keeping her in for observation, but we should be able to take her home in a day or two."

Savage studied Manning's youngest daughter. With her blonde hair and sky-blue eyes, it was easy to see why Manning and Trish had named her Summer. "What did you mean about the man who assaulted his girlfriend?"

Summer's gaze flickered between him and her dad. "It happened a few days ago. Mom volunteers at the local thrift store. There was a couple having a fight outside. When the man smacked the woman, Mom went to see if she could help. The man told her it was none of her business, but she took the woman into the store anyway, and gave her a glass of water. The man stormed off." She shrugged. "That's what mom told me anyway."

Amanda stared at her sister. “Did Mom say who this woman was?”

“No. I was just wondering if this was –” She bit her lip and petered off.

“A retaliation?” Savage finished for her.

Summer gave a worried nod.

“Could be.” Manning scratched his head, scowling. “This puts a different spin on things.”

Savage gave a thoughtful nod. It was much more likely to be the cause of the attack than some drug-addled gangbanger Manning put away months ago.

“You girls stay with your mother. Ask her if she got a name after the incident. I’m going to the station to see if I can find out who this guy was.”

Amanda nodded.

“Be careful, Dad.” Summer hugged him again. She was definitely the more tactile of the two.

Savage gave a curt nod. “I’ll drive you.”

# TWELVE

MANNING BURST through the doors of the police department. Hagan wasn't there – thank God – so Savage followed Manning in.

Savage pointed to a vacant desk. "Can I sit here?"

"Sit where you want," Manning replied. "See what CCTV footage you can find."

Savage logged in using Manning's access code, and searched through the long list of possible cameras, noting the street address and camera number. The technology had advanced in the time since his departure. He wished he could get the town committee of Hawk's Landing to agree to setting up a camera system like this. He already knew the answer. Big brother looking over their shoulder was going to be met with heavy resistance from the citizenry he protected. Regardless, he was glad to have this tool at his disposal now. Sitting at the desk with the hum of the office buzzing around him made him feel as though he was back, his old life welcoming him as if he'd never been away.

Manning dispatched a young officer to ask neighboring shops if anyone had seen anything, or if there were any private surveillance cameras in the area. There was an energy to Manning that Savage hadn't seen in a while. A purpose. He wanted to track down the man who'd attacked Trish, and nothing was going to stop him. Savage knew what that felt like. He'd had cases turn personal too.

It was never a good thing.

Savage sent the surveillance details over to Manning so he could make an official request from the central surveillance hub. Being a senior detective, gave Manning a supervisory status regarding signature authority on certain things, this happened to be one of them. He signed off on the request forms himself so there was no delay. As it turned out, there were only two cameras in the busy, suburban street, one at each end. The thrift store was located two thirds of the way down.

Summer had told them the attack had happened in the afternoon, shortly after lunch, so they had a timeframe. While they waited for the footage to download, Savage kept a nervous eye out for Hagan.

"She's on the sixth floor with the Deputy Chief," Sanchez informed them. "You want me to signal when she gets back?"

"Thanks," Savage replied.

Once the download was complete, Manning hit play on the first video. Camera 675-29384 was the one closest to the thrift store. He forwarded to noon and hit play. Nothing happened for a while. Pedestrians ambled up and down the street, grocery bags in hand, kids at their elbows. A couple of teens strolled by, hands in pockets.

Manning sped up the footage and they watched the jerky movements like some sort of weird animation, until Savage shouted, "There!"

Manning slowed it down to real time and they watched as a young couple in their twenties walked up the street. The woman was slender and willowy, with long, flyaway hair that lifted in the breeze. Her partner was stocky and heavyset, with tattoos on his forearms and a mop of unruly dark hair. He walked with a swagger, an air of disdain that Savage didn't like. Even on video, he looked like trouble.

The couple passed right under the CCTV camera, and it was clear they were arguing. The man, his face twisted with anger, yelled at the woman who had her hands in the air in an attempt to pacify him. It wasn't working. As they walked, he became more and more enraged.

Savage tensed as the young man gripped the woman's arm and swung her around to face him. She backed away, but he twisted her arm in a move designed to inflict pain.

"Nice guy." Savage shook his head at the unfolding scene. This wasn't the first time he'd done this.

Her face was now etched with fear. She shook her arm loose and pushed him away. That's when he slapped her. His palm whipped across her face, stunning her. She stumbled backwards into the glass frontage of the thrift shop, then sank down to the ground.

The door flew open and Trish ran out. Ignoring the angry man, she helped the woman to her feet. The girl was holding her cheek, a shocked expression still on her face. Her partner paced up and down, hands on hips, clearly agitated. A lot of pent-up aggression there.

Trish ushered the young woman, who was crying openly, inside. The man tried to stop her. Savage felt Manning tense as he grabbed Trish by the arm. She swung around, said something to him that made him drop his arm and back away.

"She probably threatened to call the police," Savage guessed.

Manning nodded.

The man scowled, wagged his finger at his distraught girlfriend, then stormed up the street and out of sight of the camera.

"Pull up the eastside camera," Savage said.

Manning took a note of the time, then double-clicked on the second icon. He navigated to the right time frame and hit play. "There goes the scumbag."

They could see the young man marching up the street, hands thrust in pockets, shoulders tense, head down. Eventually, he reached a Ford Cortina, pulled out a set of keys from his pocket, and opened the car door.

"Can you zoom in on the plate?" Savage asked.

Manning was already one step ahead of him. He enlarged the

image so that the car was center and foremost on the screen. Leaning forward, he squinted at the number plate. It was just barely legible.

"Got ya," he muttered.

---

LEAVING THE SQUAD ROOM, they bumped into none other than a displeased Sarah Hagan. "Savage. My office."

"What, now? I was just about to –" He pointed to Manning.

"Yes, now." Her tone left no room for discussion.

Savage glanced at Manning, then followed her into her office.

Hagan walked behind her desk, turned, and scowled at him. "What did I tell you about interfering with my investigation?"

"I'm not. I'm helping Clint track down the man who beat his wife unconscious."

That made her falter, but she didn't stop her tirade. "I'm sorry about Trish, but this isn't about that. I've just had a meeting with the Deputy Chief. He's been talking to Guy Hollander."

Shit. Hollander must have lodged a complaint.

"If this is about the country club –"

"Of course it's about the country club. What the hell did you think you were doing?"

Savage shrugged. "Talking to Hollander."

"You marched up to him in the middle of a session and accused him of being involved in Kenan Simmons' death."

"That's not how it went down, Sarah."

"Don't call me that."

He sighed. "Okay, look. I went to ask him some questions. Something you should have done at the very beginning." He knew that would piss her off. He relished that. "Kenan worked for Hollander, in an informal capacity."

"He confirmed that."

"No, he denied it."

"Dalton, you can't go around harassing our prominent citizens."

"He's a suspect in Kenan's murder. The *prime* suspect."

"No, he's not. We have nothing that links him to the murder. No evidence whatsoever."

"Have you checked his alibi?"

"There is no cause to question him."

"I disagree. He's up to his eyeballs in drugs, racketeering, prostitution, and fraudulent business practices. Every crooked road in Denver ends up at his door. Why is everyone so determined to ignore that?"

"None of that has been proven. As far as I know, he's a legitimate businessman who does a lot for the community."

"Including donating to the Police Benevolence Fund."

"Enough, Dalton." Her words sliced through him, her cheeks now bright red. "The point is, you're not supposed to be here. This is not your case. You don't even live here anymore, and you sure as hell should not be impeding this investigation."

"Kickstarting it, you mean."

Her raised voice cooled into a low growl as she glared at him, unblinking. "I'm giving you one last warning. Leave now, and I will try to forget the disruption you've caused."

"I promised Dewayne Simmons I'd figure out who killed his –"

"That's our job," she interrupted. "Not yours."

"I agree. Except you're not doing it." He was on dangerous ground now. Yet, he couldn't seem to help himself.

"That's it." She stormed to the side and stuck her head out her office door. "Sanchez. Get in here."

Sanchez entered cautiously, as if stepping on hot coals. "Yes?"

"I want you to take Sheriff Savage into custody."

"What?" Both Savage and Sanchez blurted at the same time.

Hagan ignored them. Instead, she pulled herself up to her full height of five foot seven inches. "Dalton Savage, you're under arrest."

"What charge?"

"Interfering with a police investigation. I'm sure you're well aware of your Miranda warning, but I like to do things by the book." She smirked. "You have the right to remain silent. Anything you say can and will be used against you in a court of law. You have the right to speak to an attorney, and to have an attorney present during any questioning. Do you understand your rights as I've explained them?"

"You can't be serious." Savage shook his head, butting in.

"Answer my question. Do you understand your rights?"

Savage gave a slow, barely perceptible nod of his head.

"I'm going to need you to verbalize your answer."

Savage let out a sigh. "Yes."

"Is that really necessary?" Sanchez asked. Through the glass, the rest of the department watched with rapt attention.

Hagan nodded at Sanchez. "Cuff him."

Sanchez hesitated, then shot Savage a sympathetic look. Savage bet he regretted sitting at the desk closest to Hagan's office.

He held out his hands. It wasn't Sanchez's fault his boss was a jerk. "You're making a mistake, Hagan."

"No, Dalton. You're the one who's made the mistake. You should have never come back to Denver. There's nothing for you here."

Normally, he would agree.

"What are you hiding?" Savage called over his shoulder as Sanchez led him away. "Why won't you investigate Hollander?" He saw a couple of heads turn towards Hagan before he left the squad room. "Are you in his pocket? Is that what's happening here?"

It was a lowball attempt to undermine her authority. Savage didn't care. She deserved it.

Before he got to the basement, Savage turned to Sanchez. "I'd like to call my lawyer."

# THIRTEEN

GRAYSON CARTER, otherwise known as Max "Burner" Wilson, was the only lawyer Savage knew in the city. Actually, he was the only attorney Savage knew, period.

Originally from Denver, Burner had been in Hawk's Landing for the past few months infiltrating the Crimson Angels' motorcycle club in order to investigate possible drug links to his daughter's death. He'd been instrumental in helping Savage uncover the identity of a long-acting serial killer, who'd been shot resisting arrest.

Savage had looked past Burner's vigilantism, since he'd recognized a man in search of justice. The murder of his daughter had hit him hard, as it would any parent, so Savage had given the guy a lot of leeway. More than he should have, under the circumstances. Why? Because at the back of his mind, Savage knew he'd do the same thing if it had been his kid who'd been murdered.

Sanchez let him call Burner before he was booked and his cell phone was taken away. He'd also removed his handcuffs so he could speak freely. Although they'd never been partnered, Savage had worked homicides with Sanchez in the past, and knew him to be a good cop. The respect was mutual.

"I don't know what's got into her," Sanchez said, almost apologetically. "That was way harsh, in my opinion."

Savage scrolled through his phone for Burner's number. "Appreciate it."

"I'll give you some privacy. Knock on the door when you're done."

Savage nodded. Sanchez had put him in one of the interview rooms to make the call. He dialed the number and listened while it rang.

*Please pick up.*

It kept ringing.

Crap, he wasn't going to answer.

Savage was about to hang up when a groggy voice said, "Hello?"

Relief flooded his body. "Burner, this is Dalton Savage. I need your help."

---

"NOW, this is something I never thought I'd see." Grayson Carter grinned as he stepped into the holding cell. "How are you, Sheriff?"

They shook hands.

"Glad to see you, Burner." Carter laughed at the use of his alias. "Sorry, I can't get used to Grayson."

"That's okay. I kinda liked Burner. I'm not really Grayson Carter anymore. A lot has changed in the last few years."

"I know." They sat down on the ledge that doubled as a bed and faced each other. Burner had cut his hair – although it was still long for a lawyer – and neatened up his beard. The tatts he couldn't hide. Those were with him for life.

"Who'd you piss off to get locked in here?" Burner asked.

"Lieutenant Hagan." Savage grimaced. "She's not my biggest fan."

"I can see that." Burner smirked and took out a pen and paper. "Why don't you tell me what happened."

Savage spent the next few minutes filling him in.

"Let me get this straight? She locked you up for interfering with an investigation because she holds a grudge against you."

"That's right."

"Because you rejected her four years ago?"

"Right again."

Burner chuckled. "She must have really liked you."

Savage rolled his eyes. "Can you get me out?"

"Depends. Did you interfere with the investigation?"

"I'm conducting my own investigation. I can't help it if it covers the same ground as theirs."

"Now that's tricky. Why don't you tell me what you did?"

Savage explained about Dewayne Simmons's request.

Burner's eyes widened. "You're telling me a convict that you put away, called you to find out what happened to his little brother?"

"Yep."

Burner let out a low whistle. "That's messed up, man."

"Police weren't doing anything. For some reason, nobody wants to go after Hollander."

"Guy Hollander? The same Guy Hollander who financed Connolly's development project in Hawk's Landing? The same Guy Hollander who had that thug Jonny Star on his payroll?"

"The very same."

"Well." He sat back and studied Savage. "Shit."

"As it turns out," Savage continued, "Hollander has some very influential friends, including the Deputy Chief of Police. Apparently, they're tennis buddies. As it happens, the Lieutenant is also friends with the Deputy Chief, and therefore doesn't want to touch Hollander. She won't interview him and warned me to stay away."

"Which I'm guessing you didn't."

"You guessed right. Kenan, the victim, worked for Hollander. Nothing official, just odd jobs here and there."

"Drug running?"

"Something like that. He was shot in Washington Park last week. Left to bleed out in the street. An unknown called it in around two a.m."

"You don't know who?"

"No, there were no witnesses other than this caller, and he didn't give a name or address."

"Typical."

"The only lead I have is Hollander."

"So, you went to talk to him."

"He denied knowing Kenan, of course, but I could tell he was lying. Whether it's because he's guilty or because he doesn't want to get mixed up in the investigation, I don't know."

"A guy like Hollander doesn't do his own dirty work," Burner said. "If he was responsible, he'd have a thug like Jonny Star do it for him."

"I'm looking into known associates – or rather, I was, until I ended up here." He gestured to the walls surrounding them. Sickly green and claustrophobic. Even the ceiling was green. It seemed to be holding him down.

Burner grinned. "Give me half an hour."

---

TRUE TO HIS WORD, Savage was released and walked out of the police station with Burner, less than thirty minutes later.

"How'd you manage that?" Savage asked.

"I threatened to bring up your mutual history in the discussion with the bail commissioner, as a reason for Hagan's obvious bias. She agreed to drop the charges so long as you were issued with a warning. No further interference." Burner grinned. "Consider yourself warned."

"Thank you, man." He shook Burner's hand.

"Can I drop you somewhere?"

"That's okay. I've got my car here."

"Okay, then." Burner turned toward an old, silver Mercedes C-Class Sedan parked in the visitor's section of the police parking lot. "I guess I'll be seeing ya."

Savage hesitated. After what Burner had done for him, it felt wrong to walk away. "Hey, you want to grab a beer?"

The lawyer grinned.

They arranged to meet at Savage's hotel in twenty minutes. Driving back, Savage thought about Burner. He wasn't at all like he appeared. The guy seemed to have this ability to morph into someone else. In Hawk's Landing, he'd fooled Savage and the team into believing he was one of the Crimson Angels. He'd grown his hair, got tattoos, even stolen the identity of his wife's cousin, a down-and-out biker who'd ridden with the Destroyers. There was nothing he wouldn't do to find his daughter's killer.

Now, he was back to his lawyer persona, but instead of the corporate persona Savage would have expected, Burner had a craftiness about him, a cunningness that had enabled him to blackmail Hagan into releasing him, because that was in effect what he'd done.

He chuckled to himself. She couldn't have liked that.

Back at the hotel, Savage made his way up to his room. The cell had made him feel unclean, and he wanted to shower before getting that drink. He slotted the keycard into the door and pushed it open.

*What the –?*

His room was in shambles. The closet door was open. His clothes were scattered all over the floor. The bedding had been pulled apart, the pillows upended, and his suitcase turned upside down.

At first, he thought he'd been burgled. Then he realized his room had been searched. Taking out his phone, he took some photographs of the mess.

Fifteen minutes later, he was still trying to figure out if anything had been taken when Burner called. "You coming?"

"My room's been ransacked." He spotted Manning's DVD player lying on its side, one edge caved in. That would never work again.

"What number are you?"

Savage told him.

Burner arrived a few minutes later, eyes searching around the mess. "Jeez."

"It doesn't look like anything's been taken." Savage picked his laptop up off the floor. There was also a dent in it, so he couldn't open it.

"Broken?"

Savage nodded. "Looks like it."

"Anything important on it?"

"It's my work laptop. Most of the stuff's saved on the cloud."

Burner walked into the room. "I take it you're not going to report this?"

"No point. Hagan won't need much of an excuse to arrest me again."

"Probably wise." Burner looked around. "They did a pretty thorough job. You think someone's sending you a message?"

"I'm guessing this is Hollander's work. It feels like him."

Burner gave a curt nod. "You can't stay here. I've got a spare room. You're welcome to it."

Savage hesitated. It would be better than going to another hotel where Hollander could find him. "You sure you don't mind?"

"No. Probably a good idea to be off the grid while we figure this thing out. Looks like your theory was right. If Hollander's messing with you, he's got something to hide."

Savage liked the way he'd said "we". He could use some help on this one.

# FOURTEEN

SAVAGE FOLLOWED Burner to his place in Denver's River North Art District. They passed colorful murals and intricate graffiti. Art seemed to spill from every available surface turning the neighborhood into an open-air gallery. He spotted trendy cafes and eateries, quirky shops, and vintage stores. As they drove deeper into the neighborhood, they came to an industrial area filled with converted warehouses and buildings that had been turned into art spaces and studios.

"It used to be deserted," the lawyer complained as he got out of his car. "Now it's filled with Millennials and vegetarian restaurants."

Burner pulled open a rusty garage; Burner's Harley-Davidson gleamed in the corner.

Savage snorted. "I see you decided to keep the Harley?"

A smug grin. "What can I say? I got attached to it. It's part of the new me."

Savage didn't ask what that was.

They walked into the rectangular warehouse block and took the elevator to the top floor.

Savage gazed into Burner's apartment when the elevator doors opened. "This is quite something." It was huge, spanning the entire floor. The kitchen, living, and dining area were unseparated with the bedrooms positioned at the far end. High ceilings gave it a spacious feel, and large, grille windows lacking blinds let in the large squares of sunlight. Savage admired the exposed brickwork and steel beams. It felt urban and contemporary, if a little unfinished.

His furniture was minimal, with a worn leather couch and matching armchair the center pieces in the living area, along with a flat screen television mounted to the wall. On the dining table stood a laptop, printer, and box of printer paper.

"You went back to work?" Savage asked.

"Not yet. I'm exploring some options." He didn't elaborate, and Savage didn't want to pry.

"That's the spare room." Burner gestured to the room on the left. "There's not much of a view, but the bed's comfortable."

"Appreciate it." Savage pushed open the door. The room was furnished with the basics: a bed, dresser, and closet. Leading off the bedroom was a private bathroom. There was no bedding on the bed, or any pictures on the wall.

"Don't get many guests," Burner mumbled. "Everything you need should be in the closet. I've got some cold ones in the fridge when you're settled."

"Great."

Savage shut the door and sat down on the bed, weary. He debated calling Becca, then decided against it. She'd just worry if he told her he'd been arrested and his hotel room had been ransacked.

After a quick shower, he put on some clean clothes and went to join Burner in the living room. The lawyer was watching a football game on TV, a beer on the coffee table in front of him.

"Help yourself." Burner nodded to the refrigerator.

Savage opened it and took out a beer. It felt weird to be sharing an apartment with someone, even if it was only temporary. He hadn't done that since his academy days. Even weirder was they weren't even friends. He barely knew Burner. Their paths had crossed for only a few weeks in Hawk's Landing. Now here he was, staying in the man's spare room.

"How's the little one?" Burner asked, filling the awkward silence. The commentator was talking about a costly interception.

Savage was relieved to have something to talk about. "He's got his mother firmly wrapped around his little finger."

"I'm sure."

Savage glanced up at the television. He hadn't watched football in a while.

"Take a seat," Burner said. "Then you can tell me why you're really here."

"What do you mean?"

"I know you're looking into that kid's murder, but..." Burner shook his head. "Dewayne's a convicted felon. Why help him at all?"

Since Burner had helped him get out of jail, Savage probably owed the guy an explanation. "I owe him."

"Because you arrested him?"

"No." He took a swig of his beer. "Because I killed his best friend."

Burner stared at him. "Now I'm confused.".

Savage sighed. "It started with a spree of robberies, back when I was a detective at Denver PD."

"Uh-huh."

"We knew there was a good chance this Burger King would be hit next, so my partner and I staked it out."

Burner fixed his dark gaze on Savage.

"Dewayne and this other guy Justin hit the restaurant just before closing. We were in the parking lot when they went in. Once we realized they were robbing the place, we went in after them."

"What happened?"

"Dewayne took off out the back, so my partner went after him. I stayed with Justin. I was waiting for backup when Justin made a run for it. I told him to freeze, but he turned his weapon on me. I thought he was going to fire."

"You shoot him?"

Savage nodded. "Turned out the guy had a pellet gun."

"He robbed a store with a pellet gun?"

"Yeah. And I killed him."

Burner studied him for another long moment. The football commentator was harping on about the defense taking a stand. "That's brutal, man."

Savage grunted. Burner was the only person who hadn't tried to make him feel better. He hadn't said, *it's not your fault*, or, *you couldn't have known*. Savage appreciated that.

The home team scored a touchdown and the crowd went wild. Even the commentators were shouting at each other. Burner turned down the volume. "That's why you're doing this? Because you shot his friend?"

"That's about it." Savage fell silent. Guilt washed over him, a familiar tide he couldn't suppress.

Burner frowned as he thought about this. "I'm not buying that."

Savage looked at him. "Huh?"

"I mean, that's a terrible thing, but they were criminals. You owed them nothing. There's gotta be more to this story."

He was astute, Savage gave him that much.

When Savage didn't reply, Burner said, "Why do you care so much about this guy that you put away?"

"What makes you think I care?"

Burner gave him a 'seriously?' look. "You left your fiancé and your newborn baby to come here to find out what happened to his brother."

Savage contemplated lying, then thought, what's the point? He had nothing to hide. Not from Burner, anyway.

Savage stared down at the beer in his hand. "Remember I said there were four robberies?"

"Yep."

"During the third, a woman was killed. Helen Ridley. A mother of two. She was shot in the head, point blank range. We got it all on CCTV."

"Did your man do it?"

"He says not. The perps wore masks, so it was difficult to know for sure. Dewayne swore it wasn't him, but the jury found him guilty anyway. Now he's doing life."

"You didn't think it was him?"

Savage hesitated. "I thought there was reasonable doubt. I wanted more time to investigate, but the state prosecutor was pushing for a conviction. My request for an extension was denied."

Burner gave a low whistle. "They had enough to convict."

"That they did."

"What makes you think it was someone else who shot that woman?"

"Dewayne said they were only hired for one job, the last robbery. They were contacted with instructions, given the location and time."

Burner frowned. "Contacted how?"

"A man called them out of the blue. Said he worked at that Burger King and knew a way they could make some good money fast. Dewayne's family was struggling, as was Justin's, so the boys agreed. They were nineteen at the time."

"Do you think Dewayne was telling the truth?"

"Not sure. He could have been trying to get out of the murder charge, but I don't think so. He's not that type of guy. He's not a killer."

"Everybody's a killer, given the right circumstances."

That was some statement. Then again, considering what Burner had been through, how he'd tried to hunt down his daughter's killer, it made sense.

"Any idea who set it up?" Burner asked.

"Your guess is as good as mine. We interviewed everyone who worked at the various Burger Kings but found no red flags." Savage shrugged. "We must have missed something."

There was a pause as the lawyer thought about this. Eventually, he said, "I get your motive, but I'm not sure there's much you can do about his conviction, especially with so much time having passed, but I can help you find out who killed his brother. I have a contact, an investigator I used to use when I was practicing."

"He reliable?"

"He's one of the best. Mostly financial background checks, but he's a tech whiz and can get into any system. If there's anything on Hollander out there, he'll find it."

Savage didn't want to know how many laws he was breaking by agreeing to this. He decided to chalk it up to the greater good. Hollander was not a nice guy. He deserved to be taken down. If Burner was going to help him do it, then so be it.

They talked for a while longer, and then Savage's stomach gave a loud rumble. He couldn't remember the last time he'd eaten. "Mind if I order takeout?"

Burner laughed.

They ordered a couple of pizzas and watched TV until they arrived. Savage spent the time thinking.

"There is one avenue I haven't considered," he said, once the pizzas had arrived.

Burner handed him a box. "What's that?"

Savage took it but didn't open it. "Kenan was friends with a girl from Washington Park. He walked her home the night he was shot. I was wondering about their connection. It was only because of her that he was in the area that night. As far as I know, nobody else knew he'd be there."

"You're thinking she had something to do with it?" Burner eyed him over the open pizza box, the garlicky aroma now reaching Savage's nostrils.

"Not directly, but she could have told someone. Maybe her parents?"

"Shooting your daughter's boyfriend because you don't like the look of him is pretty extreme."

"I know, but when I talked to Isobel, she mentioned her father had been in prison. Fraud, I think. Some white-collar crime. She told me she and Kenan had that in common."

"Fraud?"

"A relative in prison."

Burner took a bite of his pizza, dropped the slice back into the box and moved to his open laptop on the table. "That's easy enough to check. What's his name?"

"Angus Drake."

Burner navigated to an official legal website and did a search for the man's name. Several results popped up. He scanned them, his eyes roving down the screen. "Here we are. Angus Frederick Drake, convicted of 13 counts of securities fraud." Burner scanned the online document. "Apparently, he raised 8.5 million dollars through a vacation home investment scheme, but instead of using the money to buy homes, he used it to fund other companies he owned, pay off his mortgage in Wash Park and his daughter's private school fees, and buy a holiday house in California."

"Incredible."

"Most of the investors were from Colorado Springs and the Denver area. He got eight years but was out in four. He served his fifth under house arrest."

"A conman, but not violent.".

"Still, it's worth checking out." Burner closed his laptop and reached for the pizza again. "Kenan was probably not the type of kid he wanted his privately educated princess dating."

"She's far from a princess." Savage told him about the school visit. "In fact, Isobel was helping out at the community center when she met Kenan."

Burner looked surprised. "I take that back."

"I'll go and speak to her father."

After they ate, Burner called his investigator contact, while Savage went to his room and called Manning. He was eager to know whether his friend had tracked down his wife's attacker.

"They let you out?"

"Yeah," Savage said. "Got a lawyer friend's help." He got to the real reason for his call. "How's Trish?"

"She's conscious, but they're keeping her in for a while longer. The girls are with her."

"You manage to trace the suspect?"

"Yeah. The scumbag denied it, of course. Claimed to be out with the boys last night. The bar manager vouched for them."

"You think he's covering?"

"Must be. I'm going to talk to him tomorrow."

"Keep me posted."

"Will do."

Savage hesitated, then said, "My room at the hotel was searched yesterday. I think it was Hollander's guys."

Manning said nothing.

"You there?" Savage asked, after nearly a minute had ticked past.

"I'm here." Manning cleared his throat. "You know, you might want to think twice before pursuing this one. I know you want to help Dewayne Simmons find out what happened to his brother, but you've got a life too. If Hollander's involved – and I'm not saying he is, he's not going to want you snooping around. Is it worth risking everything to be here?"

Manning had a point, Savage couldn't deny that. Still, he'd made a promise and he intended to see it through. "I'll give it till the end of the week," he said, more to appease Manning than because he really meant it. But to be fair to Becca, he couldn't stay much longer than that.

"Be careful, Dalton."

"Always try to."

Savage hung up and stared at the undecorated wall in front of him, lost in thought. Why was everyone so damned scared of Hollander? He might be a shit of a human being, but he was still a man. Flesh and blood like everyone else. No one was untouchable. If Hollander was involved – and it was beginning to look like he was – then Savage was going to expose him. If he could just prove Hollander had Kenan killed, he'd let Denver PD clean up the mess. He didn't want the glory. He just wanted to see justice served.

For Kenan. For Dewayne.

For himself.

# FIFTEEN

A LOUD RAPPING on the door woke Savage. For a moment, he didn't know where he was. The plain white walls gave nothing away, and through the window, all he could see was the brickwork of another building. He blinked.

Manning's wife... His arrest... Burner... It all came flooding back.

"Yeah?" His voice sounded gravelly.

"My contact got back to me," Burner said, sounding muffled through the door. "I've got something."

Adrenaline swept through Savage's body, kicking his brain into action. "I'll be right out."

Pulling on some clothes, he wondered what Burner's contact had discovered. Hopefully something useful, something he could use. Something that would shed some light on Hollander's murky past.

"What time is it?" He walked into the living area.

"Seven thirty."

Burner handed him a coffee. Outside, the sun rose over the city, turning the North River into liquid gold.

"You're going to be all over this." Burner looked smug. "Guy

Hollander *was* from Philadelphia. He changed his name when he got to Denver, nearly a decade ago. He was born Rayburn Thomas Magee."

Savage spluttered. "Seriously? I can see why he changed it."

"There's more. In Philly, he worked for a man called Frank Caruso. Caruso is rumored to be part of a well-established and much feared crime family. They've been linked to drugs, racketeering, tax evasion, even murder. As in Hollander's case, the Caruso family is very well connected."

"Friends in high places."

"Exactly. There are two brothers who run the outfit. Frank is the oldest, and the one in charge. His younger brother Romano takes care of the administrative side."

"Your investigator found all this out?"

"I told you he was good. Money always leaves a trail. Bank transactions, shell companies, trusts. It's all there if you know where to look."

Savage was impressed. "What kind of law did you practice?"

"Corporate."

"Were you any good?"

"One of the best." Burner snorted. "Looking back now, I must have been insane. I put work before my family, before my marriage." At Savage's surprised look, he nodded. "Oh, yeah. That was on the rocks long before Hannah disappeared. I was a workaholic. Couldn't let it go."

"It happens." Savage thought about how certain cases had consumed him, and still did. About how he'd left Becca alone, even now, with a newborn to look after. A pang of guilt hit him in the chest.

"I'm not surprised she left me," Burner said.

"I thought you were going to look her up?"

"I did. Let's just say she's moved on."

"I'm sorry."

Burner shrugged. "Like you said. It happens."

Savage let a moment of silence hang before continuing. "So, you going to go back to corporate law?"

"No way. I'm tired of defending rich, corrupt bastards. They deserve what's coming to them."

Savage raised an eyebrow.

Burner continued, "I'm thinking about starting my own practice. Helping those who really need it."

"Admirable." Savage raised his coffee cup. "You do realize it won't pay as well."

Burner scoffed. "I don't care about the money. I'd rather do something useful with my time."

A man in search of a cause.

"Then I think it's a great idea."

Burner gave a satisfied nod.

Savage turned his thoughts back to Hollander. "Why'd Hollander leave Philly?"

"Not sure. My guy didn't find anything untoward. He may have fallen out with the Caruso brothers, but then again, he could have come here to extend the organization's influence. His MO is pretty similar. Invest in local businesses, fund community projects, make influential friends, marry the daughter of a billionaire."

Savage stared at him. "That's what Hollander did?"

"He married Selma Van Handermark, John. C. Handermark's eldest daughter. He's one of Denver's biggest landowners and one of our most prominent citizens."

The name did seem vaguely familiar. Then it struck him. "The media mogul?"

"That's the one."

Great. Not only did Hollander have money, he had major money. Money equaled power, especially in political circles. "It explains why nobody wants to go after Hollander." Savage ran a hand through his bed hair.

Burner nodded.

"How does John. C. Handermark feel about his daughter marrying a mobster?"

"You don't think Handermark got to where he is by playing by the rules, do you? Nobody's squeaky clean."

"I guess not."

This just got better and better. Savage felt like he was fighting a losing battle here. No wonder Dewayne had asked for his help. He'd needed an outsider to dig into Hollander and cut through all the political bullshit. Someone who wasn't afraid to ruffle a few feathers.

"I've got to get to the prison." Savage drained his coffee. "I want to talk to Dewayne again. He's been holding back."

"Sure." Burner stood up. "Mind if I take a look at those?" He gestured to the police folder that Savage had brought with him. Luckily, they'd been in the trunk of his car and not at the hotel when it had been searched.

"Suit yourself."

---

"DID you know who it was you were asking me to investigate?" Savage sat opposite Dewayne in the prison meeting room. Once again, they were the only two there. Visiting hours had yet to begin.

"Yeah, I knew." The slumped shoulders gave it away. Dewayne was sporting a new cut above his left eye, a deep gash held together with two tiny strips of medical tape.

"You could have warned me."

"Would you have come, if I had?"

Savage hesitated. "I would have, yes."

Dewayne gave a slow nod. "Then, I apologize. I knew Hollander's reputation. He's above the law, man. He's got connections, you know what I mean? Ain't nobody touchin' him."

Savage had come to the same conclusion. "What do you expect me to do then?"

"I don't know. Something." Dewayne sighed. His massive shoulders rose and fell. "It's not right what happened. Kenan was just a kid and they shot him like an animal and left him to die in the street."

"You don't know that for sure."

"It's Hollander, man. Who else would do that to him?"

"Drug dealers, pimps, gang bangers?" The list wasn't definitive.

"Nah, bro. He wasn't into any of that stuff."

"Unless we can get some proof, we have nothing. I can't go to the police chief on a whim. I need concrete evidence. Shady business dealings and links to organized crime are not enough."

"Hollander's a crook," Dewayne spat. "He's dirtier than most of the guys in here."

"What have you heard?"

"He's ruthless. Takes out anyone who stands in his way. One of the guys in here used to be an enforcer in Hollander's organization. He told me some stuff."

Savage leaned forward in his chair, encouraging the young prisoner to continue.

"Harassing people who wouldn't play ball, threatening folks who refused to pay up, destruction of property, even arranging little *accidents* for people he wanted out the way."

Savage frowned. "This enforcer, would he testify?"

Dewayne gave a bitter laugh. "You crazy? No way, man."

"Then there's nothing I can use." The grayness of the prison walls was getting to him. How Dewayne stood it day after day, Savage had no idea. Then again, the guy had no choice. This was his reality. Gray walls, barbed wire, guards with guns.

He thought of the wide, open spaces of Hawk's Landing, the impossibly blue sky, the misty mountain peaks. He wanted to be back there so badly it hurt.

"You gotta find something," Dewayne said. "You're the only one who can. Please. Help me get justice for my brother. Help us."

Blue skies and rolling plains would have to wait.

Savage got to his feet. "I'll see what I can do."

# SIXTEEN

SAVAGE WALKED BACK to his car, deep in thought. He had absolutely no evidence that Hollander was involved with Kenan Simmons's death. He couldn't even prove Kenan worked for the corrupt businessman. The police file Manning had given him had included Kenan's bank statements. The kid had $123 to his name. No payments had gone in, meaning no financial trail could be traced back to Hollander.

Mrs. Simmons had said her youngest son had been making good money. Cash, obviously. Impossible to trace. Maybe it was worth paying another visit to Kenan's house. He could take a look around his room.

---

MRS. SIMMONS OPENED the door with a guarded nod.

"Morning, Mrs. Simmons." He smiled, but she didn't return it. Dead eyes, forlorn of hope. What did she have to smile for? He dropped his own smile and got straight to the point. "Could I have a look at Kenan's room?"

A group of residents had accumulated in the street outside and were staring at him. He felt their hostility. Why was the white cop back? What did he want with Kenan's grieving mother?

Mrs. Simmons nodded to the onlookers as if to say, "It's alright." There were a few murmurs, and the crowd began to disperse. Tensions were high.

*Help us.*

Dewayne wanted Savage to help his community, not just his family.

Kenan's room looked like he'd just walked out. His mother hadn't touched it. "I haven't been in since he—" She petered off, hovering at the door, unable to step over the threshold.

"That's okay. I won't be long." He nodded at her to go back to the living room. Relieved, she turned and disappeared back down the corridor, leaving him alone.

Savage surveyed the room. It was typical of a young man just starting adulthood. There was a mixture of childish and adult items. A rusty toy car on a shelf, a stuffed animal with a missing eye, an NBA poster. Under the bed he found a basketball, a pitching glove, and an inappropriate magazine. Savage picked up the magazine and slid it into his jacket pocket. That was something his mother didn't need to see when she eventually got around to clearing out his bedroom.

The kid didn't have much else lying around. Some personal items. A bag with a notepad and a couple pens. A brochure from the community center entitled, *An Introduction To Computing*. Kenan was trying to better himself. Learn a new skill. So what was he doing working for Guy Hollander?

Savage searched the closet, rummaged through jacket pockets, checked in the dresser drawers but nothing turned up. Kenan was just a normal kid.

He walked back to the living room. "Thank you, Mrs. Simmons." Kenan's mother was sitting in a well-used armchair, staring at the dark television set. The pictures were all in her head. "Once again, I'm really sorry for your loss."

She gave a little nod and made to get up.

"Don't trouble yourself," Savage said. "I'll show myself out."

She sank down again and went back to her memories as Savage left through the front door.

"You gonna find out what happened to our Kenan?" came a voice from across the road.

Savage glanced up, surprised. He'd thought the crowd had gone. Instead, they were just waiting for him to reemerge. "I'm going to try."

"About time someone did something," came the retort. An elderly African American man stood on the sidewalk, hands thrust deep into his pockets.

Another spat on the ground beside him. "You five-oh?"

"No, sir. I'm a—" He hesitated. How could he get out of this quickly? "A family friend."

The elderly man said, "Yeah? What kind of friend?"

"I ain't never seen you before," a feminine voice chimed in.

*I put Dewayne Simmons in prison.* Savage couldn't imagine how well that would go down.

"Dewayne asked me to look into it."

There was a grunt. Two women joined the men. "Dewayne didn't go shooting anyone," the one said. She was Mrs. Simmons's age, but less beaten down. "You should know that."

"That's not for me to say, ma'am."

Another snort. "Well, someone should. That boy don't deserve what he got. Neither of 'em did."

Savage didn't disagree with that.

"Anyone know who Kenan was working for?" He looked around the group. All he got was blank stares.

"Kenan didn't have no job," one of the women said. "He was studying at the community center."

"I heard that." Savage searched the faces of the crowd. "His mother said he was working for a Mr. Hollander. Anyone heard that name before?"

The men shifted their feet. "I heard of him," the older one said.

"But he don't usually do business in this area." A smirk. "Nothing for him here."

Savage nodded. He was aware of many sets of eyes following him as he got into his car. The stares were less hostile now, more hopeful. In a way, that was worse.

Sighing, Savage took the magazine out of his jacket pocket and threw it on the seat next to him. Something slipped out from between the pages. Frowning, he leaned to pick it up. A coaster?

He squinted to read the name on it.

*Bascule Nightclub.*

His pulse quickened. He took out his phone and pressed the browser icon to enter the club's name into the search engine. The first link to pop up was a brief article about the establishment, built a few years ago. The picture before the actual article was that of Guy Hollander shaking the hand of some other man, both in shiny suits and plastered-wide smiles. Savage skimmed the article and found exactly what he'd been waiting for. Bascule Nightclub was owned by one of Guy Hollander's many subsidiary companies.

---

"KENAN WAS OBVIOUSLY THERE," Savage told Burner once he got back to the warehouse. "Thought I'd check it out tonight."

The lawyer nodded, leaning against the counter, coffee in hand. "Is that wise? I mean, you're already on the guy's radar."

"This is all I got."

"I'll come with you." Burner put his coffee down. "But first, I've got a question."

"About Hollander?"

"Kind of. I took a peek at that police file you left here." Burner nodded at the table. "Did you look into the victim's background?"

"Which victim? Kenan?"

"No, I'm talking way back. The robberies. Did you look into the woman who was shot?"

Savage nodded. "Of course. Helen Ridley. She was a single mom with two small kids. She was killed in one of the Burger King incidents."

"I mean her *financial* background?"

Savage frowned. "We would have run her records."

Burner shook his head. "Her bank statements aren't in the file."

Savage shrugged. "Is it important?"

"You could say that. The week before she died, she received a cash payment of fifty thousand dollars."

Fifty grand. He would have remembered that. "Do we know who it's from?"

"A shell company. The director's name is Jose Gomez."

"Can you trace this Gomez?"

Burner shot him a look. "You know how many people in America are called Jose Gomez?"

"Point taken." He gave Burner a thoughtful look. "So, what are you saying? That she got a payout? You think it had something to do with her death?" The thoughts tumbled into his brain. "You think she was targeted?"

"You're the detective." Burner spread his hands. "What I do know is that she lived at eighty-seven twenty-six Brindle Avenue, Pine Meadows."

"What's her address got to do with anything?"

"You know what's there now?"

"Nope."

"A shopping mall."

"Burner, it's been a long day. Could you just get to the point?"

Burner pushed away from the counter. "At the time of her death, Helen Ridley's house was the only property left on that site. Every other resident had sold out."

"To developers?" A bad feeling coiled in his gut.

"Yep. Except for Helen. It was the house she'd lived in with her husband, a war hero, and she didn't want to move. Too many memories. She wasn't ready to let go."

Savage stared at him. “How do you know this?”

“I spoke with Chandra, her colleague at the hair salon where she worked.”

“How did you—?” Then he got it. “Her bank statement?”

What had Burner said? Follow the money.

“Every month she received a little over two thousand dollars from Sunnydale Hair Salon in Richfield. It wasn’t a bad salary for a hair stylist, but she was popular. All the customers loved her.”

Savage shook his head. Burner certainly had a way with people. He’d gotten more information on Helen in one phone call than the entire team had over the course of the investigation.

“Anyway, Helen refused to give in. Her refusal to sell was holding up the entire multimillion dollar development.”

Savage knew where this was going. “Then, she was involved in the shooting, an apparent freak occurrence. Wrong place, wrong time.”

“Exactly.” Burner gave a grim nod. “She dies, the kids go live with their grandmother in Virginia, and the house is sold to the development company.”

“The fifty grand was an incentive to move, and when she didn’t—”

“There is no way to trace it,” Burner cut in, “but do you want to take a guess at who owned the development company?”

Savage felt sick. “Please tell me it's not Guy Hollander.”

“One and the same.”

# SEVENTEEN

"APEX HOLDINGS." Savage grit his teeth. "Why didn't I make that connection?"

"You didn't look into Helen Ridley's financial past," Burner replied. "If you had, you'd have found it."

"We didn't think to check her out. Just thought she was the victim, not the actual target."

The lawyer shrugged. "Wasn't Apex the group developing on that reservation in Hawk's Landing? Where the Native American kid was killed?"

"That's them." Savage drummed his fist on the countertop. "Douglas Connelly was running the show, but when we arrested his finance officer as well as his head of security, the company shut down the development. Hollander decided Hawk's Landing wasn't worth the trouble."

"What's happened to the site now?" Burner asked. "I didn't stick around long enough to find out. Thought I'd better get the hell out of Dodge before Rosalie and the gang found out I was an imposter." His life wouldn't be worth much if they had.

"The tribal council petitioned to use it for housing. I think they'll get it too. It is historically their land, after all."

Burner nodded.

Savage stared into the distance, lost in thought.

"Don't beat yourself up about it," Burner said. "Hollander wasn't even on your radar back then. Even if you had checked, it may not have raised any red flags."

"All four robberies were a cover up for that one isolated event." Savage paced up and down the kitchen. "Dammit, Burner. It seems so obvious now."

The lawyer didn't reply.

"Three robberies, the third culminating in Helen Ridley's murder. The fourth, a decoy designed to frame Dewayne and Justin. They were set up to fail. Right from the start, someone was manipulating them."

Burner arched an eyebrow. "Then your boy's innocent?"

"He's innocent of murder. Of that, I'm sure. He still robbed the joint."

"Which is a minor felony," Burner said. "He would have got eight, nine years at the most. Probably be out in half that."

"I need to prove it." Savage took a steadying breath, recalling the fresh scars and bruises on Dewayne's face. Life was a constant battle inside. "He doesn't deserve to be in that hell hole."

Burner just nodded. "How can I help?"

"Let's start by visiting that nightclub. Someone there might know Kenan."

---

THEY HEARD the techno beat before they even entered the club. The night air seemed to pulse with it. The queue was growing, but they didn't want to bring attention to themselves by using Savage's law enforcement ID. Instead, they waited, pretending to be regular punters.

Burner wore jeans and a leather jacket, and even though he was older than the average club goer, his biker tattoos and long hair seemed to help him blend in. Savage, clean-cut, in jeans and a T-shirt, had never felt more out of place in his life. The word "Sheriff" might as well have been written across his forehead. Thankfully, the line didn't take long. Fifteen minutes later they were inside.

The music was even louder. A DJ pranced on a raised platform like some sort of avenging angel, mixing rousing club anthems designed to whip the dancers into a frenzy. It was working, too. Below him, people gyrated on the dance floor, hands in the air, losing themselves in the heat and the rhythm and each other, along with whatever upper they'd taken.

Savage had never been one for clubbing, not even in his youth, preferring the more social atmosphere of a bar. The few times he'd been to a club, he'd hated it.

Savage grimaced as he elbowed his way through the crowd, Burner at his heels. The game plan was they'd split up and question the staff, try to find someone who knew Kenan and could verify that he'd worked for Guy Hollander. Savage nodded at Burner, and they went their separate ways.

Savage aimed for the bar. The club was busy, but not yet packed. Three bartenders swirled around each other, shaking and pouring cocktails into glasses for thirsty club goers. He ordered a beer, and when the bartender gave it to him, he leaned forward and shouted, "I'm looking for Kenan. Is he on tonight?"

"Don't know a Kenan," the bartender replied. "That'll be six dollars."

Savage handed over the money. "You sure? He told me he worked here."

"Sorry."

Picking up his beer, he moved away. On the far side of the club, he saw Burner hovering around a bunch of booths. The VIP lounge. Maybe he'd have better luck.

Savage looked around, taking in the animated atmosphere, the designated dancefloor, the strategically placed security. A bouncer stood just inside the door, keeping an eye on the crowd. All the bouncers were dressed the same. Black jeans, black T-shirt, one earpiece.

On a whim, Savage approached one. "Hey, is Kenan here tonight?"

"Kenan? Think you've got the wrong club."

"Really? Damn. He told me he worked here."

"Not here." The bouncer dismissed him, so Savage walked back into the mayhem, letting the crowd absorb him. This was a waste of time. Kenan could have just come here to party. It was a popular nightclub. He could even have brought Isobel here. She said they used to go clubbing together. Savage made a mental note to ask the Washington Park teenager about it.

He was about to head for the exit when he spotted a tall, beefy guy disappear through a door at the back of the club. Not a bouncer, he wasn't wearing the same attire, opting instead for an ill-fitting suit. This guy looked more like an enforcer, a paid thug. Savage recognized the type. And, judging by the bulge under his jacket, he was carrying.

Savage moved forward, took out his phone, and pretended to check it as he waited near to the door. Eventually, the man came back out.

Savage stopped him. "Excuse me. I'm looking for Kenan. You see him around?"

"Kenan?" The man's eyes widened involuntarily. He tried to correct it moments later, but Savage had already noticed.

*Gotcha.*

"Yeah, he told me to meet him here."

"I—I ain't seen him for a couple days." The big guy didn't like being caught off-guard and frowned. "Who wants to know?"

"That's a bummer."

"What do you want with Kenan?"

"He promised me some weed."

A suspicious gaze. "Kenan didn't deal weed."

Burner chose that moment to come up. "Hey, Fred. Long time no see." Savage went along with the ruse, returning Burner's smack on the back. The thug took a step back, watching the interaction.

"Thanks man." Savage waved his beer in the big guy's face, then moved off with Burner. They made a beeline for the exit.

"He knows Kenan," Savage said, as soon as they left the club. "He was surprised when I mentioned him."

"You think he knew he was dead?"

"That's my gut feeling, but it'll be impossible to prove. He doesn't look like the sort who'd testify."

"What do you want to do?"

Savage glanced behind him as the door swung open. Three burly bouncers burst out onto the sidewalk. "Right now, I think we should run."

Burner turned. "Shit."

They broke into a sprint and headed for Savage's car. The bouncers gave chase, but Savage and Burner were lighter on their feet and had a head start. Their pursuers weren't built for speed.

They dove into the Suburban, and Savage started the engine before Burner had closed the passenger door. With a screech of tires, they took off down the street, leaving the bouncers staring after them, their fists clenched and ready for battle.

# EIGHTEEN

"HEY, YOU GOT A DVD PLAYER?" Savage asked for the second time that week. He hadn't yet told Manning that the one he'd borrowed had been destroyed.

Burner shot him a strange look. "Yeah, in the garage. Why?"

"I want to take another look at the footage from the robberies." For the one hundredth, two hundredth, three hundredth time. He'd lost count of how often he'd watched it, hoping to spot something new. Yet, he never did. Hell, he could picture the whole thing in his mind anyway. He didn't need to watch it again. It was just something to do so that he didn't feel so damn useless.

"You got footage?"

"Yeah."

"Of all four robberies?"

He gave a nod. It was the third one he'd fixated on, though. The woman's face was ingrained in his subconscious.

"I didn't see a disc in the folder."

"It's in my car."

Burner shook his head, exasperated.

Savage shrugged. "I've watched them so many times, it slipped my mind."

Burner made a thoughtful expression, then said, "You think that's why they searched your hotel room? They were looking for the disc?"

Savage thought about Manning's smashed DVD player. "I don't know. It's from Dewayne Simmons' case, not his brother's. I came here to look into Kenan's death. Nobody could have known I had that disc."

"Except now we know Hollander could have set up Dewayne and Justin to take the fall for the robberies. Maybe he was worried about what you *did* know."

"It's possible, except the only people who knew I had the disc were my old partner and the evidence archivist." He thought for a moment. "Although, Hagan could have found out. Hagan who refused to question Hollander. Who played mixed doubles with him at their club."

"What?" Burner studied him.

"Lieutenant Hagan, she's the one in charge of homicide. She's been stalling on Kenan's case since the start. It's possible she knew about the disc."

"You think she told Hollander?"

Savage felt heat steal into his face. "I wouldn't be surprised. She's been on Hollander's side ever since I got here. Telling me what an upstanding citizen he is. Hell, she arrested me because I went to question him, something her team should have done at the very beginning."

Burner raised his eyebrows. "Sounds shady."

If what he was thinking was true, Hollander had been onto him right from the start. The scumbag had pretended not to know who he was at the country club, but Hagan could have warned him. She knew Hollander was his prime suspect. He'd told her that much himself.

Savage shook his head. "She played me right from the start. The worst part is, if I go near Hollander again, Hagan will have me arrested. If I confront her, she'll deny everything." He scuffed the base of the armchair. Cornered.

"In that case, let's focus on Dewayne Simmons," Burner said, matter-of-factly. "If we can prove he didn't pull that trigger, we might be able to prove Hollander set him up."

"How are we going to do that? I've been through the footage a thousand times."

"Let me take a look. A fresh pair of eyes always helps."

Savage gave a stiff nod and sank into the chair. "What about Kenan? I can't just let that go."

"We've got to find that 911 caller. He might have seen who the shooter was. Do you have the recording?"

"No. I asked Manning for it, but then his wife was assaulted. I'll give him a call."

After dialing his old partner's number and getting straight to the point, Manning shut him down almost immediately. "No way, Dalton. You're off the case. Besides, technically I'm retired. I don't have the authority."

"I know I'm asking a lot here, but I have nowhere else to turn. No other leads."

"I don't want to get arrested. Hagan's on the warpath. Sorry, buddy. Can't help you."

"I understand." Savage swallowed his frustration. "How's Trish?"

"She's back at home now." Manning's tone was curt. He wanted nothing to do with Savage. Hagan must have warned him off.

"I'm glad. You manage to speak to that barman? The one who gave the abusive boyfriend the alibi?"

"Yeah, it checked out. Guess we'll never know who beat her up."

"I'm sorry to hear that." That didn't sound like his ex-partner, but it was clear Manning wanted him gone. Savage had become a liability. "I'll leave you be."

"Dalton."

"Yeah?"

"Sorry I can't help." His tone was subdued.

"Take care, Manning."

"Yeah. You too."

"He's scared," Savage said, when Burner came back with the

machine. "Hagan's warned him off." He relayed what Manning had said about the recording. "I can still get it, but I'll have to request it from the 911 archives."

"Isn't it a public record?" Burner asked.

"Not if it's evidence of a crime," Savage responded. "The Freedom of Information has some reach, but not when it could potentially compromise an ongoing investigation."

Savage called the Hawk's Landing Sheriff's office. "Barbara, it's Dalton." He heard her squeal down the line. "Yeah, I'm good. Barbara, there's something I need you to do for me."

She readily agreed.

"I need a 911 telephone recording taken at 2:09 a.m. on Thursday, October ninth. Can you request it from the archives? Go about it through official channels. If possible, sooner rather than later." Her request wouldn't get back to Hagan, yet he heard her suck in a breath.

"You're not getting yourself into trouble over there, are you?"

"No, of course not." He didn't tell her he'd already been arrested once and would probably be behind bars again in the not-too-distant future, once the lieutenant found out what he was doing.

"Remember, it's not just yourself you've got to consider now."

She didn't have to tell him that. He grimaced. "I know, Barbara. Thank you."

"Okay. I'll send the audio file to your phone."

He thanked her again and ended the call.

"Let's see what you got." Burner dusted off his DVD player and connected it to the television. He opened the disc drive and took out an old Bon Jovi disc. Burner cleared his throat and put it on a shelf.

Savage chuckled and inserted the disc containing the CCTV footage. The chuckle dissolved as fast as it'd started. "This is the first robbery."

They watched the grainy footage from the street outside Burger King. A white van pulled up and two men jumped out. One tall, one stocky. Both had guns and wore ski masks to hide their faces.

"The van was stolen the week before," Savage said.

They entered the restaurant and less than five minutes later, exited. They were running, both holding bags of cash. The stocky one got behind the wheel, while the tall one dived in the back, and they sped off.

"Slick," Burner said. "In and out in under five minutes. It would take that long for the police to get there if an alarm had sounded."

Savage acknowledged this with a tilt of his head.

"Actually, the cashier did sound the alarm. The perps were long gone before the cops arrived."

They watched the second robbery. This time, it was taken from outside the Burger King itself. The two men entered the store. Once again, both wore masks, both held guns. Like before, they were in and out in record time, carrying the loot in heavy bags. The day's takings. Seamless.

"Okay, let's see the third one," Burner said.

Savage nodded to the television screen. "Here it comes."

They sat back as the events unfolded. Savage replayed them in his mind's eye as he watched. The two visuals were identical. He knew every movement, every flicker, every nuance. He knew the precise moment the woman appeared in the shot, and when she came out. When she was shot.

Afterward, Burner sat staring at the screen.

Savage turned to him. "Thoughts?"

Burner shook his head, speechless. Savage didn't blame him. It was awful to see. The woman's head exploded as she crumpled to the ground. Savage wondered if he'd become numb to it, he'd seen it so many times. The thought worried him.

Burner's voice interrupted his thoughts. "They made it seem like an afterthought."

"I know. At first, I couldn't work out why they'd shot her. It seemed so senseless. They were free and clear."

"Now we know Helen Ridley was the target all along." Burner rubbed his jawline.

Savage nodded sagely.

Burner leaned forward and squinted at the screen. Savage thought he was staring at the woman lying on the ground, blood seeping out across the tarmac, when he said, “Is that another camera over there?” He pointed at what appeared to be an auto repair shop next door to the burger joint. The roller door was shut, but above it, the tiny, bulging eye of a surveillance camera peered down. The angle was such that it might just have captured what happened in front of the restaurant.

Savage stared at the camera, adrenaline and hope now coursing through his veins.

Burner pulled out his phone. “What does it say on the awning? Mike’s Auto Repair Shop?”

Savage leaned in. The name was stenciled in gold across a dark green awning. It wasn’t easy to see from this angle, but they could just make it out. He confirmed the name and Burner searched for the shop’s number.

He couldn’t believe he’d never noticed the second camera before, despite having studied it over and over again. “It’s been a while,” Savage croaked. “The auto repair store might not be there anymore.”

Burner didn’t answer. He simply pointed to his phone. Savage paused the video footage as he waited.

“No answer.” Burner hung up. “It’s pretty late, though. Could be closed for the day.”

Savage stared at the image on the screen. “What do you say we pay Mike a visit tomorrow?”

# NINETEEN

MIKE'S AUTO Repair Shop looked a little worse for wear than it had in the footage from six years before. The green awning above the garage was faded and tatty, the gold name was barely legible, and the paintwork was peeling.

"You Mike?" Savage asked, as he and Burner walked into the garage. It stank of exhaust fumes and grease. The man working beneath the car looked up, only his head and shoulders visible, the rest of his body hidden in the inspection pit.

"Can I help you?"

"Sheriff Savage." He showed the man his ID. "This is my associate Grayson Carter."

Mike peered at them from under the car. "What do you want?" He wasn't rude, just curious.

Savage cleared his throat. "We'd like to ask you about a surveillance camera outside your garage six years ago, when the shooting took place at the Burger King across the street."

Mike frowned. "Why you askin' me about that now? I showed it to the cop at the time, but he didn't want it. Said they had enough evidence."

Savage glanced at Burner. "Which cop?"

"The one working the case. I can't remember his name." Savage's heart sank. A whole crew of officers had worked the burglaries. Mostly detectives, but a couple uniforms as well. Even Savage couldn't remember them all.

"Was it a man?"

"Yeah, shorter than you. Brown hair. Uniform."

Unfortunately, that didn't narrow it down. "White guy?"

"Yeah." Mike climbed out from the grease pit and wiped the sweat off his face, leaving a dirty smear.

"Did the detective actually see the footage?"

"Sure did. He viewed it in my office from start to finish. Terrible business, that woman getting shot and all. Especially since she had those young tykes at home."

Savage didn't need reminding. "He watched it, then told you he didn't need it?"

The man gave an impatient nod. "That's what I said."

"It doesn't make sense." Savage looked at Burner. "Why would a cop ignore evidence?"

"He might if he were covering something up," Burner murmured.

They had to see what was on the tape. Savage turned back to Mike. "You still have it?"

"I think so. It's not something you throw away, you know. I thought about taking it to the press, but then it didn't seem right, considering how that poor woman died."

Ironically, if he had taken it to the press, the outcome may have been different. Curiosity burned in Savage's gut. Burner looked equally eager.

"Can we see it?" Savage asked.

"Give me a second. I'll see if I can find it."

They followed the auto mechanic into his corner office at the back of the garage. Glass screens separated it from the main working area, so he could still look out onto what was happening while he sat at his desk. Savage noticed one other guy working on a Ford Explorer in the back, but that seemed to be the only staff Mike had.

"Just the two of you?" Savage asked, more to make conversation than anything else.

"Yeah, Timmy's my brother-in-law. We used to have a couple more guys but had to lay them off. Times are tough, you know."

Savage gave a somber nod.

"Here it is." He waved it in the air.

"You got some way of playing it?"

"Sure, give me a sec." He cleared some paperwork from off his desk, then slipped the disc into the slot in his hard drive. Judging by the chunky machine, Mike hadn't updated his computer in a long time. Just as well, they didn't make them with built-in DVD drives anymore.

The screen turned static, then cleared as the image appeared. Mike knew exactly where the action began. Both Savage and Burner leaned in.

The angle was perfect. The camera picked up the side of the van closest to the restaurant. Savage found he was holding his breath as they watched the van pull up. The tall guy got out, holding the gun. He tugged open the front door to the Burger King and darted inside, closely followed by his sidekick, the stocky man.

"The shooter is definitely African American," Burner said. "You can tell by the hand holding the gun. He's not wearing gloves."

"We never did find the weapon that killed her," Savage murmured.

"Too bad. It might've given us a couple of prints to go off or, better yet, a DNA hit."

"That's if the shooter didn't take the thirty seconds needed to clean his trail. Doesn't matter either way, there's no gun to run."

The minutes ticked by as the two men were inside the restaurant.

"This is it," Mike told them. "This is when he shoots her."

Savage tensed. He knew the timing like the back of his hand. The two men came out, one holding the money bag, the other – the taller one – pulling Helen Ridley by her hair. When he saw the coast was clear, he released her. Instead of heading back to the van, he raised his gun and shot her in the head.

Burner jumped, visibly shocked. It was worse from this angle. Closer, less fuzzy.

"Poor woman," muttered Mike, shaking his head.

Savage felt queasy, yet it was impossible to look away. He watched, transfixed, as the woman fell to the ground, a hole where her head should have been.

The perpetrator lowered his gun, then ran for the van.

"What a waste of a life," Burner mumbled, clearly moved by this clearer, more visceral footage. But Savage still stared at the screen.

Burner glanced at him. "What?"

"I know why he didn't take this footage into evidence," Savage whispered.

"Why not?" asked Mike.

Savage pointed to the screen. "Because the shooter is right-handed. You can see it clear as day."

"You can see that in the other video too," Burner pointed out.

Savage shook his head. He'd watched that footage enough times to know it frame by frame. "No. You see him shoot her, but his back is to the camera and his accomplice is blocking the view. You don't see which hand he used to pull the trigger." Savage nodded at the computer. "In this video, you can clearly see the shooter is right-handed."

"Why is that important?" Burner asked.

Savage turned to him. "Because Dewayne Simmons is left-handed."

# TWENTY

"I'VE GOT THE 911 RECORDING," Savage said when they got back to Burner's condo. Barbara, dependable as ever, had sent it through.

"Great, let's hear it." Burner took a seat on the couch.

Savage took the opposite seat and played the recording. At first, all they could hear was heavy breathing, like someone was panting.

911. *What's your emergency?*

*A boy's been shot.*

*What's your location, sir?*

*Um... Washington Park. Lilac Avenue.*

*Is the person still breathing?*

*No, ma'am. He's dead.*

*Are you with the victim?*

*No, I can just tell.*

*What is your name, sir?*

*You'd better send someone. He's lying in the street.*

*Can I take your name, sir?*

. . .

THE LINE WENT DEAD.

Burner looked up. "Can we listen to it again?"

Savage replayed it, giving Burner a chance to take it all in. The lawyer nodded as he listened. Finally, he said, "Well, he's a light-skinned male, possibly Caucasian, and appears to be in his fifties or sixties. And if I were a betting man, I'd guess ex-military."

Savage stared at him. "How'd you figure that?"

"You can hear he's a mature man by his voice. The way he calls the victim a boy shows his age."

"And the military?"

"It's the respect. He calls the 911 operator ma'am. He's concise, to the point. He can tell the kid is dead from where he's standing, which means he's got some level of experience with this type of thing. He's not panicked, yet he's just seen a murder. He's used to violence."

"You got all that from a forty second phone call?"

Burner shrugged. "Do you know how many phone calls I've analyzed in my time? Crank calls, scams, cons." He shook his head. "I've become something of an expert."

"I'll say." Savage paused to think. "So we're looking for a white man in his late fifties, with a military background who lives in the Washington Park area."

"I didn't say he lived there."

"How else would he have seen what happened?"

"He could be passing through. You said the phone wasn't his, right?"

"Yeah, it was stolen."

"So, he's also a thief. A thief with a conscience." Burner arched an eyebrow. "How many elderly white guys, ex-military, do you know steal cell phones, yet would call in a murder?"

"Is he homeless?"

"That would be my guess."

"Shit, why didn't I think of that?"

"You've had other things to worry about."

Savage glanced at him. "Hey, you're good at this."

"Thanks."

"Wanna come work for me?"

Burner chuckled. "Can you imagine how well that would go down with Rosalie and the Crimson Angels?"

"Yeah." Savage snorted. "Better not."

---

AT 5:30 A.M., Burner parked his Harley Davidson near an intersection and stored the helmet under the seat. He'd told Savage the motorcycle was part of the new him, and he hadn't been exaggerating. His undercover persona in Hawk's Landing had taught him a lot about the type of man he really was. That's why he'd kept it. He didn't want to forget.

He walked down Lilac Street, towards the location where Kenan was murdered. There wasn't much in the way of traffic. The houses were large and neat. Shutters lined the windows. People here took care of their properties, but then, they could afford to. Not like Mike, the auto repair guy, and others who were struggling to stay afloat. There was nothing faded or tatty about these houses. The vehicles parked in the trimmed driveways were high-end performance cars, their bodywork glistening in the morning dew.

Burner shivered, and it had nothing to do with the morning chill. He'd once lived in a house like this with his wife and daughter. Driven a car like this. He remembered taking Hannah to violin lessons when she was little. Boy, had that girl loved music. His wife had said it was because she'd played classical music to her in the womb. Maybe she'd been right. Hannah had wanted to play for an orchestra when she grew up. Except she never did. Grow up.

He blinked back tears and sucked in the cold air, feeling it burn a path to his chest. That was a long time ago. Another life. Back when he'd still believed in happy endings.

Burner had decided to come out early to see if he could find the man who'd placed the 911 call. Once the sun came up, the homeless population would disperse. They would no longer be in their shelters, rather seeking the warmth of a park bench or standing in line at a food bank or soup kitchen. It was now, just before dawn, that he had the best chance of finding the caller.

Burner followed Savage's directions. When he got to the spot where Kenan had died, he stood and stared down at the faint maroon smudge on the road. It was barely noticeable. In fact, it was so faint it could be mistaken for an oil stain.

The residents probably didn't even notice it anymore. They simply drove over it on their way to work or taking their kids to soccer practice or piano lessons. Nobody wanted to remember what had happened here.

He peered at the properties on either side of the street in line with the red smudge. A lush hedge ran between the two houses on the right, providing a modicum of cover. On the left, a white picket fence about waist high meant that unless the watcher had crouched down behind it, they would have been seen by the perpetrators.

Burner moved to his right. Two houses stood side by side in the sleepy, pre-dawn silence. During the day, they'd be white, bright, and highly visible, but now, they were cast in shadow, the windows dark. Only the lamps above the front doors flickered gently.

Burner studied the hedge. It was quite possible the watcher had stood in front of it, obscured by darkness, out of sight of the streetlamps and the shooter. That's what Burner would have done. He glanced down at the ground but saw nothing but a cigarette butt. He picked it up, twiddling it between his fingers. There was lipstick on it. He threw it back onto the ground.

When he was done, he gazed back down the road to where the flashing red, amber, and green lights punctuated the darkness like a colorful morse code. Beyond the intersection, a parade of shops glittered. He walked toward them. Slowly. Deliberately. Keeping his eyes peeled as he went.

This side of the street provided the most coverage. The houses were taller, two story, with large front gardens and porches. Fences and trees provided convenient hiding places and cast shaky shadows on the ground. A man could move along here with minimal visibility.

At the intersection, Burner came to a halt beside his motorcycle. The traffic was increasing now. Execs getting a head start on the day, commuters heading into the city, delivery drivers eager to miss the morning rush.

The green man flashed, and he crossed the road, heading toward the flickering strip mall. Everything was shut except for one early bird diner. It was popular, with a steady stream of people coming and going.

Burner went inside. He took a seat at the window and watched the ebb and flow of people. Suited professionals, joggers, women carrying rolled up yoga mats.

A waitress approached. "What can I get ya?"

He ordered a black coffee, then smiled at her. "I'm looking for a homeless man. Does anyone like that come in here?" Sometimes these types of diners and coffee shops gave freebies to those who couldn't afford to pay.

She frowned. "You a cop?"

"Nope, a lawyer." At least that much was true. "He's inherited some money from a relative and I'm trying to find him." A small lie, but one that would hopefully get results.

She fell for his story. "How nice. There's old Bob. He comes in every couple of days, and we give him a coffee. He always pays, though. Sits over there at the end and reads the paper. Could you mean him?"

"Possibly. I only have a last name," he lied.

"I don't know his last name, I'm afraid." Just as Burner thought.

"That's okay. Any idea where I can find Bob?"

"He sometimes sleeps around back, at the delivery entrance to the grocery store. They don't mind too much."

"Thanks, you've been very helpful."

"I hope it is him," she said before walking away. "He's a good guy. He deserves some luck."

Burner took his coffee to go and rounded the back of the strip mall.

He walked until he came to a wide loading bay, which led to the back entrance of a grocery store. The unyielding steel doors were closed, but tucked in the alcove was a figure in a dark sleeping bag.

Burner tiptoed toward him, but he wasn't ten feet away when the prone figure opened his eyes and stared directly at him. Burner flinched. The homeless guy didn't. So much for the element of surprise.

Burner gave a reassuring nod. "Hello, Bob."

# TWENTY-ONE

WHILE BURNER SEARCHED for the 911 caller, Savage put the first part of his plan into action. According to one of the uniformed officers out of the Denver PD head office, Lieutenant Hagan ran five miles every morning through Cherry Creek Park before work. The park was a natural prairie landscape to the west of the city, surrounding a large reservoir. According to his source, Hagan never missed a day. "She's a fitness nut," the officer had told him.

Savage was taking a risk intercepting her like this, but he had to find out how much she knew about Hollander's involvement in the Dewayne Simmons case, as well as his potential involvement in Kenan's murder.

"Of course, Kenan could have found out something about Helen Ridley and the robberies," Burner had said last night. Mike had given them a copy of the recording, which they'd saved on Burner's laptop. "Two brothers, one in prison, one dead. Both with ties to Hollander. What are the chances?"

Savage had to admit that was one hell of a coincidence. The problem was, Hollander was involved in so much underhanded stuff that Kenan's death might have had nothing to do with the Burger King robberies six years earlier. "Could be. I'll run it by Hagan tomorrow morning. See what she has to say about it."

"Are you sure that's a good idea? She could have you arrested."

"If we were meeting at the station, that would be a distinct possibility, but out in the middle of nowhere –" He shook his head. "I don't think she will. Besides, I want to gauge her reaction."

"You really think she's involved?"

"That's why we're doing this. I guess we'll find out."

Savage stood at the park entrance where the smooth pavement winding around the reservoir began. He rubbed his hands together to ward off the cold, watching as his breath turned to mist as he exhaled. A low haze hung over the water. Winter was coming.

Overhead, a hawk circled in search of prey, and he watched it for a while as it danced on the currents. The indigo sky faded to a pale blue, and then to a burnished orange as the sun came up.

Around 7:30, he saw Sarah Hagan's dark head bouncing up and down as she rounded the corner of the reservoir on her final stretch back to the parking lot. In her late forties, she had the figure of a much younger woman, thanks to all the running. He studied her slender silhouette, admiring the strength in her long limbs, and her steady, confident gait. It was a pity she was such a bitch.

He still couldn't believe she'd had him arrested. A fellow law enforcement officer. Who did that?

He thought back to Burner's comment the other day. *Someone with something to hide.*

"We'll see," he whispered into the chilled air.

She'd almost reached the gate when Savage stepped out from behind a tree. "Hello, Sarah."

Startled, she reared up like a horse, her running shoes sliding on the loose ground. Savage thought about letting her fall, then moved forward and caught her.

"What are you doing here?" she sputtered, fighting to regain her balance, and shake him off at the same time. Once she was stable, he let her go. Her arms were clammy with perspiration.

"I came to see you."

Hagan looked around to see if he was alone. "This is harassment."

"Relax, I just want to talk. I've got new evidence in the Dewayne Simmons case that I think you should know about."

"I wasn't on the Dewayne Simmons case. That was years ago. Long before my time." Hands on hips, she exhaled, long and slow, trying to regulate her breathing.

"I know. Dewayne has been inside for six years."

"What's this got to do with me?"

"One of the detectives on that case ignored crucial evidence that could have seen Dewayne Simmons exonerated."

Her brow wrinkled. "They made a mistake?"

"Not a mistake. It was deliberate."

"I don't understand. You're saying this officer purposely withheld evidence?"

"That's right. He viewed footage that could have provided the jury with reasonable doubt and chose to hide it. Now why would he do that?"

"I'm not familiar with the case." She brushed a strand of sweaty hair off her forehead. "If you have a problem with the way things were handled, take it up with internal affairs."

"It's your department."

"Not back then, it wasn't. Sheriff, this has nothing to do with me. The Dewayne Simmons case is closed." Not the reaction he'd been hoping for. If she was in bed with Hollander, he certainly hadn't told her about the buried evidence.

He pushed on. "I think you should reopen it."

"Now why would I do that?"

"Because Guy Hollander planned those robberies to mask a murder."

She shook her head. "What on earth are you talking about?"

"The victim, Helen Ridley, owned land that Hollander wanted to redevelop. She wouldn't sell, so he had her killed. He used the robberies to do it."

Hagan was looking at him as if he was mad. "I can't listen to this. I have to get to work." She tried to brush past him, but he put out a hand to stop her.

"Sarah, please. Just hear me out, okay?"

"Give it up, Dalton. Go home to your wife." She glanced at his left hand. "Or your girlfriend. Don't you have a newborn baby? This is not your investigation."

He wondered how she'd heard about that. "Are you going to have me arrested again?"

The barest hint of a smile played at her lips. "I might."

"Look into the victim, Sarah. You'll see what I mean. Fifty thousand dollars was paid into her account the week before she died."

Hagan fell silent, unmoving.

"We didn't check her out back then. I was part of the investigation, and we didn't check out the victim because we thought it was a random shooting. We didn't expect her to be the target."

Hagan's gaze flickered over him. "Dalton, this is madness. Hollander's an upstanding businessman. He's not going to murder someone because of a real estate deal."

"It was a multimillion-dollar mall development and Helen Ridley was the only person standing in his way."

"You've got proof that he paid this woman off?"

"It was a cash deposit."

Hagan threw her hands in the air. "Jesus."

"It was his development company, Sarah. His mall. Can't you see? The robberies were just a smokescreen, an excuse to get Helen Ridley out of the way."

"You can't bombard me with this stuff, Dalton. Where's the proof? Can you prove he organized the robberies?"

"Not yet. Hollander's smart. He gets other people to do his dirty work for him."

"Then you've got nothing?"

"I know what kind of man he is, Sarah. He did this. We've just got to find a way to prove it. With your resources—"

She held up a hand. "No. There are no resources. I'm stretched thin as it is. Even if what you're saying is true, there's nothing I can do about it. I can't reopen the case without approval from the Deputy Chief, and—"

"Then get it." He stared at her. "Get the approval."

"He'll never agree. You're accusing Guy Hollander of murder."

"His friend." Savage shot her a hard look.

"Yes, his friend! And from what I can gather, you have no evidence either, other than it was his development company. Even if they weren't friends, the Deputy Chief would be crazy to reopen the case."

Savage met her gaze head on. "He's guilty, Sarah. I know you think he's above it all, but he's not. The guy is dangerous. He's been ripping people off since he got to Denver a decade ago. Did you know Guy Hollander isn't even his real name? Perhaps you should tell the Deputy Chief that."

She rubbed her forehead. "I've got to go."

"Take a look at the case files, Sarah. You tell me if I'm crazy."

Sighing, she said, "Only to get you off my back. Jesus, Dalton. Anyone would think you've got a hard-on for this guy."

He exhaled. "Thank you."

"Don't thank me. I'm not reopening the case. You need concrete evidence before I even consider going to the DC with that."

"I'll get it."

She sighed. "Where can I reach you?"

"I'm staying at Hotel Vesta. River North Art District."

She gave a stiff nod, then turned and walked away, leaving him standing by the gate. A sharp cry rang out and he glanced up. The hawk had spotted his prey.

Savage walked back to his car and climbed in, but before he drove away, he sent a text message to Burner.

*We're in play.*

# TWENTY-TWO

THE WAITRESS SMILED at them as they ordered bacon sandwiches and more black coffee. Although the ex-soldier was in his early forties, he appeared much older. His beard was streaked with gray, his long, unkept hair straggly and in need of a wash. He sat with his hands in his lap, as though he was embarrassed to put them on the table and kept looking at Burner with a mixture of curiosity and suspicion. "Who are you again?"

"I'm a lawyer, but this isn't about the law. I'm trying to find out who shot a youngster in Wash Park last Thursday night. I think you might know something about that."

The homeless man eyed the door as if he wanted to bolt out of it. "Don't know what you mean."

"I'm not with the police. I don't care where you got the phone, I just want to know what you saw."

Bob shifted in his seat. The waitress set two steaming mugs in front of them. Burner smiled his thanks.

"How'd you know it was me?" Bob asked, quietly.

"I listened to the 911 call. The ma'am, the observational details. You gave yourself away."

Bob nodded. Burner didn't have to explain. He got it. "I was walking to the grocery store." He gave a backwards jerk of his head, indicating behind the diner. "That's where I sleep sometimes. It's sheltered from the rain."

Burner let him continue.

"I saw this kid walking down the middle of the street. He looked happy, kinda smiling to himself, like you do when you're in a good mood."

Burner nodded.

"Anyway, this car comes driving up. I didn't hear it at first, just saw the headlights."

"Make?"

"A black Hyundai SUV. Definitely electric. That thing was stealthy, man."

Burner made a mental note.

"I stepped back into the shadows. Force of habit. So, the car stops beside the kid and the window rolls down. The driver says something. I'm not sure what it was, but it could have been, 'Get in'."

"Get in? Like he knew the kid?"

"Yeah, that's what it seemed like to me."

"What happened next?"

"Nothing. The car didn't move. I waited, assuming a drug deal was going down or something."

"How long was he in there for?"

"A few minutes. I wasn't counting. Then I saw a flash inside the car, like a firecracker." He glanced down at his hands. "I knew someone had been shot."

"You recognized the sound?"

"You don't forget a sound like that." He leaned forward and reached for his cup. Burner noticed his hand was shaking.

"What then?"

Bob took a slow sip, steeling himself, then glanced up at Burner. "Then the door opened, and the kid fell out onto the street."

"They pushed him out of the car?"

A nod.

"Which side?"

"Passenger side. Same side he got in. I could tell the kid was dead, the way he slumped onto the ground. That's when I saw the blood. Gut wound." Bob shook his head. "Not much you can do about that."

Burner studied him. The homeless man seemed confident in all his answers. He wasn't drunk, or high. He seemed to have a solid grasp on reality, at least for now. There was no reason to doubt what he said. "You think there was someone else in the car with the driver? An accomplice?"

Bob rubbed his eyes. Dirty hands, uncut nails, a military tattoo on his forearm. "Don't think so but I can't be sure. I only saw one person in that car and that was the driver."

Burner's heart skipped a beat. This guy had seen the shooter. "Would you recognize him if you saw him again?"

"Nah, all I saw was a shadow. A silhouette. But one head, not two. I mean there could've been someone else in the back seat, but I don't think so."

"Okay, one shooter. How'd he get the kid out?"

"Leaned over, opened the door, then shoved him out?"

It was possible.

"I don't suppose you got a plate?"

Bob shook his shaggy head, reminding Burner of a sheep dog. "It didn't have plates."

"None at all?"

A bleary-eyed shake. "Nah."

"He must've removed them earlier." Except that was weird. "He'd have been pulled over without plates. It's risky."

The homeless guy shrugged as if to say, *that's their problem*.

It did show premeditation, however. It meant that whoever had killed Kenan had thought about it, prepared for it. They'd removed the plates to not be identified.

"This wasn't a random attack," Burner muttered, more to himself than to Bob.

"Sure wasn't. That gun had a suppressor. Whoever was in that car went there to kill that kid. I don't know what he was into, man, but it was bad. Real bad."

The waitress came back with their food. Bob dug in with the appetite of a man who hadn't had a decent meal in a long time. Burner picked at his, deep in thought.

Afterwards, they talked a bit longer. Bob was knowledgeable about current affairs. He knew a lot about the neighborhood, too. Burner suspected he could tell them a lot about what went on there after hours.

"You never saw the kid before?"

"No. I would've said. He didn't live around there."

"You said he was in a good mood. You think he met with someone?"

Another shrug, mouth full of food.

"How'd you end up on the street?" Burner asked when Bob was finishing his bacon sandwich.

Bob wiped his hands on a napkin. "Couldn't hold down a job, kept freaking out. Nobody wants to employ a nutcase. Eventually, they fired my ass. I tried flipping burgers but couldn't make the rent. In the end, I lost my apartment and started sleeping in my car. Eventually, they took that away from me too. The street was all I had left."

Burner felt bad for the guy. He'd served his country, and this is how it repaid him. "There are programs—"

The veteran raised his hand. "I know all about 'em. Cognitive behavioral therapy, they called it." He'd snorted. "Didn't do shit for me."

Burner didn't know what else to say. He couldn't help a man who didn't want to be helped. Instead, he gave Bob his business card. "If you ever need anything—" He left the rest hanging.

Bob didn't respond, but he did pocket the card.

Burner thanked him for his time, paid the tab, and left.

---

SAVAGE SAT on the low ledge outside Burner's garage and watched him drive up. He'd heard the low, deep-throated growl of the Harley-Davidson long before he'd seen it.

"How'd it go?" Savage asked, as Burner climbed off his motorcycle. "Did you find him?"

"Yeah, I found Bob. Good guy."

"Bob? That's his name?"

Burner nodded, then pulled off his helmet.

The curiosity was killing him. "Did he see who shot Kenan?"

Burner unlocked the padlock on the garage door, then rolled it up, grimacing at the ear-splitting screech. "Hang on. Let me put the Hog away."

Savage had no choice but to wait.

"The whole neighborhood knows when you get home," he commented dryly.

Burner grunted, then wheeled the motorcycle inside. He hiked the heavy machine up onto its stand, before turning to Savage. "The shooter drove up in a black Hyundai SUV. It was dark, past midnight, and the windows were tinted. He couldn't see inside."

Savage's heart sank. Dammit. "So Bob can't ID the shooter?"

Burner held up a gloved hand. "The SUV drove up alongside the kid, and the driver asked him to get in."

Savage's eyebrows shot up. "He *knew* his shooter?"

"Looks that way. Also, the SUV had no plates."

Savage's expression darkened. Premeditation. "It was an organized hit."

"Yep." Burner gave a curt nod. "The next thing, the gun goes off. Bob saw the flash inside the vehicle. Heard it too, but it was muted, like the shooter was using a silencer."

"Bob tell you that?"

"Yeah. He knows guns."

Savage was listening carefully now. "That's why there wasn't any peripheral spatter. Kenan was shot in the car."

"Correct. After the gun went off, the car door opened, and the shooter pushed or kicked Kenan out onto the street."

"Was he dead?"

"Bob says yes, and he's seen enough dead bodies to know."

Savage nodded. "He check for a pulse?"

"That's where it gets a bit sketchy. I think he did but didn't want to admit it. Doesn't want the police to look too closely at him."

"Fair enough." Savage pursed his lips. "How'd he make the 911 call?"

"A businessman left his phone in a coffee shop, and Bob picked it up. He was planning on returning it, except the owner's details weren't on the phone."

"You believe him?"

"Nah, he stole that phone. There's a lucrative market in second-hand cellphones, particularly ones that are unlocked. What he got for that phone, he could have lived off for a week."

"Except he used it to call 911, rendering it useless. He must have known the police would be all over it like a fly on shit."

"He knew."

"And he did it anyway."

Burner shrugged. "He's a good guy. What can I say?"

They walked into Burner's building together.

In the elevator, Savage said, "I'd love to pin this on Hollander, but how would he have known where Kenan was? I mean, the kid walked his girlfriend home. He wasn't there to meet anyone, to do a deal or anything nefarious. I just don't get it."

"Time to look at the girl's parents?" Burner asked.

Savage had thought about that, but then they'd found out about Hollander's mob connections in Philly. Savage thought for a moment. "Maybe. Unless Hollander was tracking him, or he'd told someone where he was going."

"Still, it's a stretch." Burner unlocked the front door to his warehouse apartment.

"Agreed. Let's rule out the folks, then we'll take another look at Hollander."

They walked into the living room, and Burner went straight to the kitchen and put on some coffee. "How'd it go with Hagan? I saw your message. Shouldn't we get to the hotel?"

"There's no rush. They won't try anything in broad daylight. We've got all afternoon to question Isobel's parents and then get to the hotel by sundown."

Burner turned to him. "You still think Hagan's dirty?"

He shrugged. "If she tells Hollander where I'm staying, we'll know. I made a reservation for today. That's where they'll come for me."

# TWENTY-THREE

THE DRAKES LIVED in a detached double-story home on Bougainvillea Close, around the corner from Claudia Dorrington, the woman who'd seen Isobel with Kenan the night he was killed.

Isobel was still at school when they knocked on the door. The teenager would not be happy when she discovered Savage had told her parents about Kenan, but he had no choice. He had to rule her family out of the investigation.

A ruddy-faced man with an expensive shirt stretched over a large paunch opened the door. "Can I help you?"

"Sheriff Savage and Grayson Carter," Savage showed his ID. "Do you mind if we come in and ask you a few questions?"

"What's this about?"

"The shooting last week."

"Oh. Sure. Come in." He held the door open for them. They stepped into a lavish hallway with subdued lighting and a vase of colorful flowers in full bloom on an antique sideboard. "We can sit in the living room."

That too was spacious and elegantly decorated. An enormous L-shaped couch took up half the room, facing a massive television mounted on the wall. A glass coffee table sat in front, with marble coasters and another vase of flowers.

"How can I help? We didn't see anything, if that's what you're here for."

"Your daughter knew the victim. Were you aware of that?" Savage had debated how to handle this, but in the end thought the direct approach was best. It would allow him to gauge Angus Drake's reaction.

"Isobel? Surely not." He looked surprised. "She would have said something."

"She was with him the night he was shot," Savage continued. "In fact, she may have been the last person to see him alive."

Angus Drake puffed out his chest. "My daughter did not know that person. I hope you're not suggesting she had anything to do with the shooting?"

"I'm not suggesting anything, Mr. Drake, but she did know him and in fact, was out with him that night. He walked her home. She didn't want me to tell you, for obvious reasons."

"But...but..." He spluttered, as if this couldn't possibly be true. "How?"

"You'll have to discuss that with your daughter, sir. She's already given me her statement. I spoke to her at the school a few days ago."

"You have no right to question my daughter without a parent present." Angry, now.

"She turned eighteen last month. Technically, she's an adult in the eyes of the law."

Angus Drake stared at him, then his shoulders slumped. "She would have told us if she'd known him."

"I'm sure she didn't want to concern you," Burner said, speaking for the first time.

"You didn't know they were friends?" asked Savage.

"Of course not."

"Did your wife?"

"Neither Marjorie nor I knew our daughter was involved with the dead person, if indeed she was."

"Kenan," said Savage. "His name was Kenan Simmons."

"Whatever. My daughter has never mentioned him."

"I knew," came a soft voice from the doorway. They all looked up as Mrs. Drake walked in. The slender woman in her early forties had fair hair brushing her shoulders and wore an apron over her clothes. There were smudges of flour on the front. Savage could see the resemblance with her daughter. They had the same brown, almond-shaped eyes.

"You knew?" Her husband stared at her. "Why didn't you say anything? The kid was gunned down less than a block away."

"Because Isobel wouldn't want me to. She doesn't know that I know." Mrs. Drake looked at Savage. He gave a small nod to show he understood.

"Good God, Marjorie. Why would you keep this from me?"

Marjorie sank down on the arm of the L-shaped couch. "Isobel's been sneaking out of her room to see Kenan a couple times a week. She's always back around one or two in the morning, and he always walks her home from the bus stop." Marjorie Drake struck Savage as a smart, observant woman who cared for her daughter.

"What the hell?" Angus Drake's cheeks became mottled. "Why didn't you tell me?"

Mrs. Drake glanced at her husband. "Because I knew this is how you'd react."

He opened his mouth and shut it again. Eventually, he turned back to Savage. "I don't want my daughter messed up in this."

"She isn't," Marjorie answered, a hard tone to her voice. "Kenan was a nice boy. I knew she wouldn't bring him home because of you, so I watched while she went out to meet him. I didn't tell her I knew, but I'm her mother. Of course I know when she sneaks out, and what time she comes home."

Angus Drake looked blank.

Savage nodded. "You didn't notice anything untoward, then. The night he was shot?"

She hesitated. "I'm not sure if this is relevant or, but I did see a black car pass by a couple of times earlier in the evening."

"What kind of car?" Savage said, quickly. Burner glanced at him.

"An SUV type. I don't know the make or model or anything. I'm not very good with cars."

Savage ground his teeth. "What was it doing?"

"Just driving around. I only noticed because I was watching the window, waiting for Isobel to get home. It stopped once, down the street. I don't know why. I saw someone get out and go around to the back. I think they got something out of the trunk, and then it drove off again."

"How many times did you see it go past?"

"Three times, I think."

"Mrs. Drake, this is very important. Did you see more than one man get out of the vehicle?"

"No, just the one." Her face creased with worry.

"Was that the shooter?" Angus Drake cut in.

Savage held up a hand. "Maybe. We can't be sure."

Mrs. Drake gasped. "If I'd known—"

"Did you see what the man looked like?" Burner turned to Mrs. Drake. "Or get the license plate number?"

"No, he was too far away." Her eyes flickered with concern. "I wish I had, but I didn't think anything of it other than it was a bit odd. I thought maybe he had car trouble or something."

"That's okay. You're doing great." Savage smiled at her.

"If that was the shooter, what was he doing circling our house?" Angus Drake shot out of his chair and began pacing up and down the living room. "Was he waiting for the kid? Waiting outside our house?"

Mrs. Drake's hand flew to her mouth. "Oh, Lord."

"I don't know, Mr. Drake. I don't even know if it was the shooter." Although, Savage would bet good money on it. What Mrs. Drake had seen was probably the perp taking off the plates and putting them in the trunk. That way he only had to drive a few blocks without them. Less chance of being noticed.

"Because if it was, how did he know that kid was going to be here? Has he been watching us, watching my daughter?"

"You think someone's been watching Isobel?" Her gaze flew to Savage. "Is my daughter in danger?"

"I don't think so, Mrs. Drake."

"But you don't know," Angus Drake hissed, turning to him.

"No, I don't, but if that was the shooter, why did they only act after Kenan had dropped Isobel off at home? If they'd wanted to target both of them, they'd have done so before she got home."

Mrs. Drake was nodding. "Yes. Yes, that makes sense."

Angus Drake grunted.

Savage glanced at Burner and shifted his gaze to the door. It was time to go. Staying here any longer would just exacerbate the issue. They had what they'd come for.

Savage stood. "Thanks for your time. If we have any more questions, we'll let you know."

Burner also got to his feet. He smiled at Mrs. Drake who was picking at her thumb nail and biting her lip. "It'll be okay."

"You find this bastard." Angus Drake said as he walked them to the door. "I don't want him anywhere near my house again."

"That's what we're trying to do, sir," Savage said. They walked out the front door and straight to the car.

"That was interesting," Burner remarked, as he slid into the passenger's seat.

Savage scowled as he started the engine. "Pity she didn't get a closer look. It would have been helpful if we could get an ID on the shooter."

Burner strapped himself in. "He's a ghost."

Savage glanced across at him. "A ghost with real bullets. That kill."

# TWENTY-FOUR

"MAYBE YOU CAN REPRESENT DEWAYNE SIMMONS," Savage said, as they sat in his hotel room, waiting for something to happen. It was nearly nine o'clock. The sky outside was an inky black adorned with only the faintest smudge of stars. You had to go to the outskirts of the city if you wanted to see them properly. Somewhere like the reservoir where Hagan went running. They'd be much brighter out there. Savage had been here since four-thirty, after they'd gotten back from the Drakes' and was beginning to go a little stir crazy.

Burner's eyebrows shot up.

"He needs a lawyer," Savage continued, turning away from the window. "Someone to present his case to the DA. He could be your first client." Burner did say he was thinking about starting his own practice.

Burner tilted his head. "I hadn't planned on starting so soon."

"No time like the present."

"I guess I could—"

"Good." Savage masked a grin. He trusted Burner. Dewayne would be in good hands.

Time seemed to drag. They discussed Dewayne's appeal. Burner thought it might work. "He's got a real shot at being exonerated."

Savage hoped so. The man deserved it. He'd more than paid for the botched robbery attempt and deserved a second chance. So did his mother.

The two ordered room service and watched an old cop show on TV. Still nothing happened. Burner read a newspaper while Savage spent a lot of time going over the events of the last few days in his head. Questioning everything.

"Maybe I'm wrong," he sighed, eventually. "Maybe Hagan isn't involved."

"Let's give it tonight," Burner said. "If nothing happens, we'll know you were wrong."

Savage shook his head. "I feel like I'm missing something. But I don't know what."

Burner put down the newspaper. "The most important factor in my book, is that whoever shot Kenan, knew where he'd be that night. Thanks to Mrs. Drake, we now know that. They were either watching him or knew his routine. Probably both, given that they were hanging around Isobel Drake's house the night of the shooting."

Savage nodded. "We also know they drive a black electric Hyundai SUV and had the foresight to remove the plates before the attack." He scratched his chin. "Why would they do that? Why not just steal a car?"

"Maybe they did and took off the plates for good measure."

Savage wasn't convinced. "A stolen vehicle... you wouldn't bother to remove the plates."

"Then maybe they did use their own car." Burner tilted his head to the side. "Or they didn't have time and had to act quickly."

"That makes more sense. If you're watching someone, waiting for them, you wouldn't have time to change cars."

"They're a one man show." Burner summed up. "Is that what we're saying?"

"Hollander wouldn't do it himself, of that I'm sure." Savage scratched his head. "And his thugs would know better than to use a vehicle registered to Hollander or one of his companies."

"He could have outsourced it to one guy. To make sure nobody else knew, not even those closest to him."

"That's possible. He hired a professional hitman to take care of Kenan."

Burner leaned back in his chair, nodding slowly. "They used a silencer, which means they have knowledge of and access to weapons. Anyone can get a gun but not many people think to get a silencer."

"A pro would."

"So could Hagan."

"You think a cop did this?"

"I don't know. All I'm saying is they have access to weapons too. They'd be able to track Kenan, either using his cellphone or a tracker. They could follow him, find out his routine."

"But Kenan got into the car. He knew his killer."

"There is that." Burner threw his hands in the air. "A guy like Kenan is unlikely to get into a cop's car."

Savage raked a hand through his hair. "Which brings us back to Hollander." He emitted a low growl of frustration, then got up and marched up and down the hotel room. "We're going around in circles."

"Let's hope your little ploy worked and Hagan told Hollander where you're staying. In which case, he'll come for you." Burner stifled a yawn. "He ransacked your room once before, and we know he doesn't like loose ends. Plus, you two have history."

Savage grimaced. "He's going to want me out of the picture. I'm the only one who's pushing this. With me gone, he's home free. With Hagan in his pocket, the investigation into Kenan's death will stall and he'll get away with it."

"Just like he has with everything else."

He never meant to use himself as bait. Savage thought grimly of Becca and Connor back in Hawk's Landing. He'd broken his promise to her. He'd said he wouldn't directly put himself in danger, but if it meant catching this guy –

Neither man slept. They turned the light off so it wouldn't show under the door, but while Burner scrolled through his cellphone,

Savage was too uptight to do anything requiring concentration, so he lay on the bed, willing something to happen.

Just before one o'clock in the morning, they heard a gentle scraping at the door. Burner, who was dozing in the chair, jumped up and hid in the bathroom like they'd planned. Savage, still lying on the bed, pretended to be asleep.

There was a soft click and the door sprung open. Savage lay dead still, his heart hammering. This was it. This was what he'd been waiting for. He squinted at the faint smidgeon of light. Was it Hagan? Or Hollander? Or someone else? One man or two? How many had they sent to kill him?

The silhouette progressed into the room. Savage tried to make out their features but couldn't. It was too dark, or the killer was wearing a ski mask or something. A shadow loomed on the wall turning the intruder into a formless giant. It reminded Savage of one of those old movies, although why he'd thought of that now, as he lay here waiting to be shot, he had no idea. One thing he knew for sure, though, the killer was alone – and holding a gun. Savage could see the suppressor extension distorted on the wall. Was this the same person who'd shot Kenan?

The killer made no sound on the plush carpeting. If Savage really had been asleep, he wouldn't have heard a thing. It would have been Game Over.

Savage waited for the intruder to make his move. Timing was everything. Too soon and the guy would get away. Too late, and he'd be a dead man. Burner would wait for his signal.

The shadowy arm rose as the killer took aim.

"Now!"

The gun discharged. Savage felt a searing pain in his side. It wasn't a direct shot, but it knocked the breath out of him. Wincing, he landed hard on the floor on the far side of the bed.

Burner burst from the bathroom. "Freeze!"

The killer, realizing it was a set-up, turned and pushed Burner out of the way. It happened so quickly, the lawyer lost his footing and ricocheted off the wall.

Savage groaned as he felt his side.

"Dalton, you okay?" Burner got to his feet and rushed around the bed.

"The vest got it," Savage wheezed. "Go after him. Find out who it is."

Burner took off after the shooter.

Groaning, Savage got up. Crap, it hurt. He turned on the bedside lamp and lifted his shirt. His fingers found the compressed bullet, still warm and compacted in the Kevlar.

Savage hobbled across the room and out into the corridor. Echoes from the stairwell told him they'd gone that way, so he stumbled in that direction. Ignoring the ache in his side, he followed Burner and the shooter, taking the stairs two at a time. He nearly lost his footing several times and was amazed when he got to the bottom in one piece. The landing was deserted.

*Where'd they go?*

Savage listened, his body still. Only his chest rose and fell in painful gasps as he caught his breath. A door slammed. He turned in that direction and pushed open a swing door to the underground parking garage.

Two shadows raced towards the ramp. One thicker, more heavyset, and Burner, about a hundred yards behind, wiry and compact. He'd never catch him. The killer had too much of a head start.

Gritting his teeth, Savage ran after them. The killer wore black and was too far away for Savage to see his face, even under the harsh fluorescent lights in the garage.

"Stop!" Burner yelled, out of breath.

The killer leaped over the exit boom and took off down the street. If only he could get a clear shot. He raised his weapon, but there were too many obstacles in the way. The contrasting light made it hard to get a bead on the runner. Burner raced after the disappearing figure while Savage, gasping for breath, struggled to keep up.

Savage stumbled up the ramp, gripping his side. He'd lost sight of the killer now but in the distance, he saw Burner's figure leap over a curb and race down the gravel road toward the dust bowl. Maybe the killer had parked there too.

As confirmation, a screech of tires could be heard up ahead. Burner was yelling into the night sky. A hazy dust cloud indicated the shooter's vehicle had taken off down the street, away from them.

"You get a plate?" Savage gasped.

"No." Burner waved his free hand after the departing vehicle. "He had them taped up. I aimed for the tires but missed."

"Shit!" Savage doubled over, coughing.

"Do you need a hospital?"

He shook his head. "Bruised ribs, that's all. I'm just pissed we let him get away."

"Sorry." Burner looked crestfallen. He was also panting hard. "I tried my best."

"Not your fault. He was quick and he had a head start." His eyes followed the route the shooter had taken, as if he'd left fiery track marks behind him.

"Also, he was wearing a ski mask," Burner said. "I couldn't see who he was."

Savage had thought as much.

"It was a sedan, I think," Burner said. "A dark color. Black, maybe navy or dark gray. Took off before I even got here. There was dust everywhere."

Savage grunted. "That's something, at least."

They'd been so close. Now the killer was in the wind.

"Well, you sure got one thing right." Burner turned to Savage. "Hagan's definitely dirty."

Savage gave a grim nod. "Seems so." He strode across the dust bowl to where the shooter's tire tracks were still engraved in the ground. "You got a light?" There were none on the outdoor parking lot, if you could even call it that.

Burner took out his phone and activated the flashlight.

"Mind if I—?"

Burner handed Savage the phone. Pointing the beam of light onto the ground, he took a long, hard look.

"Anything?"

Savage felt his pulse quicken. He stared at the tracks.

"Dalton?" Burner crouched down beside him.

*Surely not.*

"It can't be..." Dalton muttered, rubbing his eyes. He took another look, closer this time, running his finger along one of the tire tracks.

"What?"

Without answering, Savage got up. He followed the track line to the end of the parking lot, dread welling in his chest.

*Please, no.*

Except, there it was. Clear as day. He bent down and touched the indentation again, just to be sure.

Savage stood up, slowly, every atom in his body wishing it wasn't so. His voice was hoarse when he spoke. "I know who our killer is."

# TWENTY-FIVE

SAVAGE LEFT Burner at the hotel and drove back to the auto repair store. It was nearly two in the morning, but he didn't care. He had to know if he was right.

Mike and his family lived in an apartment above the garage. Savage parked in front of the building and looked for a way in. The quietness felt strange, cloying. Unnatural after the hour of frenetic activity. He was still pumped, adrenaline coursing through him, and his heart throbbed in his head as he walked around the house, looking for a way in.

On the side of the property, he spotted a steep flight of stairs leading to a front door. They were only just visible in the dim streetlight. Savage climbed them, using the railing to haul himself up, then pressed the buzzer. It seemed gratingly loud in the surrounding silence.

He waited a couple of minutes, then pushed it again. Finally, footsteps and the door swung open. A groggy Mike stood there in a robe and bare feet. When he saw who it was, he spluttered, "What the hell? Do you know what time it is?"

"I apologize for the interruption, but I have to ask you something."

Savage pulled out his phone and held it up. On it was a photograph of Savage and another man, their arms draped over each other's shoulders. They were both smiling. "Is this the officer you showed the surveillance footage to?"

Mike's tired eyes narrowed as he gazed at the photo. "Yeah, that's him."

Savage felt the bottom drop out of his world. Up until now he'd been telling himself it was some other car. That he was mistaken. It was all a horrible coincidence and that his ex-partner wasn't bent.

Except it wasn't.

"Thanks." He turned away, still clutching the railing, afraid that if he let go, he might tumble to the bottom.

"That's it?"

Savage didn't turn around. "That's it."

Mike waited a few moments, grunted, then closed the door.

Savage hobbled to his car, his head spinning. It was time to confront Manning.

---

"IT'S HIM," Savage shouted as he turned west onto the I-70. He'd called Burner on the speaker phone as soon as he got into the Suburban. "It's definitely him."

He'd know those tire tracks anywhere. Five years they'd been partners. He still remembered Manning explaining that the alignment was off, that's why the vehicle leaned to the side. They'd tried to fix it, but it kept happening. A design fault, apparently. But he loved the car too much to trade it in.

Savage put his foot down and the SUV surged forward. The more he thought about it, the more it made sense. Manning had ignored the video surveillance footage because Hollander had asked him to. He was in Hollander's pocket. The house extension, the patio, the grill. Manning hadn't saved for that on a cop's salary, he'd been accepting kickbacks. He was Hollander's man on the inside.

"Did Mike ID him?" Burner asked over the speaker.

"Yeah. There's no mistake."

"Sorry, Dalton. I know you two were close."

Once. Not anymore. Never again.

An hour ago, his ex-partner had tried to kill him.

"How'd you know it was him?"

"The tire tracks. Ford Mustang. It's heavy on the front left tire on account of the alignment being off. Always has been. Manning's had the same car for years. Loves that thing."

"*That's* how you know it's him? There could be a million drivers with faulty alignment in Denver."

"We're not looking at a million drivers. We're looking at a small pool of suspects. He's a cop, he has a service weapon, access to accessories like silencers. He could have found out where I was staying from Hagan. All he had to do was ask. She would never suspect him."

No one would. He'd been fooling everyone for years.

"What are you going to do?"

"I don't know. Speak to him, I guess. Bring him in."

"At home? In front of his wife and kids? It's nearly three o'clock."

"He just tried to kill me, Burner. I've got to go after him." He still couldn't believe it. What made a man veer so far off track that he was prepared to take a friend's life? "He buried that evidence in the Dewayne Simmons case. He's been in Hollander's pocket for years."

"You want me to provide back-up?"

Even if Burner left right then, he was still twenty-five minutes away. He'd never make it in time, and there was no way Savage was going to wait and give Manning a chance to get away. Savage thought about calling Hagan, but she'd just tell him to take it up with IA in the morning.

"No. This is something I have to do alone."

"If you're sure." Burner hesitated. "What do you want me to do?"

"Look into Manning's past. I mean way back, like before he joined the Academy."

"You think there's a connection with Hollander?"

"Maybe. There must be a reason why Manning sold out like that." Savage stared grimly ahead. It was possible that he was making excuses for the guy, looking for a justification that wasn't there, but he couldn't understand how things had gotten so out of control.

"Sure, leave it with me."

"Thanks Burner."

"Keep me posted."

How could Savage have been so blind? It would have been simple to access case files, no one would have thought twice. Manning had been on the force forever. He was one of the stalwarts, completely trustworthy.

When had he sold out to Hollander? At least six years ago, because that's when Dewayne Simmons was convicted and sent down for life. Savage gave a low whistle. God only knew how many cases had been compromised over the years. That's why there was nothing on Hollander in the files. The mobster had a guardian angel in Homicide looking out for him.

Savage flew west toward Sunnyside. It wasn't far away, maybe a ten-minute drive at this time of night. He shouldn't be far behind his shooter.

With every mile, anger built inside him. Manning was willing to let an innocent man rot in prison so he had a more comfortable retirement. So that he could build an extension on his home, put his kid through college. He knew Dewayne hadn't killed Helen Ridley, yet he'd calmly sat there and said nothing when the kid had been arrested. When his mother had broken down in court. When Kenan had watched his big brother be taken away in cuffs to serve a life sentence.

Savage turned off the freeway and wound through the suburban streets until he reached Manning's house. The windows were in darkness. Only the porch light flickered as the trees blew across it. He parked in the drive, in front of the garage. Manning's mustang was nowhere to be seen.

There was no way he'd have beaten Manning here. Manning wasn't coming home. Still, he had to check.

The buzzer echoed through the silent house. When nobody came to the door, he tried knocking. Eventually, a female voice called, "Who's there?"

"It's Dalton Savage." He tried to keep his voice even. "I need to speak to Clint."

The door opened a crack and a mass of mussed up blonde hair appeared. A pale face peeked through the gap.

"Sorry for the intrusion," he said, realizing how strange this must seem. "It's important I speak with your father."

"Dad's not back from work yet." Recognizing him from the hospital, her eyes widened. "Oh, it's you."

Savage tried to smile but failed. "You know when he'll be back?"

"He's tying up loose ends at the station. Today was his last day." She smiled, innocent and unguarded. "He's retiring."

"He hasn't been home all day?"

"No." Her forehead wrinkled. "Is something wrong?"

He had to have some reason for coming here. "I was hoping he'd help me with something, but I forgot he was retiring." Lame. How would he not know? Still, she didn't seem to notice.

"Mom's very relieved."

She wouldn't be when she finds out her husband was a corrupt cop who's been aiding and abetting a known mobster for nearly a decade.

There was an awkward pause. They were still standing at the door, him just outside on the mat. You didn't invite someone in at this time of night, not even as a courtesy.

"Give your mom my best." Savage turned away. He liked Trish and the girls and regretted the shock coming their way.

"Sure. I'll tell Dad you came by."

"Yeah. Thanks." Savage went back to his car. He contemplated waiting for Manning, but then he'd expect that and steer clear of the house.

It was possible he'd gone on the run, but Savage doubted it. It was more likely his ex-partner would come at him again. Now that

Manning knew Savage was onto him, he'd want to finish the job. He had too much to lose.

Manning didn't know about Burner's place. There, at least, Savage would be invisible.

---

HE GOT BACK to find Burner asleep on the couch.

"What happened?" Burner sat up as Savage walked inside and shut the door.

"He wasn't there. Must have known that would be the first place I'd go." Savage slumped into the armchair.

Burner stared at him, bleary-eyed. "Think he's on the run?"

"No way. He's worked too hard for this. He's not going to give it all up now. Running makes him look guilty. He'll come at me again, I know he will. I just don't know when."

"What are you going to do?"

"Find him before he finds me." Savage pointed to the laptop on the floor. "What did you find out?"

Burner jumped up, more awake now. "You're never going to believe this." He went over to his laptop and logged on. "You were right. Manning grew up in Philly."

Savage stared at him. "Seriously?"

"Yup, and guess what else?" He snorted. "You're going to love this. Hollander is his brother-in-law."

"No way."

Burner gave an emphatic nod. "Manning's wife's maiden name is Magee. Patricia Violet Magee."

"Holy shit." Savage ran a hand through his hair. Now that one, he hadn't been expecting. "He's family."

Burner nodded. "He married her right after he graduated from the Police Academy. Look, I even found their marriage certificate in the public records."

Savage peered over his shoulder.

• • •

*This is to certify that Clinton John Manning married Patricia Violet Magee on the 7th day of April, 1989.*

SAVAGE SHOOK HIS HEAD. "Well, I'll be damned. That explains a lot."

"It certainly explains why he's kept Hollander out of prison all these years."

Savage rubbed his temple. "Was this before he moved to Denver?"

"Long before. He worked for Philadelphia PD for nearly ten years, then transferred to Denver."

"Any idea why?"

"Couldn't find anything obvious. No disciplinary action, no accusations or warnings. Looks like one day, he just put in for a transfer and left."

"Was that before Hollander?"

"Manning must have been about thirty-four, thirty-five when he came here, while Hollander's only been in town the last ten years or so."

"Not Hollander's idea then. Manning was here a decade before."

"That's right. You think they waited so long to avoid suspicion?"

Savage shook his head. "No, that would be one hell of a long-term plan."

"What you gonna do?"

"I need to talk to Trish. Find out if she knew about any of this."

"If I might make a suggestion." Burner stifled another yawn. "It's late, and you've already bothered her once tonight. Why not get some shut eye and leave it until the morning?"

Savage knew Burner was right. He had to sleep, but Manning was still out there. Trish was Hollander's sister. She might know what was going on.

"He won't find you here," Burner reassured him. "Nobody knows about me." Savage got the feeling that he quite liked it that way.

"That's not what I'm worried about. I need to talk to him, find out what the hell's going on. That's all. Shit, he was my partner and he just tried to kill me."

"I know." Burner shook his head. "But he's gone to ground tonight. Talk to him tomorrow, if he shows up. The guy's not under arrest, and we can't prove he was at the hotel tonight." They hadn't bothered to call the cops. They didn't want to have to explain what happened.

Savage scratched his head. "He might go back to his normal life and pretend like none of this ever happened. Deny everything."

"He might," Burner agreed. "You're the only person who knows he's the killer."

Savage shivered. He didn't normally get those, but an icy chill shot down his spine. It left him with a terrible feeling of dread. Burner was right. They could pick this up after he got some rest. Nothing else was going to happen tonight. "Okay, let's sleep on it."

But sleep didn't come. As he tossed and turned, Savage thought about Manning and Hollander. Brothers-in-law. Clinton had kept that quiet. A familial bond. That's why his old partner had been passing on information. Hollander may have even threatened him, threatened his family.

He froze.

The attack on Trish. What if that was Hollander too? It could have been a warning directed at Manning. Play ball or else. Would the ruthless scumbag send someone to beat up his own sister?

Savage threw off the covers and sat up again. He had to talk to Manning. There might still be something he could do, some way of helping his friend and ex-partner. A way to put this right.

# TWENTY-SIX

THE NEXT MORNING, Savage went to see Trish. He knew Manning wouldn't be there. Going home was far too risky. The retired cop wouldn't return until the threat was neutralized.

Trish's hopeful face appeared at the door. "Have you found him?"

"No, I'm sorry." He hesitated. "Do you mind if I come in? There's something I want to talk to you about."

She frowned, but beckoned him in. Her eyes were red-rimmed and puffy, like she hadn't slept and the bruises from her attack were turning yellow "Is this about Clinton?"

He gave a tight nod. She led him into the kitchen and gestured for him to sit down. "What is it?"

Savage turned to face her. "Do you think he could be with your brother?"

She stiffened. "Why would you say that? I haven't spoken to my brother in nearly ten years."

If Savage were still part of Denver PD, he could check her calls, but now he was on his own. No phone traces, no call logs, no bank statements. Savage wasn't sure whether he believed her or not. She looked sincere, but the flash of fear in her eyes made him doubt her.

"Why is that?" he asked.

"We—We don't get along."

"You haven't spoken to him, even though you go to the same country club."

Her eyes hardened, chest heaving quicker, breaths shallower. "Look, I don't like my brother very much, and I have no idea why you think my husband may be with him."

"Because your husband is working for him."

"What do you mean? Clint is—was a police detective. My brother is a... crook."

"Clint is unofficially working for Guy Hollander. He was his inside man in the police force."

"I can't believe that."

"I'm sorry to have to tell you this, Trish, but Clint was passing on sensitive information about police investigations. That's a criminal offense."

She paled. "Clint wouldn't do that."

"I'm afraid I have proof."

Her eyes widened. "What kind of proof? Clint is an honorable man. He wouldn't do these things!"

Savage maintained a calm demeanor. "Can you call your brother and ask if Clint is with him? I need to know, Trish. If he's being coerced, maybe I can help him."

Her eyes filled with tears. "Is that what happened? Is Clinton in trouble because of something my brother did?"

"I don't know." Savage shook his head. "That's why I need to talk to him. Can you make the call?"

Trish hesitated, then nodded. Taking out her cell phone she scrolled through her contact list then hit the call button. Holding it to her ear, Savage could see her hand trembling. He wished he could tell her it was going to be alright, but he couldn't. It might never be alright again.

"Ray, it's Trish." He noticed she'd called him by his original name. Clearly Guy hadn't stuck with her. "Is Clinton with you?"

There was silence as she listened to what Hollander had to say.

"Well, if you haven't seen him, do you know where he might be?"

She paused to let him speak again.

"No, he hasn't come home. I'm getting worried."

Her expression remained unchanged from the moment she'd hit the call button.

"You said you'd leave us alone, and now I find out my brother's been working for you."

Savage gave his head a frantic shake, but it was too late. The damage had been done.

Trish faltered. "He's... here. He's helping me find Clinton."

*Crap.*

There goes the element of surprise.

"Don't lie to me, Ray. If something's happened to him, I'm going to hold you personally responsible."

Savage watched her expression harden. "Find him, Ray. Find him and send him home."

Then she hung up.

"Your brother doesn't know where he is?"

"No, and he denied they were working together, but he was lying. This is because of him, I just know." She dropped her head into her hands. When she looked up, her eyes were wet with tears. "It's always been this way. Ray's ambitious—too ambitious—and that makes him do things that aren't always..."

"Legal?"

She scoffed. "I don't understand my brother, Dalton. Never have. Even when we were kids, he was looking for ways to make money and exploit people. We weren't close. When we finished school, we went our separate ways. When I went to college, he started working for the Carusos."

The Philadelphia crime family.

"Is he still working for them?" Savage asked.

"I don't know. When he moved to Denver ten years ago, he swore he'd severed ties with that family. Said he wanted nothing more to do with them. That he was starting anew. I wanted to believe him, but it became obvious he was up to his old tricks again." She shook her head. "That's when we argued. I told him I didn't want anything to do with him and his money-making schemes. He got offended and stormed out. Since then, we've had minimal contact."

Except the same couldn't be said for Manning.

"Thanks, Trish." He put his hand on her shoulder. "Try not to worry. I'll see if I can find him. There must be a way to trace his cell phone or something." Hope flared in her eyes, and he hated himself for it.

"You'll let me know when you find him?"

"Of course."

She squeezed his hand. "Thanks, Dalton. He's lucky to have a friend like you."

Yeah, right. A friend he'd tried to kill.

---

GUY HOLLANDER ENDED the call with his sister and slipped his phone into his back pocket. Then he punched the wall. White hot daggers of pain vibrated down his arm, feeding his anger.

*Damn you, Savage.*

That man had a habit of poking his nose where it didn't belong. Why'd he have to come here to Denver, to *his* city, and cause trouble. Wasn't it enough that he took down the drug running side of his organization and kicked him out of that shitty little backwater? Crusher, Jonny Star – his two best men, rotting in prison right now. Because of *him*.

Hollander growled and inspected his knuckle. Blood trickled down his fingers. He flexed his hand. It was because of Savage that Manning had gone underground. Somehow Savage had figured out Manning was dirty. That they were related.

Where the hell was the little weasel? He'd never liked Manning. Even when Trish had married him, he'd thought the rookie cop was a brown-noser. Turned out that brown-noser had been his best secret weapon over the course of the last decade. Funny how things turned out.

Except now Manning had vanished. Trish was looking for him. Savage was hunting him. And what Manning knew could do some serious damage. The dickhead could bring down the whole organization.

He'd thought after Roberto had beaten up Trish, Manning would toe the line. For a while, he'd seemed to. He'd resigned from the police force – which Hollander wasn't happy about, but he let slide – and he'd attempted to take out Savage. Except, he'd failed. Worse, he'd given himself away in the process.

Manning had outrun his usefulness. If people thought he was dirty, he was of no use to the organization. Normally, he'd have people like that taken care of. That knowledge was dangerous. Except Manning was family, so he got special dispensation.

Not anymore.

Hollander ground his teeth. His brown-nosing brother-in-law was a liability. Once Savage got hold of him, Manning would tell him everything. He was weak like that. Pathetic. He had no balls. He might even try to make a deal. That would be worse. That could not be allowed.

He took out his phone again and called Winston Fremont, a finance guy who worked in one of his subsidiary companies. Winston picked up almost immediately. It wasn't often he got a direct call from the boss.

"Winston, do you still have that cousin in Robbery?"

The man's voice was gruff and concise in his ear. "Yeah, Len."

"Great. I think it's time we gave Len a call. I need a trace on someone's cell phone. If you can't get his location, I need to know where he last was."

"Sure, boss. What's his name?"

"Clinton Manning. Let me know when you have something."

"Will do."

Ending the call, Hollander stared out of the window. The sun reflected off the high-rises making them gleam like mirrors. In the distance, the North River snaked through the city like a silver serpent. This was *his* town. Nobody was going to take that away from him.

# TWENTY-SEVEN

ON THE WAY back to Burner's, Savage called Becca. Maybe it was the close call with Manning, maybe the situation was getting to him, but he needed to talk to her and hear her voice. She'd always been there for him, and when things got complicated, she was the one he went to.

"I'm trying to wrap things up here," he said. "I've got one thing I need to do, then I can come home."

"How long will it take?"

"A couple days, if I'm lucky. I've got to find someone. He's gone missing."

Her steady breathing filled a silence before she spoke again. "That could take a while, couldn't it?"

"I hope not. I miss you guys." He couldn't disguise the longing in his voice.

"We miss you too." She hesitated again. "Dalton, what's going on?"

"It's complicated, but I know who framed Dewayne Simmons and why. We're working on getting him released."

"We?"

"Yeah, me and Burner. You remember him? He lives in Denver now."

"The one who rode with the Crimson Angels."

"That's him. He's helping me out. He might even be able to assist Dewayne with his appeal."

"That's great news, but who's gone missing?"

He hesitated. "The killer. I think he's on the run." There was no way he could tell her Manning was coming after him.

"Is it Hollander?"

He was surprised she remembered his name. "Hollander's the puppet master, but he had help. Someone on the inside."

"Oh?"

"Yeah." He sighed. No point in hiding it now. "My old partner."

"He's been helping Hollander?"

"He's been feeding him information, hiding evidence, skewing investigations. It's been going on for years."

"Have you spoken to him about it?" Her voice was strained.

"Not yet. He disappeared."

She let out a defeated breath of air. "Be careful, Dalton." He heard the fear in her voice and wanted to ease her mind, but he couldn't.

"I will." That he could promise, at least. "How are you two doing?"

"We're fine. Connor's always hungry, and I'm sure he's grown a few inches since you last saw him."

Savage was hit with a wave of longing so strong it took his breath away. "Give him a kiss for me."

"Of course."

He heard the doorbell in the background.

"Oh, there's the door. I gotta go. Call me later, okay?"

He promised he would, and with a hurried, "Love you," she ended the call.

---

SAVAGE GOT BACK to Burner's place in the River North Art District just as the lawyer was leaving. He was on his Harley, backing out of the garage. It was strange seeing him on the gleaming chrome motorcycle, dressed in jeans and a leather jacket. It reminded him of Rosalie's gang and how Burner had so seamlessly integrated with them.

Burner turned to see Savage come in and asked, "How'd it go with Trish?"

Savage told him what had happened. "Now Hollander knows we're onto Manning."

Burner frowned. "You think Hollander will be looking for you too?"

"Maybe. Manning is a liability for him. If he talks, it could blow Hollander's reputation out of the water."

"Surely, he'll go after Manning, then? Not you."

Burner had a point. Would Hollander try to take out his brother-in-law? Given what Savage knew about the mobster, the answer was yes.

"Even more reason for me to find him," Savage said. "He might be able to testify against him, and we can put that crooked scumbag away for good."

Burner gave a hopeful nod. "Let me know if you need any help. I'm on my way to see Dewayne Simmons. I decided to take his case. He doesn't know yet, but I'll explain it to him when I see him."

Savage managed a smile. "Have you spoken to the DA?"

"Not yet. I'm going to collate all the evidence, then hit him with it."

"You've got a copy of the disc?"

"Got that locked away, and another copy on my laptop. I want to hear Dewayne's side of the story, just so I'm clear on the facts, and then I'll go and see the DA."

Savage massaged his bruised ribs. At least that was one thing they could put right.

---

THE SUN WAS at its zenith when Savage arrived at the Denver PD. He pulled into the police parking lot and saw Sanchez leaning against his patrol car, smoking. He nodded at Savage and said, "Manning isn't here. He retired."

"I know. I'm here to see Hagan."

Sanchez coughed on a lungful of smoke. "You're kidding?"

"It's important."

"It's not a good idea. She's in a shit mood today, God knows why." He flicked his cigarette onto the ground. A halo of sparks exploded around it before he smothered it with his foot. "You're asking for trouble, Savage. And it's my ass that's going to have to put the cuffs on you."

"Have you ever thought of changing desks?" Savage shot back as he strode past and entered the building. He would have taken the stairs, they were usually quicker than the ancient elevator, but not with his side aching like this. The bullet had caused an interesting magenta bruise on his side that spread out like an ugly claw over his ribcage. It wasn't pretty. Still, it could have been far, far worse.

He stepped out of the elevator and moved toward Hagan's office.

She noticed him from the moment he entered the floor. Her dark scowl indicated she wasn't pleased to see him. "If you're here for me, it's going to have to wait. I'm busy."

"This'll only take a minute." He didn't move from her doorway.

Sighing, she beckoned him in. "I keep waiting to hear that the DA is reconsidering Dewayne Simmons case, but—" She spread her hands and gave him a blank look.

"Funny you should say that." Savage sat down on the chair opposite. It was easier than standing. "His lawyer is on his way to see him right now."

She arched an eyebrow.

"Anyway, that's not why I'm here. I found the officer who buried the evidence."

Genuine curiosity etched her face. Her silence encouraged him to continue.

"He's still working here. Or was, until yesterday."

"You're telling me one of my officers is corrupt."

"That's exactly what I'm telling you. Clinton Manning has been feeding information on active investigations to mob boss Guy Hollander for years." At her look, he held up a hand. "Yeah, yeah. You can say he's one of Denver's most prominent citizens, but we all know he's just a mobster in a fancy suit."

She closed her mouth.

Savage continued. "Every case Hollander was involved in fell flat. Not enough evidence. Witnesses disappearing. Crime scene contamination. If you look closely, Manning was on the team every time."

"Clinton Manning?" She stared at him. "Don't you think I'd know whether one of my detectives was dirty?"

"How would you know? No offense, Sarah, but he was my partner for years and I didn't know." Savage pulled a DVD from his pocket. "This is camera footage of the third Burger King robbery. The one where Helen Ridley got shot. I know it wasn't on your watch, but you might want to take a look. It clearly shows the shooter as being right-handed."

Her eyes dropped to the DVD. "This is the evidence Manning buried?"

"It is. The store owner confirmed it was Manning he showed it to. He positively ID'd him from a photograph. There is no mistake."

Hagan was silent for a moment. "Why are you giving this to me? Manning has retired. You're really going to dredge this up? Ruin your old partner's reputation? Stop his pension?"

"Dewayne Simmons has served six years for a crime he didn't commit because of Manning, and God knows how many other cases have been compromised. Word of this gets out and you're going to have a whole bunch of appeals on your hands. Internal Affairs is going to question every case Manning ever worked on. Like it or not, Lieutenant, this *is* your problem, now."

She swallowed. It would be her reputation in the toilet. "Dalton—"

"Watch the footage."

She stood from her desk and closed the office door, then turned back to look at him. Say for argument's sake you're right. What am I supposed to do about it?"

"He tried to kill me last night, Sarah."

"What?" She sank into her chair.

"He broke into my hotel room and tried to shoot me. Luckily, I was wearing a vest." He pulled his shirt to the side and displayed the colorful bruise.

Hagan winced. "You wear a vest in bed?"

"No." He scowled at her. "I was expecting him, or rather, I was expecting Hollander."

Hagan shook her head, confused. "You thought Hollander was going to kill you?"

"Yeah." He hesitated. "Don't take this the wrong way, Sarah, but you're the only person I told where I was staying. Nobody else knew."

There was a silence as his words struck home. He watched her cheeks turn pink. "You thought I told Hollander? You thought I was dirty?"

"I didn't know, that's why I told you where I was staying."

"It was a test?" The pink deepened to red.

He gave a curt nod. "When Manning turned up at my hotel, I knew you weren't involved. He'd gotten the information while he was here, at the station."

"He asked me where you were staying. Said you had a DVD player that belonged to him, or something."

"He said that to track me down."

She dropped her head into her hands. He'd never seen her look so deflated. "Okay, let's take this one step at a time. How'd you know it was Manning who shot you? Did you see him?"

"Not exactly. It was dark and he wore a ski mask."

She glanced up. "Then how do you know?"

"I chased him to his car. The tire tracks match his Ford Mustang."

"You guessed it was him based on tire tracks in a hotel parking lot?"

"It's a dirt parking lot and I know his car."

"That's thin, Sheriff. You know how many cars' tracks there would be in a parking lot? That'll never stand up."

"They were fresh. I saw him drive off."

"Did you identify his car?"

"It was a dark sedan. He drives a navy blue Ford Mustang. The plates were covered."

She sat back in her chair and exhaled. "Let me get this straight. A man in a mask breaks into your hotel room and tries to shoot you. He flees, but you go in pursuit. He escapes in a dark car with the plates covered, leaving track marks in the dirt?"

"That's about it."

"So, you've got no actual proof that it was Manning who shot you?"

Savage hid his disappointment. He'd hoped for more from Hagan. They'd never seen eye to eye, but he'd hoped she'd have more faith in him than this.

"Lieutenant, I'm right about this. I have the bullet. We could send it to forensics." Even though he doubted Manning had used his service weapon.

She thought for a moment, then said, "I'm not ruining a man's life without damn good reason. I don't doubt you were shot, and if you haven't reported it to the police, you should. But we're going to need more than that."

He got to his feet, grimacing against the pain. "You're making a mistake. Manning is dirty. Hollander killed Helen Ridley, and you're letting them get away with it."

Her mouth was a thin line. "Get out, Dalton. Before I arrest you. Again."

# TWENTY-EIGHT

SAVAGE WENT BACK to Burner's but instead of going inside, he took a walk around the block to try and calm down. Even the pain in his side didn't put him off his stride.

Damn Hagan. Why was she so goddamn stubborn?

The South Platte River that ran through the district was not pretty. Controlled by a man-made canal, it sliced through the industrial landscape like a silver scar. A graffiti-strewn concrete wall prevented cars from driving over the edge, but it was low enough to see over, and the fast-running water did make him feel more grounded.

On either side of the river was open land, building sites or container lots. The two-lane road that ran alongside the river wasn't busy. Occasionally a truck would rumble past, or a pickup with crates on the back. Working vehicles. It was hard to believe that one day this would be transformed into luxury apartments, studios, and boutiques with waterfront views.

He'd been walking for a mile when Burner called. "Hey, someone wants to talk to you." Savage knew who it was before Dewayne came on the line.

"I wanted to thank you, man. What you've done for me and my family is huge." The relief was evident in Dewayne's voice.

"You're not out yet, but there is a good chance the DA will accept the new evidence. Burn—I mean Carter—is going to see what he can do."

"You listened to me. You believed me when nobody else did."

Savage took a deep breath. The air smelled like dust with a faint hint of sewage. "I hope it works out, Dewayne."

"Thank you."

Savage accepted the young man's praises, then ended the call. Some of the tension in his body dissolved, as if swept away by the river. One good thing had come out of this. If Burner worked his magic with the DA, hopefully Mrs. Simmons would get one of her boys back.

Hanging up, he saw he had missed a call from Becca. That was strange. Even if he'd been on the call with Dewayne, it should have notified him another was waiting.

He dialed her back, but there was no answer.

It rang again. He smiled and glanced down to see Manning's home phone number. He answered it, pulse escalating. "Hello?"

"Dalton, it's Trish."

His heart sank. "Hey Trish. I don't have any news right now."

"That's not why I'm calling." She sounded upbeat, happy even. "Clinton messaged me."

"He did? What did he say?" Savage found he was holding his breath.

"He's sorry for not saying goodbye but he had to go away for a few days to tie up some loose ends. He'll be home soon."

"Did he say where he was going?"

"No, but isn't that great? He's okay. I was so worried."

"Sure, that's great. I still need to talk to him urgently. Did you tell him I was looking for him?"

"I did, but he said everything will be resolved when he gets back."

*What did that mean?*

"Okay, thanks."

He pocketed his phone and stared into the rushing water. What could have taken him away for a few days? What loose ends did he need to tie up? How would everything be resolved when he got back?

Then he knew.

An icy chill shot through him.

*Becca.*

Fumbling, he called her back. No answer.

*Shit.*

He tried one more time.

*Pick up, dammit.*

Nothing.

Heart hammering, he turned back towards Burner's place. Manning hadn't gone home last night. It was a six-and-a-half-hour drive to Hawk's Landing. It had been 2 a.m. when he'd gone to Manning's house. It had been 8:30 when he'd spoken to Becca this morning.

*Oh, there's the door. I gotta go*

He broke into a cold sweat.

*Dear God, no.*

Savage broke into a run.

---

DEPUTY REBECCA SINCLAIR was out on patrol when her colleague James Thorpe called. "You're out by Buxton Heights, aren't you?"

"Yeah, just turned onto Carnegie."

"Can you swing by the boss's place? He wants us to check on Becca and the baby."

Sinclair had known Thorpe for over a year, since he'd first started working at the Hawk's Landing Sheriff's Department, and she could tell by the timbre of his voice that this was serious.

"Did he say why?"

"No, just that it was urgent. She's not answering her phone. Can you go there now?"

"Turning around as we speak." With a screech of tires, she executed a perfect U-turn and sped off towards the Sheriff's neighborhood. "My ETA is ten minutes. How about you?"

"I'm leaving now, so make that twenty."

"See you there."

She put her foot down, feeling the cruiser press forward. A car pulled out in front of her, dawdling. A swift blast of the sirens and she swept past, unwilling to break her speed. Savage never asked for favors. Not unless it was an emergency.

Sinclair had been second-in-command while Savage was on paternity leave. James Thorpe was Acting Sheriff, and he was good at it. Level-headed and precise, he made thoughtful decisions and didn't rush into anything, but he didn't have the split-second intuition that Savage had, or the ability to read a situation and predict the outcome. He didn't have ten years of homicide experience either, and it showed. Not in the day-to-day activities, but when at a crime scene or dealing with angry residents, drunk troublemakers, or outlaw motorcyclists. Still, they were managing well, all things considered.

Last week they'd had a showdown at Mac's Roadhouse, a rough biker bar on the Durango Road. It could have gotten messy, but they'd managed to resolve it without any blood being shed, thanks in a big part to the Sheriff's friend, Zeb, who rode with the Angels. She was taking that as a win. Sadly, the perp, a hot-headed club member called Billy Ray, had beaten a prostitute half to death at a local whorehouse in the trailer park, and worse still, the victim, a twenty-four-year-old called Mary-Lou, was refusing to press charges.

There were some parts of Sinclair's job that frustrated the hell out of her, but she couldn't control what other people did. In her mind, Billy Ray should be hung, drawn and quartered for what he'd done to Mary-Lou. A night in a cell and a warning was nowhere near punishment enough. Still, if the vic didn't want to go to trial, there was nothing they could do.

The road to Dalton Savage's house came up faster than expected, and Sinclair cut her speed to take the corner. Her tires screeched as they fought for traction. That's when she saw the smoke. It billowed up into the air like a funeral pyre, and it was coming from the Sheriff's house.

"Shit!"

She floored it up the street towards the swirling plume, only to find Savage's house ablaze. Ramping the pavement outside, she jumped from the car and sprinted towards the house.

"Becca!" she yelled, standing at the downstairs windows. Flames licked at the blinds, making entry impossible. "Becca! Are you in there?"

No reply.

Heart thumping, she ran around to the back of the house. The kitchen door led out to the back yard. Maybe she could get in that way. Flinging open the garden gate, she raced up the path to the door. It was locked.

"Becca!" She pounded on it with her fists.

Still nothing.

*Goddammit.*

She had to get in somehow. Becca might be unconscious in there, unable to get to the baby. Oh, God. Connor.

Using her shoulder, she ran at the door. It didn't budge. The kitchen window was closed, but peering inside, she could see the flames hadn't made their way to the back of the house yet.

Looking around her, she grabbed an ornamental rock and hurled it against the window, causing the glass to shatter. After scraping the remaining shards off the sill with her gun, she holstered it and swung her leg over to enter the house.

Dropping down onto the kitchen floor, she got her bearings. Smoke was seeping into the room, so she grabbed a tea towel and tied it around her nose and mouth. There wasn't much time. "Becca!"

Nothing.

Where the hell was she? Sinclair ran down the corridor from the kitchen to the living room. She got as far as the living room door, but then had to stop. The smoke was too strong. Holding her breath, she glanced into the living room but didn't see anyone lying on the floor unconscious. The room was clear.

Thank God for that. Eyes watering, she retreated and ran down the hallway to the main bedroom, but that was empty too. The bed, however, was unmade, the sheets still pulled back as if Becca had just left it. The baby cot against the wall was empty too.

*Thank God.*

Relief made her legs wobble. Becca wasn't home.

She heard a crash and a dark smog puffed into the bedroom. The fire was progressing. The thick smoke made it harder to breathe. Sinclair backtracked down the corridor, hands on the walls as visibility was so bad. Coughing, she paused to check the second bedroom, which Becca and the Sheriff had turned into a nursery. It was empty too.

"Sinclair!" came Thorpe's voice from the kitchen. "Are you in there?"

"Coming," she tried to reply, but the words caught in her throat as smoke made it impossible to speak. Spluttering and gasping, she only just made it to the kitchen before she was overwhelmed.

"Rebecca!" yelled Thorpe, as she buckled over, spasms clenching at her lungs. He dragged her up off the floor and pushed her over the window. She fell onto the grass on the other side. Blinded by hot tears, lungs tightening with smoke, she lay there, wheezing.

Thorpe towered over her. "What the hell were you thinking? You could have died!"

"Can you give me a moment?" she choked, eyes streaming.

"That was foolish."

"I had to check they weren't in there."

He shook his head. Another spasm wracked her body, and she could taste the acrid smoke in her mouth. After that, she gulped in lungfuls of sweet, fresh air and managed to get her coughing under control."

"You okay?" Thorpe asked.

"I will be." She shook her head. "I checked every room. They're definitely not in there."

"Thank God."

Sirens could be heard coming up the road.

"I called the Fire Department when I saw the flames," he said. "The paramedics are on their way too. They'll check you out." She smiled her thanks. That was James, always by the book. Unlike her, who'd dashed inside without thinking.

She swiped at her eyes. "I didn't want to wait in case they were in there."

He patted her on the back. "You did good. I'm sorry I shouted at you. It's just—" He faded out.

"I know." He was worried. She got that.

They went around to the front of the house where the fire engine had stopped, and men were rushing to get the hoses out to douse the flames. Fire Chief Mason O'Riley, a gruff but competent man, came over. "Anyone inside?"

"Not that we saw," Thorpe told him. "My deputy here did a quick check."

O'Riley glanced at Sinclair, taking in her disheveled appearance. "That was a brave thing to do. We'll see if we can get this blaze under control, but it might be too far gone." As he spoke, jets of water sprung from the giant hoses and pounded the flames that were now creeping up the walls and licking the roof. Wood and plasterboard disintegrated, exposing the inside of the house.

The smoke pyre got worse, and the whole house seemed to sizzle and crackle in an angry fervor. Awestruck neighbors came out of their homes and gathered on the street to watch.

"What happened?" asked one.

"No idea."

"Were they home?" hissed another.

Sinclair dusted herself off and approached the group. "Anyone here know where Becca and Connor are?"

They stared at her. She must have looked like a chimney sweep, but she was still a deputy. Flashing her badge, she tried again. "Anyone know the owners?"

A few nods. A timid woman in her forties came forward. "I know them, but I don't think Becca was home. Usually, she's out hanging up laundry or playing with the baby in the garden, but I haven't seen her all day."

"Do you know where she went?"

"No, sorry."

Sinclair went back to Thorpe. "We should put a trace on her phone. I don't know what happened here, but she could be in danger. Her and the baby."

Thorpe nodded. "Get Littleton on that. I'm going to call the boss."

She watched him walk away, his chin jutting out. That was one job she was glad she didn't have to do.

# TWENTY-NINE

SAVAGE SPED ALONG HIGHWAY 285, listening to the V-8 engine scream as he pushed the Suburban to its limits. He had the blue light going, but the sound was off. It was a six-and-a-half-hour drive. He hoped to hell he was wrong about Manning, but that bad feeling in his gut kept getting worse.

His dashboard lit up as Thorpe's call came through on the car's Bluetooth. "About time," he muttered, even though it had been less than an hour since he'd called his deputy. This was his Acting Sheriff calling to tell him everything was fine, and Becca and Connor were safe and sound.

He answered the incoming call. "Savage."

"Your house is on fire, boss, but Becca and the baby aren't there."

Savage thought he'd misheard. "What?"

"Sinclair went in to take a look. I swear they weren't there."

His house was on fire? What the hell was going on? He broke into a cold sweat. "Where are they?"

"I don't know. We're trying to find them. Littleton's running a trace on her cellphone now."

"How bad is the fire?" Maybe it was just a small one, something the fire department could put out, with minimal damage.

"Pretty bad, Sheriff."

Technically, he wasn't the sheriff while he was on paternity leave. Thorpe was. But he didn't correct him. His mind was galloping through possible reasons for the fire. Becca left the oven on. The gas exploded. Electricity shorted out. "Do they know how it started?"

"Not yet. Once the Fire Department gets it under control, they'll do an assessment."

"It's still burning?"

Thorpe hesitated. "Yeah, it's still burning. The Fire Chief doesn't know if they can save it."

Savage's heart sank. This was Manning's doing. He'd kidnapped Becca and the baby to get to him. He was going to use them as a get out of jail free card. His life back in exchange for theirs. It made sense.

He thumped his fist on the steering wheel. Why hadn't he seen this coming? He could have warned Becca, prepared her for what might happen. Looking back now, it should have been obvious.

"Let me know as soon as you trace her," he snapped, then regretted it. "Sorry, I'm on edge. I'm on my way back, still five hours out. I should be there before dawn."

Thorpe let out a long exhale and asked, "Do you know who did this?"

"Yeah. I think a man named Clinton Manning took Becca and Connor and set fire to the house."

"You think they've been abducted?"

"If it's Manning, he's taken them. He'll also have turned her phone off or destroyed it so you can't trace it. I still want her last known location."

"I'll call you as soon as we've got something," Thorpe said. "Who is this guy?"

"An ex-cop from Denver who's got a grudge against me. He's taken them to get to me. To punish me." Savage shook his head. Becca and Connor were his Achilles heel, his weakness. Any madman out for vengeance would know that to get to him, all they had to do was to use his family. It was a rookie error, and one he might pay for dearly.

"Um..." He could tell Thorpe didn't know where to go from there. This was too big for him, for his experience. "What do you want me to do, Sheriff?"

"He's driving a Ford Mustang, navy blue. The plate number you should be able to get from the DMV. Put out an APB. Hopefully someone's seen him."

"Will do." The confidence was back. Thorpe had direction now, he knew what to do. It was familiar territory. "You want us to trace Manning's cell too?"

"Sure, although he probably won't have it on." Manning was too smart for that. Still, he might turn it on for a second to look up something or make a call, and then they'd nab him.

Glancing at his GPS, he figured he had covered almost a third of the distance, which meant he had a little over two hundred miles to go. He'd have to slow down to go through the ridge, but in a couple hours, he should be home. What was left of it, anyway.

Manning.

*Please don't hurt them.*

That was the only thought going through his mind. Over and over again.

He took a deep breath, forcing himself to remain calm. If he panicked, he was useless. Panic clouded the brain, slowed his reactions, and he needed to be at his best to find Manning and get his family back.

Manning wanted something. That was leverage Savage could use. He wanted his life back. No actual charges had been brought against him. Hagan had been reluctant to pursue it since Manning had retired. If Savage played his cards right, maybe they could resolve this.

Manning had a wife and two daughters who he loved. He wouldn't want to give them up. He'd built an extension on his house, a pool, a grill. He wanted to live to enjoy those things. Savage could use that.

He exhaled slowly. All was not lost. He just had to wait for

Manning to contact him, which his ex-partner would do sooner or later. The man was looking for a way out, and Savage would give it to him. If they could just talk, they could resolve this.

All he had to do was wait.

---

SAVAGE MADE the journey in just under five hours. The sun had set behind the mountains, and a faint smog hung over the town. The fire had been burning since before he'd left Denver. Even though he knew this, he wasn't prepared for what he found.

Two fire engines, three police vehicles, and a forensic van were parked on his street, their headlights illuminating the site where his house used to be. In its place was a smoldering mass of charred remains.

Climbing out of his car, he stumbled toward the soft-glowing cinders as if in a daze. Most of the fire had been put out, only a small section of embers still flickered in the darkness. A team of specialists in fire-proof gear were rifling through the remnants, taking samples, and trying to figure out where the fire originated.

The Fire Chief approached Savage and placed a hand on his shoulder. "We couldn't save it." Savage recognized him but couldn't remember his name. "It was too far gone when we arrived."

"You're sure there was nobody inside?" His voice wobbled with tension. The thought of Becca and Connor being burned alive... Hell, he couldn't even go there.

"Doesn't look like it. Your deputy got inside before it got too bad and said it was empty, and we haven't found any... remains."

Savage looked around and spotted a very dirty Sinclair talking to one of the other fire officers, notebook in hand. He thanked the Chief and walked over to join her. Up close, she looked ragged. Her clothes were sooty, her face smudged, even her hair was stringy and tinged with gray that he knew to be ash. She was also still coughing.

"Find anything?" he asked, giving her a pat on the back.

Sinclair shot him a weak smile. "House was empty. They weren't inside when it started. I made sure."

"Thank you." He squeezed her shoulder, weak with relief. Sinclair had risked her life to make sure his family were okay. "Any idea how it started?"

Sinclair had a minor coughing fit so the fire officer said, "We found an accelerant in the living room. Looks like it was deliberate."

He clenched his fists.

*Damn it, Manning. I'm going to get you.*

They'd been partners, for God's sake. They were supposed to have had each other's backs. Ten years they'd worked homicides together. Savage had met his wife, his daughters, the damn dog. Manning had attempted to kill him. He'd kidnapped his family and burned down his house. What the hell was going on?

He watched the forensic specialists trawl through the wreckage, and when his eyes started burning, he walked wearily back to his car. He'd kept his phone in his pocket the whole time, but it had remained silent.

"Where are you staying?" Sinclair asked, coming up behind him. It was midnight, and there was nothing more they could do here.

"No idea." Savage turned and gazed at what was left of his house. A hundred memories wiped away in the blink of an eye. His life with Becca. Connor. Everything they'd built together had been reduced to a smoldering mess of twisted metal, burned wood, and ash. He blinked away the tears that threatened, figuring it must be the smoke, and turned back to Sinclair. "I'll find a hotel."

"You can stay at my place."

Savage blinked, surprised. "Don't put yourself out."

"I'm not. I've got a spare room. You're welcome to it. I'm going back to the station, anyway. I've got to write this up." She nodded behind her. "I won't be back till morning."

He hesitated. As much as he didn't want to impose, it did seem like the easiest option. "If you're sure?"

"Absolutely. The spare key is under the potted money tree around the side of the house." At his blank look, she said, "It's the one with the twisted trunk. See you later. I'll let you know if we find Becca or Manning."

He nodded. Once his deputy was gone, Savage got into his car and rested his head back on the headrest. All he could see when he closed his eyes were burning embers. He hadn't slept for nearly thirty-two hours, and he was beginning to feel it. Yet, he couldn't give in. Becca and his son needed him.

Where were they now? Were they okay? Was Connor alright?

He longed to see them. To hold them. He wanted to smell Connor's sweet scent and hold Becca's hand. His family.

*Nothing* was more important than his family.

---

SINCLAIR LIVED in a two-bedroom bungalow on the western edge of Hawk's Landing, ten minutes from the main street. It was a modest house, smaller than most on her street, but it was well-kept, with a neat front porch overlooking a small garden. He parked in the driveway next to the house.

What did she call it? A money tree? Savage got the flashlight out of the glove compartment and used it to look around. Sinclair had a bunch of potted plants along the side of the house, but it wasn't hard to find. His eye immediately caught the twisted stems entwining, as if in an embrace. Lifting the pot closest to the tree, he found the spare key underneath.

Savage let himself in. It was pitch dark inside, so he fumbled around for a light switch. The interior was as tidy as the exterior, with cream walls, a newish-looking carpet, and an array of silver-plated photo frames on a wooden side cabinet. He took a moment to study them.

Sinclair with her arms around a young woman, possibly her sister. An elderly couple sitting outside on a deck, happy smiles on their wrinkled faces. The third photograph was of Sinclair on a beach with a dark-haired man. They looked like they'd just emerged from the water. Wet hair, sparkling eyes, and careless smiles. Savage wondered who he was. Sinclair had never mentioned a boyfriend, and he didn't think she was seeing anyone. Then he turned away. It was none of his business.

He found the spare room and sat down on the bed, weary with exhaustion. Why didn't Manning call? It was the only way forward, for both of them. What was he waiting for?

His stomach rumbled. He couldn't remember when he'd last eaten. Or slept, for that matter. Feeling like an intruder, he wandered into the kitchen. Sinclair wouldn't mind if he made a sandwich. He had no appetite, but he knew he had to eat to keep his strength up. Becca and his son needed him.

Opening the refrigerator, he found some cheese, lettuce, and a tomato. Grabbing some bread, he made a sandwich and took it into the living room. He ate, phone beside him, but no matter how hard he glared at it, it didn't ring.

Using Sinclair's house phone to keep his line free, he called the station. Thorpe picked up.

"Any news?"

"No, sir. You were right about Becca's cell. It's not showing a signal. He must have turned it off."

Savage grunted. Manning would know better than to allow them to track her. "What about his?"

"Same thing."

Tiredness made his eyes sting. "How about the Mustang?"

"Nothing yet, but we've got every law patrolman in the county looking for it. If he's on the road, we'll find it."

"Thanks, Thorpe. How's Sinclair doing?"

"Still coughing. Thinking about sending her home."

"Do it," he said. "She needs to rest."

Thorpe said he would, promised to let him know as soon as they got something, then hung up. Savage was left alone in a strange house, with only his simmering rage to keep him company.

After he'd eaten, Savage called another ex-cop, Zebadiah Swift.

Despite the late hour, Zeb was still awake and answered after a couple of rings. "Yeah?"

"It's Savage."

Zeb grunted. "Anyone would think we're friends the way you keep calling me."

Savage didn't respond to that. "I need your help."

"What do you mean?"

"You're still riding with the Angels, right?"

"Yeah?" There was a hesitancy in his voice, like he didn't want to know where this was going.

"I'm looking for a man, an ex-cop called Manning. He abducted Becca and my son."

"You're shitting me?"

"I wish I was. The son of a bitch burned my house to the ground, just to teach me a lesson."

"I heard there was an inferno in town. That was you?"

"Yeah."

"Shit, man. What do you want me to do?"

"Manning's taken them somewhere, and I need to find out where. Sitting around is killing me. Can you help?"

"I can get a message to the guys, if that's what you mean. We'll keep a lookout, let you know if we see him."

"That's all I ask."

"Give me the details."

Savage gave him Manning's full name, a brief description, and the make and model of his vehicle, along with the license plate.

"Got it. It's late, not many of the guys will be out now, but we'll do what we can."

"Thanks, man. I owe you."

There was a pause. "Your deputies did a fine job with Billy Ray. They didn't make a fuss. Rosalie appreciated that. I figure this is the least we can do." There was nothing more to say. The clock was ticking. Every minute Becca and Connor were gone put them at risk.

"Talk soon," Zeb said, and ended the call.

---

SAVAGE WAS HALF asleep on the couch when a shrill, incessant noise from the television jolted him awake. He'd put on some game show to distract himself while he waited, but he'd fallen asleep anyway. Rubbing the grit from his eyes, he looked around for the remote. That's when he realized it was his phone. He'd changed the ringtone and hiked up the volume so he wouldn't miss it.

Snatching it up, he almost shouted, "Hello?"

"I have your girlfriend and your son."

The anger surged, but he fought to keep his voice even. "Manning, if you hurt them—" The words died in his throat.

"Relax. They're fine. We need to talk."

Savage managed to get his heart rate under control. They were alive. Manning hadn't harmed them. He closed his eyes, letting that sink in.

"Dalton?"

He shook his head, finding his voice again. "I agree. Where?"

"I'll give you the coordinates."

Clever. It meant that if Savage was with anyone, he wouldn't be able to tell them where he was going. They'd have to look them up.

"Shoot."

Manning read out the coordinates and Savage wrote them down on a notepad Sinclair kept beside the phone. "Got it." He ripped off the top sheet and studied it. The numbers meant nothing to him.

"You there now?"

"Yeah. Make sure you come alone. Any hint of backup and they die. You got that, *partner*?"

Savage bristled but forced himself to remain calm. "Reading you loud and clear. *Partner*." He couldn't wait until this was over and he could have it out with Manning. His blood boiled with pent-up fury.

"Just you wait," he muttered as he hung up the phone. "Just you fucking wait."

# THIRTY

SINCLAIR GOT HOME JUST as the sky was lightening in the east. Every muscle in her body ached. Her eyes burned from the smoke, and she had a lingering cough that wouldn't quit. The paramedic said it would take some time for her lungs to clear. All she wanted to do was take a hot shower and fall into bed.

Strange, Savage's car wasn't outside. Maybe he'd decided not to stay, after all. Lifting the potted plant at the side of the house, she noticed the spare key was gone. He must have come inside.

She let herself in. There was an empty coffee cup on the table and the television was on, but no sign of Savage.

"Hello? Dalton, are you here?" She rarely called him by his first name, but Sheriff didn't seem appropriate since he was on leave and Thorpe had assumed that title.

There was no answer. She checked the spare room, just in case he'd left his car somewhere and gone to bed, but it was empty. There was no sign he'd even been there. No dent in the bedding, the pillows were smooth, and the light was off.

Frowning, she took out her phone and called his number. It rang, but he didn't pick up. That too was weird. Savage always answered his phone, even when off duty. There's no way he wouldn't answer now, since he was waiting for news of Becca and Connor, or the man who'd taken them.

Unless he had a lead.

She walked around the house wondering what it could be. If Savage was following up on something, he might not be able to pick up, but if that was the case, he damn well should have told them where he was going. He might need backup.

Maybe he called Thorpe after she'd left. Even though it was only a ten-minute drive home, he could have called then. But Thorpe was as clueless as she was.

"No, he hasn't spoken to me about it," Thorpe said.

"You want me to try and call him?"

"Yeah, he might answer if it's you. I can't believe he'd go off on his own like this."

Thorpe said he'd be in touch.

While she stood in the living room deciding what to do, her house phone rang. It was so unexpected that it made her jump. Nobody called her on that phone, let alone in the middle of the night.

She rushed over to it, still clutching her cell. "Hello?"

"Who's this?" came the abrupt reply. She didn't recognize the voice.

"Deputy Sinclair. Who's *this*?"

"This is Zeb Swift. I'm looking for Dalton. I mean, Sheriff Savage."

Zeb? That ex-cop who ran the trailer park and rode with the Crimson Angels.? He'd been there when they'd arrested Billy Ray. It was thanks to him the situation hadn't gone to hell in a handbasket.

She softened her tone. "He's not here. I just got home, and he's gone."

"Gone where?" There was concern in his voice, and she remembered the Sheriff telling her that Zeb had saved his life once.

"I don't know." She paused. "Can I help at all?"

"He asked me to get the Angels to look out for his man. Manning, is it?"

"Yeah." Her heart beat faster "You got something?"

"Maybe. One of the boys saw a dark blue Mustang turn off Durango Road this morning, headed to Apple Tree Farm."

"That old place. It's empty, isn't it?"

"Closed down last winter. Would make a good hideout."

"I'm on my way." Sinclair grabbed her keys off the counter and headed back out the door. Her hot shower would have to wait.

---

SAVAGE RACED up the road to Apple Tree Farm, the Suburban kicking up dust and dirt behind him. The road was dry and uneven, and as he bounced over the potholes, he wondered in what state he'd find Becca and Connor.

*Please let them be okay.*

If Manning had hurt them in any way... If he'd touched one hair on his baby's head... Savage gripped the wheel until his knuckles turned white. Then, not even God could help him.

As he got closer, he noticed Manning's Mustang parked outside the deserted farmhouse. It was still early, the sun only just up, but there was more than enough light to see up ahead.

The farmhouse wasn't large, under a thousand square feet, and consisted of one bedroom, a living room and a wide porch that spanned the whole front of the house. The owners used to sell farm produce out of it before they were forced to close.

Savage drove right up to the door and skidded to a stop. There was no need for stealth. Manning knew he was coming. This wasn't an extraction. This was a negotiation. Manning's freedom for his family. Taking out his cellphone, he opened the Voice Memo app, and pressed record. If Manning was going to bargain with him, he wanted it recorded.

Climbing out of the SUV, he made a big show of tucking his Glock into the back of his jeans. Hopefully Manning would focus on that and forget about his phone. The air carried a hint of coolness still clinging to the remnants of the night. His breath came out misty as he marched up the steps to the front door. It opened before he made it to the top.

"Get your hands up." Manning pointed his gun at Savage. The two men stared at each other. Manning looked older. He'd aged ten years in the last forty-eight hours. The lines around his eyes were deeper, more distinct, and his hair was mussed, displaying more gray than Savage had noticed when it had been slicked back.

To be fair, Savage had probably aged too. He hadn't slept in two days and the worry was making him physically ill.

"Manning." He put his hands in the air. "What have you done with Becca and Connor?"

"They're fine."

Savage shook his head. "I need to see them."

"Not yet." Manning waved the gun at him. "Keep your hands where I can see 'em."

Savage knew the drill. He kept his hands raised while Manning patted him down. His ex-partner gave a soft "tsk" as he retrieved the Glock, but he left Savage's phone in his pocket.

"Hands behind your back." Savage complied, wincing at the twinge in his side, and Manning cuffed him.

"That from my bullet?" he asked, noticing the flash of pain cross Savage's face.

Savage chose to ignore that question. "Aren't you supposed to hand those in when you retire? Along with your service pistol?"

"Shut up." Manning gestured to one of the two wooden chairs that had been left behind in the farmhouse. "Sit down."

It was awkward with his hands behind his back, and his ribs were on fire, but he managed. Only once Savage sat down did Manning relax his arm.

Savage fixed his gaze on him. "Why are you doing this?"

"You know why." Manning flipped a chair around and straddled it.

"I know Trish is Guy Hollander's sister, and you've been helping him for years, right back to the Burger King robberies. I know you buried surveillance footage that would prove Dewayne Simmons couldn't have shot Helen Ridley. I know you let an innocent man go to prison."

Manning shrugged. "I couldn't let you look too closely at the victim. If you had, you might have seen the payment into her account, and where she lived. Then it would only be a short leap to Hollander."

"He told you to set up Dewayne as the fall guy?"

Manning nodded. "It had to be someone a jury would believe was capable of murder."

"A poor black kid from Five Points who was so desperate for money he agreed to rob a burger joint?"

"It was a good plan. And it worked, too, until you came along asking questions." Manning shook his head. "Why couldn't you just stay gone? It would have saved all this"—He waved his gun around, an annoyed expression etching his features.

"Because it didn't feel right. Even back then, it didn't feel right. The investigation was too rushed. The state prosecutor was pushing for a conviction. We needed more time."

Manning smirked. "You've always been such a boy scout. Dalton Savage never bends the rules, never cuts corners. Well, I've got news for you, pal. The real world isn't like that. Some of us don't have the luxury to do what we want."

"What does Hollander have over you?" Savage asked, quietly.

Manning gave a heartless laugh. "You mean apart from being family?"

"He must have something on you. Did he threaten Trish? The girls?"

Manning leaned forward, resting his arms on the back of the chair, gun in his right hand. "Guy Hollander is not a man you say no to. He can be very persuasive."

"He had Trish beaten up, didn't he? Was that him being persuasive?" Savage could see in Manning's eyes he was right. "All that bullshit about the abusive boyfriend outside the shop. That was all for show. You knew all along it was Hollander."

Manning clenched his jaw. "Trish was a warning. It's not the first time, either. I tried to say no once before and you know what happened? My daughter was run off the road. She was in a brace for three months."

"You should have gone to Hagan."

"I couldn't. I'd have to confess to all of it. Internal Affairs would eat me for breakfast. I'd lose everything. Not to mention the reputation of the department." Manning stared at the gun in his hand. "I was trapped. I had no choice but to do as he said."

Savage studied him. Hollander had whittled him down to a shell of his former self. The jovial cop that Savage had known was long gone.

"After Trish was attacked, I knew I had to get rid of you. If you weren't around, the case would remain closed. That's why I went to your hotel, but I guess you were expecting that."

"Yeah. I thought Hagan was dirty and that she'd tell Hollander where I was staying. But it was you all along."

"Can't believe I fell for that. I underestimated you, Dalton. Won't happen again."

"We can still make this right." Savage leaned forward in his chair. "If you testify against Hollander, we can put him away."

"We've been through this. I'll lose my pension."

"You'll be free of Hollander."

"I'll be in prison. You know what happens to cops inside."

"He's looking for you."

Manning swallowed. "What do you mean?"

"Trish called him. She wanted to know if you were with him. He's coming for you, Manning. Even if you kill me, you still have to answer to him."

Manning hesitated. "I'll take my chances. He knows I won't talk."

"Does he? You've never been in the firing line before. Hagan knows you were the one who ignored the DVD footage of the robbery."

Manning scowled. "What did she say?"

Savage thought about lying, but then decided against it. He was here to do a deal with Manning. To get his family back. Not make

Manning feel like he had no way out. "She wants more proof before she goes to IA."

He exhaled. "That's good."

Savage pressed home his advantage. "Listen, Clint. Let's make a deal. You give me Becca and Connor, and we walk away from this. You go back to Denver, live out your retirement in your nice house with Trish. See your grandchildren enter the world. We'll forget this ever happened."

"I wish I could do that, buddy." Savage saw real anguish in his ex-partner's face and knew it was futile. Savage knew too much. As long as he was alive, Manning—or rather Hollander—was at risk. And while Manning might let it go, Hollander certainly wouldn't.

"You're going to kill me? Is that how this ends?"

"I really am sorry. I didn't want it to be this way, Dalton, but you couldn't take a hint. I told you to leave it, to go home, but you wouldn't listen. You're too damn stubborn. It's just like before with those damn drug peddling motorcyclists. You were supposed to die then, but you dodged that bullet too."

Savage furrowed his brows in thought. Then, he got it. "In the mountains? That was you?"

"That was Hollander. You were making life difficult for him. He told me to get rid of you. I tried to do it quickly, but one of your guys took out my sniper." He shook his head. "Fucking nine lives, you've got."

Savage tried one more time. "It doesn't have to be this way. You can make a deal. Immunity for Hollander. You can be free of him. Of his hold over you."

"Don't think I haven't considered that, but there is no proof Hollander did anything illegal. You said it yourself, Hagan has nothing. I'd only be implicating myself."

Savage ground his teeth. Manning was right. Hollander never got his hands dirty. It was Manning who'd organized his attempted assassination in the mountains. It was Manning who'd come after him in the hotel room. It was Manning who'd kidnapped Savage's family and held him at gunpoint.

"Did you hire those thugs who robbed the burger joints and killed Helen Ridley?"

"No. I had nothing to do with that, but when I saw the video, I knew it couldn't be submitted into evidence. So yeah, I ignored it. I have no idea who pulled the trigger."

"You could argue that you were coerced. That Hollander beat up your wife and threatened your family if you didn't comply."

"Please. Hollander has connections. Here. Back in Philly. He's not the only one, you know. There's a whole organization behind him."

Savage remembered something Burner had told him. "The Caruso brothers?"

A solemn nod. "Those guys don't screw around. If we bring Hollander down, they're going to come after us. There's no escaping people like that. It only ends one way. At least like this, I have a shot."

"You do this and you're home free?"

He nodded. "I'm out. I'm retired. They have no more use for me."

"How'd you know they won't take you out?"

"I don't, but it's the best chance I've got. I take care of you and retire quietly."

Savage let out a slow breath. "Where are Becca and Connor, Clinton? Let me see them. Please?"

"In the bedroom. They're fine. I've given them a light sedative, but that's all." That would explain why he hadn't heard Connor crying.

"I want to see them."

Manning shook his head. "I can't allow it. Once you're dead, they'll be released. Don't worry, I'm not a monster." That was something, at least. Then he stood. "I'm sorry about this, Dalton. If there was any other way..." But the decision had been made. Savage knew it was only a matter of time before Manning would pull the trigger.

That's when he heard the thunder.

# THIRTY-ONE

"WHAT THE HELL IS THAT?" Manning turned and looked out of the window.

"Sounds like the Crimson Angels." Savage watched Manning warily. "Local outlaw motorcycle gang. Sometimes, they use this farm as an informal meeting place."

"Seriously?" Manning growled in frustration. "I suppose you're going to tell me this is a coincidence."

Savage shrugged. "I don't know why they're here."

Manning marched up to him and pressed the gun against his temple. "Is this you?" he shouted. "Did you tell them to come?"

"No, of course not," Savage yelled back. "Do you think I want to risk Becca and the baby's life? I came because I wanted to make a deal. Your life for theirs."

Manning didn't know what to do. He kept walking to the window, then turning away, then turning back again. The encroaching roar grew louder. Savage could see the swirling dust from where he was sitting. He'd been in Manning's position before. When the Angels arrived en masse, they were a formidable sight.

"Go," Savage said. "Go now. You can leave through the back. There's still time."

Manning's eyes narrowed as he watched through the window. "They're armed. They're surrounding the farmhouse." He swung back to Savage. "You told them. Somehow, you told them to come here." Overcome by a fit of rage, Manning grabbed Savage by the front of his shirt and hauled him to his feet. With his hands cuffed behind his back, Savage was powerless to resist. "You're coming with me."

He stumbled forward. "Where?"

Manning opened the front door and pulled Savage out onto the porch. The cold metal barrel of Manning's gun pressed against his temple. He knew the safety was off. Tensing, he tried not to move. One twitch of Manning's finger and he'd be history.

He tasted sweat on his upper lip and for the first time since this had started, Savage felt afraid. Afraid he wasn't going to see Becca and his son again. Afraid he was going to die here, in front of this outlaw motorcycle gang, at the hands of his former partner who intended to become his murderer.

Zebadiah Swift stepped from the circle, a Mossberg 590 pump-action shotgun in his hands. He pointed it at Manning. "Let him go."

Savage shot him a grateful look, but would Manning back down? The leather and chrome semi-circle watched menacingly, weapons at the ready. If all hell broke loose, both he and Manning would get peppered with bullets. He noticed Rosalie Weston, the President of the club, was absent. Scooter, her VP, was riding in pole position, but it was clear that Zeb had organized this little show of strength.

Manning pressed the pistol harder against his head. Savage closed his eyes. At any moment, he expected a bullet to blast through his brain. He wasn't backing down.

"Get back, or he dies," Manning warned the outlaw bikers. His ex-partner had no intention of letting him live. Hollander's orders. If Manning wanted his life back, he had no choice but to do it.

He opened his eyes and in his peripheral vision, Savage saw a crouching Thorpe and Sinclair sneak around the back of the farmhouse. Manning, focused on Zeb, hadn't noticed. Savage let out a ragged breath. If they could get into the farmhouse undetected, they could rescue Becca and Connor. Then they'd only have Manning to deal with.

"Get back," Manning warned. The bikers didn't budge. Nearly twenty leather-clad, tattooed, armed men glared back at him. It was a stand-off. He felt Manning tremble, the gun digging deeper into his skin. The retired Denver cop was on edge, desperate. There was no telling what he might do.

"Stand down," Savage croaked, as sweat trickled down his face. He did not want to die here. Not when help was so close. Getting the bikers to stand down would buy him the time he needed for his deputies to enter the farmhouse. "Do as he says."

There was a low murmur, and slowly, the circle eased backwards. Another few yards and Manning would be able to reach his car, with Savage in tow.

---

ACTING SHERIFF JAMES THORPE levered open the backdoor to the farmhouse. It creaked, then gave, but whatever noise they made was absorbed by the scene out front. "You get Becca and Connor," he whispered, as they snuck inside. "I'll get the Sheriff."

Sinclair gave a quick nod and took off down the corridor. Thorpe followed, keeping low as he snuck towards the front room. He'd seen Manning pull Savage out onto the porch. Mouth dry, he tiptoed across the living room to the open front door. Hiding behind it, Thorpe pushed his glasses back up his nose and gathered himself together. One more step and Manning would see him.

Acting Sheriff was a huge honor, and one Thorpe wasn't about to turn down, but he couldn't wait for Savage to get back from paternity leave. Thorpe knew he didn't have what it took to be Sheriff, and that wasn't a bad thing. His skills lay elsewhere. He was a data guy.

Statistics and figures were his passion, and he loved reading maps and satellite images, and tracing suspects' online footprints.

Fieldwork was okay, but he wasn't a natural. Not like Savage. He was thin and weedy. Growing up, he hadn't been particularly athletic. He'd had to learn those skills, work on his fitness. Even now, after ten years in law enforcement, he still felt uneasy pulling a gun on a suspect.

"They're not here," Sinclair hissed, coming up behind him.

"What?" Thorpe turned, distracted.

"Becca and the baby. They're not here."

Thorpe shook his head, her words registering. "Then where are they?"

"I don't know. You'll have to ask him." She gestured to Manning, who stood with his back to them, one hand gripping Savage's arm, the other pressing a gun against his head.

*Here we go.*

Taking a deep breath, Thorpe stepped out from behind the door. Fighting to keep his hand steady, and in his most authoritative voice, he barked, "Manning, drop the gun."

Manning spun around and pulled the trigger. Thorpe saw the gun discharge as if in slow motion. Manning's finger tightening... the hammer drawing back ... the flash burning as the bullet flew from the gun. He tried to hit the deck but wasn't fast enough. A searing pain tore through his shoulder. He yelped and dropped the gun, falling to his knees. Blood oozed from his shoulder, spreading out over his shirt.

Thorpe clutched his shoulder, gritting his teeth. His glasses had fallen to the ground and cracked, but he didn't care. He'd never been shot before. Not without a vest. Last year, while on a mountain rescue, he'd been shot several times in the torso while wearing his vest. He'd been knocked unconscious but had survived with no real injuries other than bruised and fractured ribs.

This was different. It felt like someone had shoved a red-hot poker into his shoulder. Eyes watering, he looked up and through blurry vision, saw Sinclair dive from behind the door and go for Manning's gun. They wrestled, the gun waving frantically in the air like an unmanned water hose. Thorpe could only watch from the ground. It hurt too much to move.

The gun went off. Without his glasses, Thorpe wasn't sure who'd pulled the trigger, Sinclair or Manning. The bullet whizzed upwards into the steel-gray sky while Manning tried to twist it out of Sinclair's hand. She wasn't giving it up, though, a look of grim determination on her face. He knew that look. Manning had a fight on his hands.

Savage, finally getting to his feet, charged head-first like a raging bull into Manning and Sinclair, his arms still cuffed behind his back. All three of them went sprawling across the porch, although Manning somehow managed to retain his grip on the gun.

Thorpe watched, horrified, as Manning turned it on Savage. A shot sounded. Deafeningly loud. His ears rang.

"No!" Sinclair got to her knees, lunged toward Savage, but it was Manning who fell. Thorpe stared, confused, as blood ran down Manning's face. It was only then he realized it was Manning who had been shot, not Savage.

Savage lay on the ground, breathless, but unharmed.

Thorpe looked at the bikers. Zeb stood ten yards away, a smoking shotgun in his hand.

# THIRTY-TWO

"BECCA? CONNOR?" Savage called, once Sinclair had made sure Manning was dead.

"They're not here," she told him, undoing his cuffs.

"What?" He scrambled to his feet, stepped over a pale Thorpe, and ran into the farmhouse. "How could they not be here? Manning said they were in the bedroom." It wasn't a big property, just the living room, bedroom, and kitchen. They were all empty. There was no furniture inside the house aside from the old chairs, which they'd sat on, a dirty mug in the sink and a torn lampshade in the bedroom. Savage stood in the center of the living room and looked around in a panic. "Where are they?"

Zeb came into the house. "You okay?"

"The bastard's holding Becca and Connor somewhere else." Savage heard the anxiety in his own voice. He'd believed Manning, which was a stupid error of judgment. He ought to have known the dirty cop wouldn't bring his only leverage here, where he was meeting Savage.

Zeb's eyes grew wide. "What? They aren't here?"

Savage shook his head. Desperation welled inside him, followed closely by a seething rage. "If he hurt them—"

"He didn't," Zeb said calmly. "He was using them to get to you. Remember that. He's got them stashed away somewhere, probably a motel room."

"We've got to find them." Savage bent down and inspected Manning's body. He pulled out his wallet, but there was nothing other than a few notes and some credit cards. No phone.

"He must have been staying somewhere," Zeb said.

Sinclair was inspecting Thorpe's shoulder wound. The Acting Sheriff had managed to prop himself up against the wall. "It's just a flesh wound, you were lucky. Might need a couple stitches, but you'll live." He gave a weak nod. "I'll call an ambulance. We'll get you to the hospital."

Savage felt around in Manning's jacket. In the inside pocket he found a white plastic card with a metallic strip on one side.

"Looks like a keycard," Zeb said.

Savage turned it over, heart sinking. "No name."

"If he got the room in Hawk's Landing, there are only a handful of possibilities," Sinclair said, looking up. "And I know for a fact it's not the Boulder Creek Hotel, because I studied those keycards earlier this year when Douglas Connelly was staying there. They don't look like that."

"She's right," Thorpe said.

"I can help," Zeb offered.

Thorpe shook his head. "I don't think that's possible, Mr. Swift. You're going to have to come down to the station and give a statement." He nodded at the hole in Manning's head. "Sinclair, take his rifle."

Zeb, who knew the drill better than most, sighed. "Can't it wait? There's a woman and a child out there. We need all hands on deck."

Thorpe hesitated.

Zeb looked at Savage. "Dalton?"

"Thorpe's Acting Sheriff, Zeb. While I appreciate what you did here tonight, we've gotta follow protocol." Zeb scowled, but he handed his rifle to Sinclair. Thorpe got to his feet, leaving a bloody handprint on the wall.

"What about them?" Sinclair nodded to the bikers.

"Let them go," Savage said. "We can't have them running all over town." Thorpe nodded as if this had been his decision too.

Sinclair strode outside to pass it on. He heard her thanking them for their help in both finding Manning and their show of numbers. As the motorcyclists were leaving, another patrol vehicle raced up the dirt road, its siren rising above the Harley engines.

"Littleton," Sinclair said, exhaling as a slender man in a deputy uniform got out of the car.

Littleton had barely put the car in park before leaping out and rushing over. "Barbara called me. What happened?"

Sinclair filled him in while Savage walked toward the Suburban, reaching into his pocket for his phone. It was time to give Hagan a call. It was late, but Trish and the girls deserved to know their father wasn't coming home. Plus, they might know where Manning was staying and, therefore, where he was keeping his hostages.

"I'm going to get started," he called over his shoulder. Every moment counted. Becca could be tied up or hurt, and who was looking after Connor? When was the last time he ate? Was he warm enough? He was practically a newborn, only a couple of weeks old.

His worry must have shown in his face, because Sinclair said, "I'll help. You take above the railway line, I'll take below.

Savage grunted his thanks. The line divided the town roughly into two, with the northern section more affluent than the south, which also bordered the reservation.

Sinclair nodded. "Littleton can tie this up and take Zeb in. Thorpe, you've got to get to the hospital and have that looked at."

Littleton, still absorbing everything, nodded.

As Savage left Apple Tree Farm, he passed two ambulances and a beat-up station wagon coming the other way. He lifted his hand at the occupants as he passed. Ray and Pearl were a husband-and-wife forensic team who had worked at some of their other crime scenes. They were quick, discreet, and had about fifty years of combined experience working in a big city. The crime scene was in good hands.

Their evidence would back up what had happened and confirm Zeb's role in the shooting. There'd be an investigation, of course, but Zeb had saved his life in front of about twenty witnesses. Defending another's life with deadly force applied to civilians as much as it did to police, although the opportunity, or willingness, to do so was far less. Thankfully for Savage, Zeb was a combination of both worlds. There would be some legalities to hurdle, but Savage would be in Zeb's corner every step of the way. A life debt demands as much.

SARAH HAGAN ANSWERED the phone on the second ring. "For Pete's sake, Savage, haven't you left yet?" He was beginning to doubt she had any other setting apart from rude.

"Actually, yes." He turned onto Durango Road heading toward town. "I'm back in Hawk's Landing."

"So why are you calling me?"

"I've got a situation here. It involves Manning."

"Manning?" Her tone was now more concerned than before.

Savage explained what had happened. He told her everything, starting with how Manning had abducted Becca and Connor, burned his house down, threatened to kill him, and finally, been shot by a member of the public.

There was a moment's silence as Hagan digested this. "Jeez, Dalton. How do you get yourself into this shit? Where's your girlfriend and son now?" He liked that she jumped to the important part. There was no hostility in her voice, no resentment. Not anymore. Not now that their lives were at stake.

"I don't know." Savage's voice cracked. The strain was getting to him. He fought to keep it together. "We're looking for them. We found a hotel keycard on Manning, but it could be anywhere."

"Have you tried looking up her last location?"

"He turned her phone off almost immediately."

"I'm not sure what I can do."

"I need you to authorize a search of his house. Talk to his wife, Trish, and see if she knows where he was staying."

Savage heard scratching. "Give me his address and I'll get on it. Damn Manning for losing it like that. What the hell was he thinking?"

"He's related to Guy Hollander," Savage said. "Real name Ray Magee. Manning's his brother-in-law."

"Holy crap. Guy Hollander is his wife's brother?"

"Estranged. She claims they haven't spoken in years, but obviously the same can't be said for Manning."

He heard her groan. "This is going to be a shit storm, isn't it?" Savage knew she was thinking ahead to the internal investigation into Manning's corruption and the failure of the department to put a stop to it.

"Manning is dead, Sarah. Maybe this doesn't have to end in a shit storm."

"We can only hope," she said wearily. "Otherwise, I'm going to have to reopen all Manning's cases. The entire department is going to come under scrutiny. Every case we've ever worked. Every lousy murdering scumbag we've put away is going to use this as their get out of jail free card."

Savage wouldn't want to be in Hagan's shoes right now. "Maybe when you're reviewing those cases, you can get Hollander on something. He deserves to be behind bars."

She grunted. "The guy's cleaner than a virgin's honeypot." That was Sarah Hagan.

Savage pulled into the parking lot of the Budget Hotel. That was really its name. "I've gotta go. I'll talk to you later." He ended the call.

The Budget Hotel lived up to its name. It was Hawk's Landing's cheapest hotel, and while Savage had never stayed there, he'd been in several times to look for criminals, fugitives, or Johns who'd forked out for a room because they couldn't take their girl back to their own home. The narrow building had a dingy lobby and a tattooed teenager behind the front desk. There was a distinct smell of dope in the air.

"Yeah?" The teenage receptionist grunted.

Savage showed him the keycard. "This one of yours?"

The kid stared at it, then shook his head. "Nah. Ours have the hotel name on it." He took one out of a drawer at his hip and held it up so Savage could see. "See. Totally different."

"I see." Savage wanted to be sure. "You don't have a guest named Clinton Manning staying here, do you?"

"Don't recall the name."

"Could you take a look?"

The kid's eyes narrowed. He must be stoned, but he was cautious. Maybe he was used to the cops asking questions about his clientele. "Who are you?"

Savage slapped his ID against the glass partition. The kid nearly fell off his swivel chair. "One moment, Sheriff, sir." He fired up a computer and clicked the mouse a couple of times, then shook his head, keeping his bloodshot eyes low. "No, sir. There's no one by that name staying here."

Savage gave a curt nod and left.

---

THE FLAMINGO HOTEL, stupidly named since he'd never seen a flamingo in Hawk's Landing, was located closer to the railway line. It had three stars as opposed to the Budget Hotel's two and was pretty decent if you ignored the freight train that came thundering past at three every morning. They didn't put that in the brochure.

Savage walked up to the reception desk. "Hi Tallulah." A local girl who lived on the reservation, she'd been friends with one of the victims in the last case he'd worked on.

"Hey Sheriff," she replied with a smile. "Is there something wrong?" People just assumed that when they saw him coming.

"This one of yours?" He held up the keycard.

"Could be. We do use blank ones like that. Let me check." Savage waited while she ran the card through the card reader. If it belonged to this hotel, the reader would read and verify the information on the magnetic strip. "No, sorry. It doesn't recognize it."

His heart sank. "You're sure? It's not a glitch."

She did it again, then shook her head. "Not one of ours. Where'd you find it?"

He didn't tell her it was on a dead body. "I'm looking for a guest named Clinton Manning. Can you check if he's staying here?"

Unlike the Budget guy, she didn't question it, immediately tapping away at the keyboard. After a second, she looked up. "Sorry, Sheriff. There's no one with that name staying here." She paused, as if unsure whether to say something, then added, "But sometimes the guests don't use their real name."

"Don't you ask for ID?"

"Not if they pay cash in advance."

He dug in his pocket for the photograph and showed it to her. "This is the man. Do you recognize him?"

Tallulah studied the picture. "Sorry, I haven't seen him. If I do, I'll call the Sheriff's department." There wasn't any chance of that happening, but he nodded anyway.

*Damn you, Manning.*

Savage got back into his car and pounded the steering wheel until his hands hurt. Now what? He'd covered the two hotels on this side of the tracks. Taking out his phone he texted Sinclair. "Any luck?"

He waited a few minutes but got no reply.

Tiredness made his eyes gritty, and he blinked to clear them. Tears welled, catching him by surprise. Dropping his head, he let them fall. He couldn't lose Becca and Connor. Life without them was unthinkable.

Savage took a deep breath. He couldn't let the bastard get the better of him. He had to believe they were still alive, that Manning hadn't hurt them. Zeb was right. His ex-partner might have been a dirty, conniving scumbag, but he'd needed them to lure Savage in. He would have kept them alive for insurance, just in case Savage didn't play ball.

He exhaled, rubbed his eyes, and started the SUV. Not knowing what to do, he drove back to the Sheriff's station.

# THIRTY-THREE

"ANYTHING?" Savage asked Sinclair as he walked into the Sheriff's station. Not wanting to go into his old office, which was now Thorpe's, he perched on the edge of Sinclair's desk. Outside, the sun was fighting its way through the clouds, throwing pale beams across the floor. The sounds of the office were reassuring, and though he was exhausted, he'd rather be here than back at Sinclair's, by himself.

Littleton was at his desk writing reports and keeping an eye on the phone data, in case Becca turned on her cell again. Savage had given him the recording to file as evidence. It would help back up Zeb's statement and prove Manning's role in all this, but it still didn't implicate Guy Hollander. Savage had listened to it, and while Manning had talked about being trapped, and having no choice, he hadn't offered any concrete evidence of Hollander's involvement. The mobster's defense lawyer would just argue Manning was paranoid, and deny he'd been threatened or intimidated in any way. They couldn't prove Hollander had been involved in Manning's daughter's accident, or Trish's attack. Savage sighed. The word of a clearly disturbed man who wasn't alive to testify wouldn't go far.

Barbara Wright, the station administrator, was making coffee and force feeding them cookies from a large tin. “You need to keep your strength up,” she said.

Sinclair stifled a yawn, or maybe it was a cough. “I visited all three hotels on my side of the tracks and nobody recognized him. The keycard didn’t match either. I think we’re going to have to look further out.”

“You mean Durango?” Littleton glanced up. “It’s five times the size of Hawk’s Landing. There are a couple hundred hotels.” Durango, a town with a population of twenty thousand, was nestled at the base of the San Juan Mountains eighteen miles from Hawk’s Landing.

“I know, but if they're not here—” She fell into her chair.

“Then, they must be there.” Savage moved off her desk and started pacing up and down by the window.

“Here, drink this.” Barbara elbowed him out of the way to get to Sinclair. “You look terrible, and I don’t like the sound of that cough.”

Savage stopped pacing and took a good look at his deputy. He’d been so caught up in his own drama that he hadn’t noticed that her clothes were still filthy and although she’d cleaned her face, there were black smudges along her hairline and down her neck. Her eyes were bloodshot, and she looked like she was about to drop.

Guilt gnawed at him. Sinclair was going all out to help him. They all were. Littleton had been working all night. Poor Thorpe had been shot by Manning. Zeb had killed a man. All because of him. He took a steadying breath. “I’m sorry. You look beat. Why don’t you go home and get some sleep?”

She raised her head and he saw a glimmer in her eyes. She wasn’t done yet. “No way. Not while they’re still out there. You need all the help you can get.”

“Thanks, Sinclair.”

She waved her hand in the air like it was nothing. “Let’s call Shelby at the Durango Sheriff’s office. He’s got a team of deputies. Maybe they can help.”

“Good idea.” It still wouldn’t be enough, but it was better than nothing. At least they’d cover more ground.

Barbara, who was getting to know the Durango Sheriff pretty well, said, "I'll call him right now."

Savage shot her a grateful smile. "I'm not going to stand around here twiddling my thumbs. I'll get over there and start searching."

He was about to leave, when his phone rang. Everybody jumped.

"Sorry." He turned it back down before answering. "Sarah?" Maybe Hagan had some news.

"You find them yet?" was the first thing that she said.

"Not yet. You speak with Trish?"

"Yeah. Nice family. Pity he's screwed them up so badly."

Savage didn't reply. He imagined it had been a total shock to Trish and the girls. They wouldn't have known about their father's involvement with organized crime, or his desperate attempt to save himself and the life he'd built.

"She hasn't spoken to her husband since that message he sent her just after he left. The one that said he'd be gone for a couple days."

He closed his eyes.

"His daughter *did* though."

He opened his eyes. "When?"

"Last night. He called the house. She said he sounded strange, like he was sad." Savage's brain went into overdrive. That would have been the night before he met Manning at Apple Tree Farm. Maybe his old partner had had an inkling it would all go wrong. Or maybe he was just feeling conflicted that he had to kill Savage and kidnapped an innocent woman and baby.

"Sad?"

"Yeah, he told her he loved them, and that he hoped to be back soon. He was obviously upset about something."

"About having to kill me," he said bitterly. Becca and Connor would have been with him at the time. "Did she say anything else?"

"Actually, yes, and this might help you. When she asked where he was, he said at a ski lodge. He said it was nice, and he'd take the family there one day."

There were only three ski resorts near Durango. That narrowed it down. "I gotta go. Thanks, Hagan."

He hung up and turned to the others. "He told his daughter he was staying at a ski lodge." Durango had great skiing in winter. Three resorts and 300,000 acres of backcountry. Right now, there was no snow, but it would come.

Sinclair jumped up, all signs of exhaustion vanishing in her excitement. "Let's split up. You take Purgatory, Littleton and I will take West Mountain. Tell Shelby to cover Silver Mountain."

"Purgatory is too far north. I doubt he'd go there. I'll meet you guys at West Mountain. Shelby can send a couple of deputies to Silver Mountain, just in case." They raced out of the station. Savage leaped into his car, put the siren on and his foot down.

"I'm coming, Becca," he whispered, as he flew along the Durango Road, past Mac's Roadhouse, toward the next town. "Hang in there. I'm coming."

---

HE'D JUST REACHED the outskirts of Durango when the radio crackled. "Savage, Shelby. Pick up."

"This is Savage."

"We found 'em."

The Suburban veered across the road as Savage went weak with relief. He skidded to a stop on the shoulder, shaking.

"Where? Are they—"

"They're alive, Dalton."

"Oh, thank God." Emotion welled in his throat, and he choked on his words. "W—Where are they?"

"Silver Mountain. I sent a patrolman to take a look. The receptionist recognized him from the photograph your deputy sent over. Manning was here, but not under his own name. He used his wife's."

Savage wiped his face that was suddenly wet with tears. He hadn't even realized he was crying. "I'll be there in ten."

Savage screeched to a halt outside the main entrance to the Silver Mountain resort three miles north of Durango. Sheriff Shelby was already there with an ambulance and the patrol vehicle. Racing into the lobby, he looked around but couldn't see anyone.

"Hello?"

Where the hell were they?

A young woman in her twenties appeared, her cheeks flushed. "I'm sorry, sir. You'll have to wait. We have an emergency."

"I'm Sheriff Savage," he snapped, barely keeping his voice from shaking. "Where are they?"

"Second floor. R—Room 203."

Savage took off at a sprint. His heart was pounding so fast he thought it might explode. Racing up the stairs, he rounded the corner and nearly collided with Shelby on the landing.

"Is she there? Have you got them?"

Shelby put his hand on Savage's shoulder. "Yeah, we've got them. They're okay. A little dehydrated, especially the baby, but they're alive." Savage stumbled into the room. A uniformed deputy was helping Becca to her feet while two paramedics leaned over a small carry cot. Savage lurched toward it. "Is he okay?"

Connor lay still, his eyes closed. Savage gripped the paramedic's arm. "Is he—?"

"We've gotta get him hooked up to some fluids. He's badly dehydrated, but he should pull through. Vitals are strong. He's a tough little guy." A sob of relief escaped Savage as he watched them take his son out to the ambulance. Then he turned to Becca, and she fell into his arms, sobbing. "Oh, God, Dalton. I was so worried. I thought we were going to die here."

"I was never going to let that happen," he whispered, stroking her head.

"I was so scared. Is Connor going to be okay?" Her eyes darted to the cot where he'd lain. Empty now, other than a blanket that had been wrapped around his tiny form. "I couldn't get to him. I—" She petered off as tears sprung to her eyes and ran down her cheeks.

"Shh... He's going to be fine." Savage held her against him. "Everything is going to be fine."

"What about Manning? What if he comes back?"

"He's not coming back, Becca."

She pulled away. "You mean?"

"He's dead."

"You—?" Her eyes widened.

"Not me. Zeb."

"Zeb?" He saw the confusion in her eyes, then she shook her head and hugged him again. It didn't matter.

"I'll explain later. Right now, let's get Connor to the hospital." She nodded and buried her face on his shoulder.

# THIRTY-FOUR

SAVAGE WALKED into the Sheriff's department the next day, feeling better than he had in weeks. Connor was doing well, having spent the night under observation in the pediatric wing of the hospital. The little champ had rallied after being fed intravenous fluids and electrolytes and was back to his normal vocal self. Savage had just spent a couple hours there before coming into the station. They wanted to keep him in for the day but told Savage he could take him home this afternoon.

Home. Now that was a sore point. He and Becca had moved into Sinclair's spare room until they figured out what they were going to do. She'd offered, and they'd been too exhausted last night to refuse. His own house resembled the remnants of a bonfire, and he hadn't even called the insurance company yet.

Of course, Sinclair's was only temporary. He'd have to look around for a more permanent place, but right now he just wanted to be somewhere quiet with his family, while he tied up loose ends.

Zeb had given Littleton a statement and was awaiting a court date. Since he had a permit to carry a concealed weapon and had used it in self-defense – or rather Savage's defense – he was unlikely to be charged. They had confiscated his gun, but he'd get it back after he was cleared.

Thorpe was back, his shoulder in a sling. "Are you sure you don't want your office back, boss?" he said, as Savage sat down on the other side of Sinclair's desk.

"You're the Acting Sheriff, Thorpe. You stay where you are."

"Okay." With a nervous nod, he went back to his desk.

"How's Becca?" Barbara asked, after he'd told her about Connor.

"She's okay. I've left her to sleep. She needs rest."

Barbara gave a knowing nod. "I'm going to make you a warm stew for supper," she told him. "I'll bring it to you later."

"You don't have to do that."

"I want to." She looked almost offended. "None of you have time to cook."

That was Barbara. He wouldn't talk her out of it, and it did sound good.

Hagan had been shocked to get the voice recording of the showdown with Manning. They'd talked after he'd gotten back to Sinclair's, and she'd promised to listen to it and call him this morning. The search had turned up a few things, but she hadn't gone into detail. "It might be nothing," she'd told him. "I'll get back to you in the morning." He'd been too tired to argue.

Now, he jumped as the phone rang. "You've got to change that ringtone," Barbara admonished, walking away with her hand on her chest. "Nearly gives me a heart attack every time it goes off."

"Sorry." He picked it up. "Hey Sarah."

"You sound chipper this morning."

"I am feeling much better." He sensed her smile, and thought, that's a first. He could be wrong. She was probably scowling down the line at him, as usual.

"I've got some good news."

"About the recording? Can we use it to nab Hollander?"

"Well, no. I've run it past our legal team, and they say it's a no-go. There's not enough evidence to arrest him. We could bring him in for questioning, but the Deputy Chief doesn't think that's a good idea."

"He wouldn't," grunted Savage. Typical. "What else you got?"

She hesitated. "We think Manning was being blackmailed."

That was news.

"By whom?"

"Kenan Simmons."

"What? No way."

"We found a note in his garbage can. It's in Kenan's handwriting."

"What does it say?"

"I know about you and H."

"You and Hollander?" He thought for a moment. "Kenan found out that Manning was dirty, and that he was giving information to Hollander. Could that be why they met in Wash Park?"

"We're not sure when this was written. It could have been weeks ago."

"Have you checked Manning's phone records? Maybe Kenan called him and demanded money."

"We're doing that now."

"Keep me posted."

"Will do." She hesitated again. "There's one more thing, Dalton."

"Yeah?"

"We found gunshot residue in Trish's car, along with traces of blood spatter. She says she doesn't know how they got there."

Savage went cold. "What model is the car?"

"It's a Hyundai Tucson."

Manning had taken Trish's car when he'd shot Kenan.

"Sarah," he said. "I need you to meet a man named Bob."

---

"SO, MANNING KILLED THAT KID?" Thorpe asked, coming out of his office. "The one you went up to Denver for?"

"Seems like it. Kenan was blackmailing him. We don't know all the details yet, but it looks like Manning tracked him to his friend's house, waited until he was walking back to the bus stop, then pulled over to confront him. Maybe he offered him money, or to make a deal. Kenan got into the car and a few seconds later, Manning shot him."

"That poor kid," Barbara whispered. "He had no idea what kind of man he was dealing with."

"Ironic, since it was the same man who'd helped convict his brother to life in prison."

Sinclair shook her head. "What a mess. If only he hadn't tried to blackmail him. He'd still be alive today."

Choices. That's one thing Savage had learned. In the end, it all boiled down to choices.

"What are you going to do now?" Sinclair asked.

"I'm going to go back to Denver." At their look of surprise, he chuckled. "Dewayne Simmons is being released. The DA reviewed the new evidence and he's being exonerated."

"What evidence was that?" Littleton asked. Savage forgot his team knew nothing of the investigation in Denver.

"We found surveillance footage that proves the shooter in the robbery six years ago was right-handed. Dewayne Simmons is left-handed. It couldn't have been him."

"Are you going to meet him?" Sinclair asked, smiling.

"Yeah, I'd like to be there when he walks out."

They were still talking about the case when the door to the front lobby opened, and like a blast of cold air, in walked Guy Hollander.

# THIRTY-FIVE

GUY HOLLANDER SMILED at the surprise on the Sheriff's rugged face. Good. That would teach him to be complacent. You couldn't be complacent in their line of work. It made you vulnerable.

"How'd you get in here," Savage growled.

"The door was wide open." Hollander tsked. "Terrible security, but then I don't suppose you need to worry in a small town like this."

A female deputy – pretty, with a model's figure – drew her weapon and aimed it at him. He put his hands in the air. "Easy, hot stuff. I'm just here to talk." She didn't move.

A skinny man rushed out of an adjoining office, hand on his holster. While a geeky kid sat and stared at them from behind his desk. The poor guy looked terrified.

"I'm unarmed, in case you were wondering."

Savage nodded to the skinny man who let go of his gun, walked over somewhat hesitantly, and patted him down. Hollander tried not to flinch. He didn't like other people's hands on him. "If you're finished..." He glanced at the skinny guy who straightened up and nodded at Savage.

"He's clean."

"I think it's time you and I talked, don't you?" Hollander fixed his gaze on Savage.

"Take the office," the skinny man offered. Hollander wondered at the strange arrangement, then he remembered Manning saying something about Savage being on paternity leave. He didn't think much of the Acting Sheriff. Still, appearances could be deceiving.

He followed Savage into the office and closed the door.

"What do you want, Hollander?"

"Such hostility," Hollander murmured, looking around. "Nice place you got here. It's a pretty town too. I've never been to Hawk's Landing before."

"No, you sent your thug Jonny Star to do your dirty work for you."

Hollander tried not to smile. He was in control now, not like when Savage had taken him by surprise at the country club. "I don't know who you mean."

"Yes, you do." Savage didn't sit, so neither did he. Instead, they faced each other like two silverbacks. Hollander almost expected the Sheriff to start beating his chest, such was the tension in the air. "What are you doing here?"

"I heard about Clinton. I wanted to see if there was anything I could do. Trish is very upset."

"You've spoken to Trish?"

"Of course. She is my sister." Hollander didn't mind playing the part of the doting brother.

"Trish knows her husband was working for you."

Hollander gave a soft snort. "Clinton was a police detective. He didn't work for me."

"No, he was just feeding you information. He was your eyes and ears inside the police department. He kept you apprised of everything, didn't he?"

"Don't be absurd." Hollander kept his voice low and even. Savage would not get a rise out of him. "I'm sorry to hear he cracked like he did, he was a good man. I'd like to know when his body is going to be released."

"Are you going to take him back to Denver?"

"To his wife, yes. He deserves to be buried there."

"I can't tell you that. You'll have to speak to the Acting Sheriff."

"Oh, yes. That's right. You're on paternity leave."

Savage's eyes narrowed. "Yes."

"How is your son? I heard he had a close call. I can't believe Clinton abducted them like that. He must have really hated you." Savage's jaw popped and Hollander knew he was getting to him.

"I think he was more scared of you."

He gave a dry laugh. "Bullshit. He knew he could count on me. You, on the other hand, threatened to expose his mistake."

"Mistake? Is that what we're calling it?"

Hollander gave Savage the wide-eyed stare he was so good at. "Oh, yes. Clinton told me he'd messed up. He'd ignored evidence that later would turn out to be important. You'd threatened to go to his boss, who'd have called Internal Affairs. After thirty years of service, my brother-in-law would have ended up with nothing. It's no wonder he snapped."

"He snapped because he knew you'd kill him if he didn't take me out."

Hollander clicked his tongue. "Sheriff, I hope you haven't bought into his madness. I had nothing to do with his actions. He wanted you off his back, pure and simple. That's what a jury is going to think."

There, he'd said it. Savage had to know it was fruitless going after him. Nothing he had would stand up in court. Nothing.

"Did you know Clinton shot Kenan Simmons, your employee?"

Hollander stared at him. He hadn't been expecting that. What the hell? Why had Clinton done that?

"I told you, Kenan didn't work for me."

"Yeah, right." The gleam in Savage's eye told Hollander the Sheriff didn't believe him. So what? It had no bearing on anything. It was just something else to add to Manning's sordid criminal history.

"Why would a police detective shoot a kid like Kenan? I don't get it."

Savage frowned. "You really don't know?"

"No, I had no idea." He was genuinely puzzled. "Will you enlighten me?"

Savage rolled his eyes. "Because of his connection to you. Kenan was blackmailing him."

Hollander narrowly prevented himself from laughing. "Shit. Clinton really lost his mind, didn't he? You know, I had a friend who did that once. Turns out he had early onset dementia. Maybe Clint had that."

The Sheriff put his hands on his hips. Hollander sensed he was losing it. "If there's nothing else, I think you should leave now."

"I'll leave, if you let me know when I can take my brother-in-law's body home."

"Give me a number where I can reach you."

Hollander gave a slow, ominous grin. "Oh, I'm sure you already have it. Speak soon, Sheriff. And give my regards to Becca."

---

"WHAT DID HE MEAN, 'give my regards to Becca?'" Sinclair asked, as Savage came out of the office. They were all staring at him.

"It was obviously a threat. He asked how Connor was too."

Thorpe shook his head. "That man is dangerous."

"I know."

"What did he say?" Sinclair asked. "Did he admit to having that woman shot?"

"No, he didn't admit to anything. That's not his style. In fact, he denied any knowledge of Manning's corruption. Said he was as shocked as anyone that he went off the rails like that. Even had the gall to suggest he might be suffering from early onset dementia." He clenched his jaw.

Sinclair shook her head.

Barbara came in sheepishly. "I'm so sorry. It's my fault he waltzed in here. I was so relieved that Becca and the baby were alright that I left it open."

"That's alright." Savage and Thorpe spoke at the same time. Savage cleared his throat. "It was an honest mistake. Don't beat yourself up about it. Hollander wasn't here to cause trouble, he just wanted to let me know it would be useless going after him."

"Is that true?" Littleton asked. "Is it useless?"

The conversation he'd had with Zeb a few weeks ago came back to haunt him.

*No one is untouchable, Zeb.*

*I think you'll find this guy is the exception.*

# THIRTY-SIX

SAVAGE GAZED out of the helicopter window and squeezed Becca's hand. It was a week after the kidnapping, and she was still vulnerable. He'd never seen Becca this insecure. She was usually so strong, the one others went to with their problems, but he knew it would take time for the horror of what had happened to fade.

The snowy white peaks sparkled in the mid-morning sun. Below, the city of Colorado Springs sprawled out over the plains. It was the nearest city to the Colorado State Penitentiary, where Dewayne Simmons had served his time.

"Will we make it in time?" Becca asked, as the chopper dipped.

"I hope so. He's being released at noon. Burner's going to meet us at the airport." Colorado Springs was half a day's drive from Hawk's Landing, so they'd opted to fly, wanting to spend as little time away from Connor as possible. The Durango FBI field office had offered them a lift.

"He'll be okay with Jasmine, won't he?" she asked, for the umpteenth time since they'd left a gurgling Connor at Jasmine Hatch's house. His son showed no ill-effects from the dehydration he'd suffered after he'd been abducted.

Savage had known Jasmine for several years now, since he'd first gotten to Hawk's Landing. In fact, one of his first cases had been investigating her daughter's murder. Olivia had been killed after trying to bring to light scandal with far reaching implications for the environment and the inhabitants of Hawk's Landing and its surrounding neighbors. The tragedy brought him together with Hatch. For all of the subsequent fallout, he would never regret having shared that time with her. As a result, he was still in the good graces of her family, Jasmine's special coffee being one of the perks.

He smiled at her. "Jasmine has raised two daughters and two grandchildren. Connor couldn't be in better hands." Besides, her partner, Jed Russel, was ex-101st Airborne Division and would die before he let anything happen to her or her kin. But he didn't tell Becca that. She didn't know how close he'd come to Jed, Jasmine, or her daughter Rachel. He'd played down their relationship, and over time it had become as insignificant as he'd wanted it to be.

"If you're sure." Her earnest blue eyes fluttered to the window. They were descending rapidly now, the rotor blades throbbing loudly making it difficult to hear each other. Another ten minutes and they'd be on the ground.

A smiling Burner was waiting for them inside the terminal. Savage pumped his hand. "Thank you," he said. "I have to admit, until you called and said he'd been exonerated, I still had my doubts you could pull it off."

Burner shot him a look that said, *please, this is me we're talking about*. Then he turned to embrace Becca. "I heard what happened. Thank God you're alright."

"I am." She smiled bravely, but Savage could see the cracks. This was the second time his job had put her in danger. Last year, a man called Axle Weston had run her off the road and she'd ended up in a ditch with a severe concussion. She'd been pregnant at the time.

Now this.

Becca was only human. He might think she was built differently, since she was always there for him, but this had frightened her. He didn't know how much more she could take.

He pushed the worry aside and focused on Burner. "We'd better get a move on if we're going to make it."

"Car's waiting."

They followed him out of the terminal and into the multi-story parking lot. Burner got behind the wheel of his silver Mercedes and waited until they'd buckled themselves in. "We've got an hour. Plenty of time."

Colorado State Penitentiary was in a remote area forty miles west of Colorado Springs, surrounded by desert landscapes and rugged terrain. They set off, Burner driving as fast as he could, staying ten miles within the speed limit. Forty minutes later, they saw the sprawling maximum security complex come into view.

BECCA SHIVERED. "WHAT AN AWFUL PLACE."

"It houses some of the most dangerous and high-risk offenders in the state," Savage told her. It had a reputation for being one of the most violent prisons in the state too, but he didn't say that. "Dewayne spent six years here, for a crime he didn't commit."

"Tragic." She shook her head. "It must have had an effect on him."

Savage thought of the tattoos that covered the inmate's finely honed physique. Of the cuts and bruises. "He's got scars," he said quietly. And they weren't just on the surface.

They drove up to the electric gates, and he saw Becca glance up at the control towers on either side, both with armed guards in them. The facility was monitored 24/7 by top range surveillance cameras. There were an inordinate number of correctional officers who controlled the movement of the inmates.

Burner stopped the car. "This is as far as we go," he said. "They'll bring him out."

All three of them got out of the car. A cold wind blew off the mountains, chilling them. Becca pulled her coat tighter around her. At five minutes to noon, they saw a prison van approach the gate. The multiple buildings were so spread out, they had to transport him to the exit.

"Right on time," Burner murmured.

The hulking form of Dewayne Simmons, escorted by two uniformed prison guards, walked toward the gate. He was dressed in casual clothes, jeans, a T-shirt, and an oversized hooded top that made him look even bigger than he was, and that was saying something. No jacket. Probably what his mother had brought him on her latest visit.

Mrs. Simmons wasn't here. She had no means of getting to the prison, and they hadn't had time to arrange anything. But her boy would be home soon. Savage would see to it personally.

At the gate, the officers turned to Dewayne, gave him a curt nod, and gestured to another guard standing by the gate armed with an automatic rifle. There was a loud clunk, as the electronic bolt was released, and the guard opened the gate. It screeched apart, just wide enough for a man to walk through.

Dewayne hesitated, unsure whether to proceed or not. It was clear that he couldn't wrap his head around the fact that he'd been exonerated. It must have felt surreal. After six years of hell, he was free.

Savage gave an encouraging nod and Dewayne, meeting his eye, began to walk. He made it through the gate, which closed immediately behind him, the electric bolt slotting back into place. On the way in, that sound must seem like the end of the world, but now it signified everything Dewayne was leaving behind.

Savage grinned and walked up to shake his hand. "Hey Dewayne. We thought you might need a ride."

Dewayne Simmons began to cry.

# THIRTY-SEVEN

CONNOR REACHED up for his bottle, his little hands chubby and eager. Savage gave it to him, smiling. The baby put it straight in his mouth.

"You're right," Savage said to Becca. "He has grown."

They were still at Sinclair's place, but she was at the station most of the time, only coming home to sleep. He hadn't appreciated just how hard she worked before now. The girl had no life.

Becca perched at the end of the bed. "You did a good thing, Dalton, proving Dewayne's innocence." She'd been quiet on the drive home, and he knew she was reflecting on what had happened. "I understand why you did it now."

He turned to look at her. "I'm sorry you and Connor got involved. I didn't mean for that to happen."

"Obviously, but you couldn't have foreseen that. Manning was desperate, I see that now."

He should have foreseen it. He'd been so caught up in Manning's attempt to kill him, that he'd forgotten he had an Achilles heel. His family.

"Hollander had him by the balls. There was nowhere to turn. If Zeb hadn't shot him, Hollander probably would have. I'm almost certain that's why he came here."

Becca's eyes widened. "Guy Hollander came here? To Hawk's Landing? Why didn't you tell me?"

He shook his head. "I guess I just forgot. He walked into the sheriff's station cool as a cucumber. I still can't believe the audacity of the man."

"What did he come for?"

"To gloat, among other things." He wasn't going to tell her he'd made a subtle threat towards them.

*Give my regards to Becca.*

One thing was for sure, though. He'd have to keep watching over his shoulder. As long as he left Hollander alone, Savage felt the mobster would leave him alone. That was the way it went.

Savage was content to do that. For now. He'd had enough excitement. There'd be time to dedicate to Hollander later. No man was untouchable.

"You can't put him away?"

"Got nothing on him. The guy's squeaky clean. Never gets his hands dirty."

She gave a knowing nod. "He's smart, isn't he?"

"Very." He pressed his lips together.

*But I'm smarter.*

"I'm glad he's gone back to Denver." She heaved a sigh of relief. "Hopefully, we'll never see him again."

"I second that." Connor sucked hungrily on the bottle as if in agreement. Savage smiled and said, "Hey, you know that old place out on the Durango Road, Apple Tree Farm?"

"Wasn't that where—?"

"Yeah, but that's not why I'm mentioning it."

"Oh?" Her eyebrows rose.

"It's abandoned. The bank foreclosed and the owners have moved out. I think I can get a pretty good deal on it."

"It's pretty run down, if I remember correctly." She tilted her head to the side. "What are you proposing? That we buy it?"

"Maybe. I thought I'd go out there this afternoon and take a good look around. It's only one bedroom, but there's plenty of land. We could add an extra room, make it a bit bigger."

"We'd need to." She pursed her lips. "It does have pretty views of the mountains."

He smiled. "That it does."

She broke into a grin. "Let's go take a look."

---

THE FARMHOUSE WAS in better shape than they'd thought. The foundations were solid, the frame itself was made of hard-wearing timber and despite the peeling paint and rusty window frames, wasn't in too bad a condition.

Becca stood on the back porch and gazed up at the purple-hued mountains. They had the lightest sprinkling of snow on them, but it would get heavier as winter approached. She took a deep breath, then exhaled. "This is perfect."

Later that day, Savage went to the bank and bought the property. He was now the proud owner of Apple Tree Farm.

That evening, he, Becca, and Sinclair celebrated with a glass of champagne. Barbara had dropped off yet another one of her pot roasts, and Connor slept peacefully in his brand-new cot in the spare room.

"You'll have to furnish it before you can move in," Sinclair said.

"We're going to take a trip into Durango tomorrow," Becca told her. "We need to buy everything."

Sinclair cringed. "I can't imagine what it must be like to lose everything in a fire."

"It sucks," Becca said, "but it does make you realize that the most important things are not material possessions." She smiled at Savage.

"I couldn't agree more."

They were just finishing up when Savage's phone rang. He excused himself to answer it.

"Dalton, it's Sarah Hagan." So she was back on informal terms, was she? He grinned to himself.

"I've got some news."

"Oh, yeah?"

"Guy Hollander was shot and killed today in a drive-by."

Savage felt the world tilt. "Come again?"

"He was gunned down, Dalton, in the middle of the fucking day. Someone took him out."

"Shit. When did this happen?"

"About five hours ago." Hagan hesitated. "You don't have any idea who did this, do you?"

"No, of course not. You don't think I had anything to do with it?"

She sighed. "No, I don't."

"No leads, then?"

She snorted. "Strangely enough, there were no eyewitnesses. Nobody seems to have seen a goddamn thing."

"Convenient."

"Yeah. Any ideas?"

"Could be his Philly connections? I heard he was mixed up with some serious mafioso types over there."

"Could be. In that case, we'll never find 'em."

"Sorry, Sarah. Thanks for letting me know."

"Sure." She hesitated. "Dalton?"

"Yeah."

"Sorry."

"What for?"

"You know. Everything."

Savage bet that hurt to say.

"Forget about it," he said.

He heard her exhale. "Okay, I'd better go. Be seein' ya."

"Yeah. See you, Sarah."

. . .

"WHAT WAS THAT ABOUT?" Becca asked, as he returned to the table.

"That was my old Lieutenant in Denver." He looked at Sinclair. "Guy Hollander was gunned down in the street this afternoon."

Becca gasped. "Oh, no. You don't think—?"

Although he hadn't said anything to Hagan, he'd had exactly the same thought.

*Dewayne Simmons.*

"You think this was Dewayne?" Sinclair stared at him. "The man you got exonerated."

"I don't know."

God knows, the ex-con had reason enough to want Hollander dead. The mobster had framed him and sent him away for six years. Caused his mother untold heartbreak. Manipulated Manning into doing his dirty work for him, which resulted in his kid brother getting shot and left to bleed out on the street.

Somehow, Savage didn't think Dewayne Simmons was going to let anyone screw him over again. Prison had taught him that much.

"Dewayne wouldn't have done this." Becca started clearing the plates off the table. "He's not the murdering type."

"Revenge is a powerful motive," Savage said. He'd seen men kill for less.

"What are you going to do?" Sinclair asked.

Becca shot him an anxious look.

"Nothing." He smiled at her. "It's not my case. It's got nothing to do with me."

"You think Denver PD will catch him?" Sinclair got up to help Becca.

"We don't know that it is him." Savage picked up the empty pot roast dish to take it back to the kitchen. "It could be anyone. I'm sure Hollander had a lot of enemies." He thought about Derek Edwards, the man from Arvada, who'd had to rebuild his life after his business went bust. There must be others. "You piss off that many people, and someone's bound to come back at you."

Maybe it was Dewayne. Maybe not.

He didn't want to know.

***

Dalton Savage returns soon in ***THE FROST KILLER***! Click the link below to pre-order your copy now!
https://www.amazon.com/dp/B0CBL896W1

Join the L.T. Ryan reader family & receive a free copy of the Rachel Hatch story, *Fractured*. Click the link below to get started:
https://ltryan.com/rachel-hatch-newsletter-signup-1

Join the L.T. Ryan private reader's group on Facebook here: https://www.facebook.com/groups/1727449564174357

LOVE SAVAGE? Hatch? Noble? Get your very own L.T. Ryan merchandise today! Click the link below to find coffee mugs, t-shirts, and even signed copies of your favorite L.T. Ryan thrillers! https://ltryan.ink/EvG_

# ALSO BY L.T. RYAN

**Find All of L.T. Ryan's Books on Amazon Today!**

**The Jack Noble Series**

*The Recruit (free)*

*The First Deception (Prequel 1)*

*Noble Beginnings*

*A Deadly Distance*

*Ripple Effect (Bear Logan)*

*Thin Line*

*Noble Intentions*

*When Dead in Greece*

*Noble Retribution*

*Noble Betrayal*

*Never Go Home*

*Beyond Betrayal (Clarissa Abbot)*

*Noble Judgment*

*Never Cry Mercy*

*Deadline*

*End Game*

*Noble Ultimatum*

*Noble Legend*

*Noble Revenge*

*Never Look Back (Coming Soon)*

**Bear Logan Series**

*Ripple Effect*

*Blowback*

*Take Down*

*Deep State*

**Bear & Mandy Logan Series**

*Close to Home*

*Under the Surface*

*The Last Stop*

*Over the Edge*

*Between the Lies (Coming Soon)*

**Rachel Hatch Series**

*Drift*

*Downburst*

*Fever Burn*

*Smoke Signal*

*Firewalk*

*Whitewater*

*Aftershock*

*Whirlwind*

*Tsunami*

*Fastrope*

*Sidewinder (Coming Soon)*

**Mitch Tanner Series**

*The Depth of Darkness*

*Into The Darkness*

*Deliver Us From Darkness*

**Cassie Quinn Series**

*Path of Bones*

*Whisper of Bones*

*Symphony of Bones*

*Etched in Shadow*

*Concealed in Shadow*

*Betrayed in Shadow*

*Born from Ashes*

**Blake Brier Series**

*Unmasked*

*Unleashed*

*Uncharted*

*Drawpoint*

*Contrail*

*Detachment*

*Clear*

*Quarry (Coming Soon)*

**Dalton Savage Series**

*Savage Grounds*

*Scorched Earth*

*Cold Sky*

*The Frost Killer (Coming Soon)*

**Maddie Castle Series**

*The Handler*

*Tracking Justice*

*Hunting Grounds (Coming Soon)*

**Affliction Z Series**

*Affliction Z: Patient Zero*

*Affliction Z: Abandoned Hope*

*Affliction Z: Descended in Blood*

*Affliction Z : Fractured Part 1*

*Affliction Z: Fractured Part 2 (Fall 2021)*

# ABOUT THE AUTHOR

**L.T. RYAN** is a *Wall Street Journal*, *USA Today*, and Amazon bestselling author of several mysteries and thrillers, including the *Wall Street Journal* bestselling Jack Noble and Rachel Hatch series. With over eight million books sold, when he's not penning his next adventure, L.T. enjoys traveling, hiking, riding his Peloton, and spending time with his wife, daughter and four dogs at their home in central Virginia.

* Sign up for his newsletter to hear the latest goings on and receive some free content ➜ https://ltryan.com/jack-noble-newsletter-signup-1
* Join LT's private readers' group ➜ https://www.facebook.com/groups/1727449564174357
* Follow on Instagram ➜ @ltryanauthor
* Visit the website ➜ https://ltryan.com
* Send an email ➜ contact@ltryan.com
* Find on Goodreads ➜ http://www.goodreads.com/author/show/6151659.L_T_Ryan

***

**BIBA PEARCE** is a British crime writer and author of the Kenzie Gilmore, Dalton Savage and DCI Rob Miller series.

Biba grew up in post-apartheid Southern Africa. As a child, she lived on the wild eastern coast and explored the sub-tropical forests and surfed in shark-infested waters.

Now a full-time writer, Biba lives in leafy Surrey and when she isn't writing, can be found walking through the countryside or kayaking on the river Thames.

Visit her at bibapearce.com and join her mailing list to be notified about new releases, updates and special subscriber-only deals.

Made in United States
Troutdale, OR
08/19/2023